THE COMPLETE CASES OF ANNE MARSH

Arthur Leo Zagat

ARTHUR LEO ZAGAT

THE COMPLETE CASES OF

ANNE MARSH ™

ARTHUR LEO ZAGAT

ILLUSTRATIONS BY

AMOS SEWELL

STEEGER BOOKS • 2019

TABLE OF CONTENTS

DAUGHTER OF DISHONOR

THIS ARRESTINGLY DIFFERENT,
DRAMATIC STORY OF A GIRL,
FORCED OUTSIDE THE LAW IN
ORDER TO CHAMPION THE CAUSE
OF ROBBED AND RUINED MEN, IS
THE FIRST OF A SERIES THAT
PROMISES TO MARK A NEW HIGH
IN DETECTIVE ENTERTAINMENT.
THE REMARKABLE, VITALLY ALIVE
CHARACTER OF ANNE MARSH,
THE GIRL ROBIN HOOD OF
THESE STORIES, IS DESTINED TO
BECOME A PARAMOUNT FIGURE IN
AMERICAN DETECTIVE FICTION.

ANNE MARSH laughed for the pure joy of living as the hood of her roadster lifted to the long climb of Bolton Turnpike over Lane Hill. For a moment the height's thickly wooded summit was a black, jagged line against the sky's gold-spangled velvet—then the forest crowded in close to the zigzagging incline. In minutes now the purring car would breast over the ridge. Anne would see the vast sprawl of Laneville's lights in the valley far below, and she would be almost home.

Home! In front of the high, dignified portal of the old house Dad would be waiting, iron-grey, stalwart, his strong, seamed countenance immobile except for the dancing glow in his deep-set grey eyes. They wouldn't kiss. His big hand would engulf her small one in the firm grasp of wordless comradeship, and palm to palm a warm tingle would run through then both of a love somehow too deep and real for caresses.

Then the phone would commence a flurry of dating for the Christmas holidays and the door-bell would start ringing. It was good to be coming home!

The road was a white ribbon twisting out of the blackness of the pines that dropped on Anne's left to a sightless, almost sheer descent. The wind....

Anne's heel stamped hard down the brake pedal!

A figure appeared from the shadows—

—a fist slashed at Ryan's gun...

THE STEERING wheel fought her. The car skidded, slewed sickingly, screamed to a stop. In the headlight's beam Anne saw a dark, prostrate form in the road and beyond it a sedan grotesquely pitched forward on a broken front wheel like some gargantuan animal beaten to its

knees. Startled pity seized her. She reached for the door-handle....

A burly figure lurched out of the shadow of the other car and the seemingly injured man was on his feet. Astonishment held the girl rigid as the two rushed toward either side of her roadster, blued automatics showing in their gloved hands. She glimpsed brutish faces half-hidden by hat-brims pulled low; thin-lipped, cruel mouths. Kidnapers!

"All right, buddy." The roadster door was open and a voice was growling at her. "Hop out. We need this buggy of yours." The fellow's gun threatened her.

"No argument." Anne managed to keep fright out of her voice. "I can't find words to refuse you." She slid along seat leather to the man, thrust a shapely leg down to the running board, reached the ground. He backed cautiously away, his weapon unwavering, and grunted, "It's a dame!"

"A skirt!" This was a new voice, thin, almost effeminate. The speaker, springing lithely out of the sedan, was undersized, snakily slight even in his bundling of sweater and overcoat, and what Anne could see, sallow white in the glare of her headlights. "Let's look her over." But it was the bag he held in his hand that held her eyes.

It was small, brown. Two thick straps ran around it to a steel fastening at the top that was locked shut by a padlock, and a coiled chain chalked, as the newcomer pattered toward her. She had seen bags like that before, fastened to the wrists of bank messengers.

A manacle swung at the end of the chain. It was locked shut but it encircled no one's wrist and its bright steel was dulled by a red stain.

"We got to get going," a hoarse voice growled. "Get back in the boat, sweetheart."

"No," Anne moaned. "You can have the car, but…."

"Damn right we can have the car, and you're coming with us." An arm lashed out and biting fingers dug into her arm, forcing her backwards, lifting her to the running board.

Anne's scream was cut short by harsh glove-wool across her face. Her futile fists hammered against a barrel chest, and the cold metal edge of the roadster floor scraped the back of her thighs as she was shoved back onto it.

Something plunked against the car and ice spray showered over her. Suddenly the fierce grip on her was gone as her captor whirled, snarling. Another snowball flashed out of the tree murk, staggered the bag-holder, and then the underbrush was alive with scattered rustlings, with the thudding of many footfalls as if from a dozen scattered directions.

"Don't shoot, fellows," a voice bellowed, somewhere in the darkness. "You'll hit the girl. Don't shoot till you get near enough to aim straight."

The thugs crouched, their guns up, quivering. "The bulls," some one grunted. "Sneaked up on us...." Shots pounded, and Anne rolled, squirming across the car floor. She lifted to the wheel. A burly form lurched in, reaching for her. She jerked away, slid out of the opposite door and was down on road-ice again as the car plunged away.

A maelstrom of spurting snow made hazy the dark shapes tumbling into the car's wide seat. It slewed to pass the wrecked sedan, twisted vainly to take the road again. Tortured rubber shrieked hideously, and a scream of terror flickered through the gloom. After a heart-stopping moment there came from below the sound of a cataclysmic detonation. Then—the silence of sudden death.

ANNE STARED down into the abyss with dilated pupils. Her icy lips moved. "Skidded. Through the fence."

An arm was around her waist, holding her firmly, somehow gently. "Steady," a voice sounded in her ear. "Steady. Head up!"

Anne pulled chill air into her lungs. "It—it was horrible." She shuddered.

"Not as bad as what they did in Bolton. Shot two men down without warning and chopped the money-bag loose." Anne looked up to see a face that was wan in the winter light, but clean-cut, blunt-jawed and powerful. "Messy as hell. But they didn't have corporation lawyers to tell them how to steal neatly." There was something grim in the youthful tones, something bleak and bitter.

Anne scarcely heard him. She disengaged herself. "I'm all right now," she murmured. "Thanks to you and your friends." She glanced around. "But where are they?"

He shrugged. "I haven't any friends with me." The slight pause before the last two words made them an afterthought, seemed to give the first part of his statement a queer emphasis. "There's just me."

Anne saw then that he was not only alone but also unarmed. "But—but you shouted to them. I heard them."

The youth chuckled dryly. "Snowballs make a lot of noise in the brush."

"Oh!" the girl gasped, comprehension dawning on her. "There were three of them and you...." She recalled flame lashing into the woods, orange-red flame that had been the trail of lethal lead. "They might have killed you!"

"They might have. But all this is not getting you home. Where were you going?"

"Laneville. We can walk down the hill. I live in the first house across Waley's Creek."

"You're the Marsh girl, then!" His interruption was sharp. "Webster Marsh is your father, the president of Union Light & Power. First citizen of Laneville. Treasurer of the Community Chest and—Damn! If I'd known!"

There was sudden enmity in his eyes. At the corner of his compressed mouth a tiny, heart-shaped scar was abruptly an angry red. "What do you mean?" Anne exclaimed.

He wasn't listening to her. He had twisted aside. From the direction of Laneville a far-off, melancholy howl crescendoed to an eerie climax, died away, rose again to become the pulse-stirring wail of an oncoming siren.

"Listen!" Anne's rescuer snapped fiercely at her. "If you think you owe me anything forget you've seen me. I was never here." Then suddenly he had clutched her to him—and was gone into the black screen of the woods. Gone! But on Anne's lips his kiss burned like white fire.

Headlight glare struck each needle of the evergreens into startling distinctness, blinded her as she whirled to it. "There it is!" someone shouted and brakes squealed.

Men in blue uniforms came out of the glare, past the wrecked sedan. Rifle-barrels splintered the light. "What's happened here? Where's Slinky Collins and his rats?"

THE POLICEMAN turned, saw what it was she had indicated. "Get down there, boys, and see if any of the snakes are still alive." He turned back to her. She saw a gold badge on his breast. "You're lucky they heard us coming, miss. Collins has picked women up before, on his getaways, but he didn't take them far. There wasn't any chance of help for you, up here, if we hadn't got the word from Bolton and shot right out. Nobody ever comes up in these woods in winter."

"No," Anne said with stiff lips. "Nobody."

"That's why they made for here. There's caves in there, and gullies, where we wouldn't have found them in a thousand years."

"I'll be going back, Cap," a toneless, unexcited voice interrupted from behind Anne. "You don't need me here and I want to find out what that call from the Marsh place meant."

"The Marsh—," Anne whirled. "What call?"

The stocky man was not in uniform. "What's that to— Oh, you're Miss Marsh!" There was no expression in his pinched, pointed visage, least of all in the cold, odorless eyes that peered out of slits between drooped lashless lids. "You're Anne Marsh. You're driving home from college for the year-end vacation."

The way he said it hinted at an intimate knowledge of her affairs. But Anne couldn't resent that now. "What's the matter at my home?"

"I don't know. Some woman phoned for help from there just as the Collins flash came in on the teletype. Captain Porter yelled for me to come along and...."

"Dad!" Apprehension clutched at her throat. "Something's happened to Dad! What are you waiting for? Come on."

"Wait, Ryan. I want to question Miss Marsh."

"That can wait, Cap." The detective's face was still mask-like, hut he must have understood the anxiety rocking her. "She won't run away." Then they were going past the sedan, past a big police car, were in a two-seater that whirred almost catlike to turn back toward Laneville and spurt into fast motion. It climbed over the ridge, pounded down the steep ramp on the other side.

"Hurry," the girl moaned. "Please hurry."

"Fast as I dare go," the plainclothes-man grunted. Then, "They come at you out of the woods? Hopped you before you saw them?"

The question jerked Anne back to the terror just passed. "No. They—" She checked herself. "What makes you say that?"

"There was tracks coming out of the woods. Who made them?"

"Who?" Who was he, the youth who had saved her? What was he doing in those woods the Captain had called a crook's sanctuary? "I—One of them. One of the bandits. I remember now.... Two of them stopped me and the other came out from the trees."

"That's funny. The tracks I mean laid over the imprints of your roadster's tires after it drove away." He seemed quite casual, but his eyes were boring into her suddenly. "You're sure there was no one else there?"

"Sure? I'm not sure of anything. It was all a nightmare. But hurry. Why can't you go faster? Something's happened to my father!"

Anne leaped from the car before it had quite stopped, flew up steps to the porch. The door opened. Faith's wrinkled face was white as the apron wrapped around her.

"Where's Dad?" the girl exclaimed.

The aged woman pointed wordlessly up the stairs rising from the lobby. Voices rumbled up there and a shadow moved across yellow light that Anne knew poured out of her father's study. A black shadow, gaunt, and somehow fearful as the shadow of Death himself.

And death was in the room, waiting for her. Webster Marsh was a dreadful, still heap on the floor and over the desk-edge above him little drops of colorless liquid dribbled from an overturned tumbler to splash on his colorless face. The acrid smell of peach blossoms stung Anne's nostrils.

CHAPTER TWO
MURDER WITHIN THE LAW

THE **SICK-SWEET** odor of funeral flowers hung in the study, reminiscent of the one pitiful wreath that had rested on the lonely coffin in the living room below. Laneville had averted its head from the funeral. Of all Anne Marsh's fair-weather friends there had not been one to attempt comfort in her bereavement.

Anne was very pathetic in the lustreless black of mourning, very frail and very tiny in the high-backed chair before the great desk from whose mahogany top Faith had polished away the stain left by the spilled poison draught. With bloodless fingers the orphaned girl touched first one, then another of the three papers on that desk-top.

The first, was a clipping from the editorial page of the Laneville *Courier;*

NIL NISI BONUM

It is an age-old tradition that of the dead one must say "nothing but good." But sometimes the sad necessity comes to violate the merciful rule, and the suicide of Webster Marsh forces such a necessity upon us.

Because he despoiled the Community Chest to which our charitably disposed gave all they could afford in this time of depression, Laneville's poor went without their Christmas baskets yesterday. Because he who was trusted above all others in our city violated that trust, all next year our hospitals must curtail their services, our orphanages shut their gates, our welfare services suspend their doles, the starving be left to starve.

The failure, a fortnight ago, of Union Light & Power added

a heavy load to the demands upon these institutions of neigh-
borliness. Thanks to Webster Marsh they will not be able to
meet that need.

Today the grave receives Laneville's shame. But as long as
poverty remains unrelieved in this city, as long as the naked ate
unclothed and the hungry unfed, the soul of Webster Marsh
will have no peace.

Anne's fingers, her dreary eyes, went on to the next
paper. It too was a clipping, from the news columns this
time;

LIGHT COMPANY TO BE REORGANIZED
Syndicate Takes Over Assets

Approximately half of the employees of the defunct Union
Light & Power Company were assured of continued employment today when the court accepted the offer of a group of
prominent citizens of Laneville to purchase the utility's physical plant and continue curtailed services.

The sum to be paid for the corporation's property, while large,
will be sufficient to liquidate only the mortgage bonds. The
unsecured loons, including that illegally made by Webster
Marsh with funds of the Community Chest, are now definitely
valueless.

The syndicate is composed of John Simpson, Dr. Thomas
Wayne, Frederick Harris, John Lawton, Donald Reynolds, and
Fulton Zander. The eminence of these gentlemen in Laneville's
business and civic life assures the community efficient service.

"And an enormous profit to line their own pockets,"
Anne muttered. "A profit stolen from the mouths of the
starving. Dad! You fought them all your life, but they
smashed you at the end."

"Here's your breakfast, Miss Anne." The girl turned to the querulous thin voice at the door. Faith was coming in, a tray in her hands.

THE DRINK sent revivifying warmth through her, the toast crunched crisply. "Faith! I know what happened now. They swindled him and killed him. They killed him just as surely as if they had put the poison in his drink with their own hands."

"Hush, dear. You mustn't say things like that."

"No, Faith, I'm not crazy. Look here. Look at the letter I found in this little secret drawer in the desk." Anne picked up the third of the papers that had been before her. "Let me read it to you."

"It's from John Simpson, president of the First National Bank, and it's marked confidential. It's dated October sixteenth.

" 'My dear Webster', it begins. 'I have bad news for you. I've repeated to our friends the gist of our conversation yesterday. I told them about our board's insistence on payment of the bank's big loan to your company by the end of the month, and that it meant collapse unless you could find funds elsewhere. I told them that you had put all your personal fortune into the pot, even pledged your home, in an effort to stave off the situation till December fifteenth when the Bank would again have funds available to replace the loan with enough additional to meet your needs. I appealed to them to subscribe to the deficit till that time.

" 'It was useless. The fall in the market had tied all of them up, as it has me. There's nothing left to do. The company must fail unless you can lay your hands on more money for the short period it will be needed.

" 'My suggestion recurs to me—but of course you are right. While morally justifiable that would be illegal. However, I have a hunch that you will find a way to save the great institution you have built up....' "

"I—What's that all about?" Faith looked confused. "What's in it that makes you so excited?"

"Don't you understand? Don't you see? The bank called its loan, but Simpson promised Dad that the company could have the money back by the fifteenth of December— and hinted that he use the Community Chest money during the period between. It is always distributed the Saturday before Christmas and that would be time enough to get it back—*if the bank kept its promise!* Father didn't like the idea, tried to get funds elsewhere, was refused. Simpson emphasized his suggestion in this letter. Dad had to take the chance to save the company, to save all the hundreds of people who work for it and own stock in it. And then the bank, Simpson himself, *reneged on its promise.*

"They all said in October they had no money. The market is ever so much lower today, but today Simpson and Wayne and Harris and the rest of them had enough to buy the properties at a third of their value. It's as plain as—as a safe that's been blown open. The whole thing was a put-up scheme. They wrecked the company, murdered Dad with his own hand, and now they're dividing the loot. Those highly esteemed citizens are thieves, killers, as surely as Slinky Collins was. But he was messy with his guns and his knives. They stole and killed within the law, neatly...."

Where had she heard a bleak and bitter young voice saying something very like that? A new twinge twisted Anne's heartstrings.

"Why don't you tell the police about it? Why don't you have them arrested?"

"I can't. There isn't any law against what they did. The law doesn't call it murder. It calls it finance, business.... *What's that?*"

THE SOUND of hammering came up from below. Faith's skinny hand went to her breast.

"It—it's the marshal," she whispered. "Tacking up an attachment notice. He—they—they're-going to sell the house at auction, and everything in it. I didn't want to tell you he was here till you ate something."

Old Faith's tortured accents trailed away. The hammering rang out in the agonized silence.

A bell shrilled, clamorous, the ringing of the telephone on the desk.

Faith snatched the receiver from its cradle, got it awkwardly to her ear. "Hello," she quavered. "Hello." She looked frightened. "New York is calling. Your Aunt Frances."

"Talk to her." Anne's direction was the merest whisper of breathed sound. "You talk to her."

"Hello, Mrs. Works. Miss Anne says I should talk to you... She's—she's layin' down!

"Yes! Yes!... All right, I'll tell her."

Then, to Anne: "She says she's sorry she had a big party on and she couldn't come out to the funeral. She says you should come to live with her. She needs a social secretary and you could have the job. She says you'll have a room, and your meals and clothes, and Sundays to yourself."

New York, Anne thought. Escape from the accusing eyes of the poor in Laneville, from the icy, unrecognizing stares of her erstwhile friends. Security of a sort, and a chance to forget and to be forgotten.

Tack-tack-tack the hammer went, and stopped. Someone dragged furniture across the floor, arranging it for sale. The sale would leave nothing but her clothes and her roadster.

"What shall I tell her, Miss Anne?"

A sentence stood out from the dingy newsprint on the desk, letters of black fire. *"As long as the naked are unclothed and the hungry unfed the soul of Webster Marsh will have no peace."*

Anne Marsh's livid lips twisted and suddenly she was no longer frail, no longer pathetic. Her eyes were hard, sinister.

"Tell her I'm staying in Laneville. Tell her I have something to do here. Tell her the only friend I have in all the world is going to help me."

"She says 'no thank you,' Mrs. Works," Faith said into the receiver. But Anne didn't hear her. Anne was reading the list of names in the news clipping, reading them as if to impress each name on her memory forever.

CHAPTER THREE

"COME INTO MY PARLOR," SAID THE SPIDER

PERHAPS IT was the spice-and-vanilla aroma of Faith Parker's baking, and the witchery of her cooking that made the success of the little tavern by Bolton Turnpike, just the other side of the bridge over Waley's Creek. Perhaps it was the dimly lighted quietness of the place, the tempting semi-isolation of the booths lining its walls, the gay freshness of the spring flowers on each table and each chintz-curtained window-sill. Perhaps, more than all these, it was Anne Marsh's wistful smile, her shy but sincere welcome to each newcomer as she sat at her desk near the kitchen door.

At any rate the patronage of the Tavern had grown steadily as the snow melted from Lane Hill. Nightly the line of parked cars outside had lengthened. By spring one simply didn't belong if one went home from theater or party without a visit to the Tavern.

There was a little space between Anne's desk and the nearest tables. To one or two of the highly observant it seemed queer that she seemed always to be listening, no matter how busy the Tavern was. She couldn't possibly hear anything of the low-toned conversations, the whispered confidences the very atmosphere of the place seemed somehow to encourage.

If the keen-eyed ones had watched closely enough they might have seen Anne's hand move, once in a while, under the edge of that desk, almost as if she were throwing a switch. If their ears had been as keen as their eyes they might then have heard voices whispering from somewhere under that desk. Voices that came from one or another of the shadow-shrouded booths where tongues might wag a little loosely, perhaps, in fancied security from eavesdropping.

Hidden microphones, concealed wires, a speaker tuned low almost to inaudibility! The Tavern was not quite what it seemed. Those hours in the attic workshop with her father had not been wasted ones for Anne Marsh.

She was listening now to the buttery, fat-drowned tones of John Simpson. He had ordered a double portion of waffles doused in maple syrup, a pot of Faith's ambrosial coffee. Fulton Zander, his emaciated, bespectacled attorney, was pecking at a salad and listening to his client, his hatchet face as acidulous as the vinegar with which he had doused the greens. Anne could see them—in a ceiling mirror that seemed only to be part of the clever decorations of the restaurant.

"You're an insufferable fusser, Fulton," Simpson mumbled from a full mouth. "That safe in my bedroom's as good a place for it as the bank's vaults. Besides, no one knows I took it home."

"The servants."

"Mae gave the girls the day and night off when she left for New York this morning. There's only the butler, Spencer, and he was downstairs in the pantry when I put the stuff away."

"Spencer! Deaf as a door post and alone in the house with ten thousand dollars. You're a fool, John."

"All right. I'm a fool. But there isn't anything to do about it now. I'll just have to rely on Molly Day. Say, I haven't tasted waffles like these since…."

But the speaker under Anne's desk was silent, "Take the desk, Hannah," she called to a pert, black-eyed little minx who was head waitress. "I have a headache and I'm going inside to lie down."

The single-roomed lean-to that was the living quarters of the Tavern's owners had only one entrance, a door out of the bustling kitchen full in the view of Faith and her assistants. There was something like adoration in the sweating, swarthy faces that watched the slim girl slip through it, and in the seamed countenance of their task-mistress something else.

Within the dark bedroom, bureau drawers scraped open, thudded shut. The hinges of a closet door creaked softly. A head was silhouetted against the one window, peering out, a head on which a cap was pulled down low and whose chin was buried in a turned-up coat collar.

From underneath that iron-barred window a gully-side dropped sheer for twenty feet to where Waley's Creek was shrouded by clustered high bushes. Even had it been possible for one to get through the firmly set rods guarding the aperture a straight fall down awaited him.

Black-gloved fingers tugged at the bars in a certain order. Inside the room there was the barely perceptible scrape of wood on wood, and abruptly a dank, earthy odor. Momentarily a dark square showed in the vagueness of the floor, was jogged by a blacker shape. Again there was the furtive scrape of wood on wood and the floor was solid again.

The bushes at the margin of Waley's Creek rustled momentarily. A shadow flitted over an apparently natural line of stepping stones across the streamlet's ripple—the shadow of a slender boy. A minute later an unlighted roadster purred along Bolton Turnpike, toward the sleeping city of Laneville.

THE SIMPSON MANSION, arrogantly set back on a terraced lawn in a section of Laneville where property values were highest, was as pompous in its pillared pseudo-Colonialism as its owner. High columns stalked across its front, but its drabber rear rose straight and unornamented in starglow from a moonless sky. There was something ominous in its pale sheen to the slitted eyes of the youthful figure crouched tensely in the scant concealment of a high back fence.

A little muscle twitched in Anne Marsh's cheek. "Dad," she murmured. "For you...."

No light showed from the house Anne watched. But she knew that the lower-floor doors and windows, the windows that could be reached by climbing the columns at the front, were not only locked but wired with an alarm that would ring in the not distant police station at the first illicit touch. The second story openings at the rear here were unwired—because they were high from the ground.

Anne fumbled inside her jacket, brought out a compact bundle of slender, hollow tubes, each minutely thinner than the next. Swift, deft motions, long rehearsed, fitted the steel rods together, end to end, as a fishing rod is joined.

Now she was close against the base of the house, and the rod was quivering all its long length as it lifted, slowly, slowly, till at last it was upright, till at last its hook bit into a wooden sill.

Anne had been often a guest with her father in this house, knew it intimately, almost, as she knew her own. That window was not haphazardly selected. Her rubber-soled feet clinging to the wall, her gloved hands clutching the rod she had devised, she climbed to it, attained it at last, crouched, breathing hard but soundlessly, on its narrow ledge.

This was easy! The sash went up too noiselessly, as if it had been oiled especially for her. The thick rug received her without a sound, and the stab of her tiny flashlight showed that the doors were shut, the door to the corridor and the one to the bathroom that connected with Mae Simpson's room.

The air was tainted, faintly, with tobacco-odor. The flicking beam fingered luxurious furnishings, a silk-covered bed, paintings of nudes on the wall. But where was the safe?

Wait! One of the pictures, the one over the night table, showed a well-rounded woman stretched full length on a white bearskin, a white ostrich-feather fan spread under beckoning, seductive eyes. Molly Day—the fan-dancer! "I'll have to rely on Molly Day," the banker had said....

Anne darted to that picture, lifted it away from the wall. The round black door of a countersunk safe stared at her.

From the capacious pockets sewn in the lining of her jacket the prowler lifted a stethoscope. The sound of the combination dial, turning under her fingers, was a rasping rush in the earpieces. Tumblers fell into place with pounding jars. In the workshop under her own bedroom floor through which her secret exit led she had practised hours for this moment. The door swung open!

Anne ripped the listening device from her ears, stowed it away.

She flicked her flashlight into the gaping hole behind that door, saw a paper-banded bundle of currency, reached for it—and froze....

Vaguely, terrifyingly, motor-roar surged through the night, the thunderous roar of the squad car that had mounted Lane Hill. Nearer, appallingly nearer. And suddenly a door bell was ringing, a knocker was banging somewhere below and a hoarse voice was shouting some unintelligible summons.

MOMENTARILY ALL of Anne but her brain was rigid in the grip of nightmare terror. Caught!—but how?

The pencil-thin beam of her flashlight, jerked askew in that first instant's realization of failure, answered her. A snapped copper filament hung in that beam, a threadlike wire that came out of the wall just over the safe. Its other part coiled from the back of the picture of the nude! In moving the canvas she had herself called the police to her capture!

The realization galvanized Anne into action. She snatched up the money, thrust it into her pocket, whirled and darted to the window. Her rod still hung, swinging in a slight breeze, from the window-sill. Her eyes plumbed the darkness below.

No one, yet. Anne heaved out on the sill. From within there was the loud creak of opening hinges, a high-pitched, old man's voice. They were in the house, were running up the stairs!

The girl slid down the rod, struck the ground, leaped away. Terror lent her wings to hurtle across the back-yard, to scramble ever the fence. She came down sprawling on the other side. Waited, heart in throat, for the shout that would show she had been seen.

"Clancy," someone bellowed. "That you?"

"Shut up, you ape! He'll hear us down here."

"Hell. Foster an' Corbett's got him inside there."

Anne was on her feet again, was darting into the lightless alley between the two houses fronting on Vallon Place. Luck was with her. Before the stupid police knew their bird was flown she would be in her roadster, would be halfway to Waley's Creek.

A shadow came alive, leaped to meet her! Fingers dug into her arm and a harsh palm went across her mouth, stifling her scream. She went down to her knees under the powerful thrust.

CHAPTER FOUR
THE PAY-OFF

ANNE MARSH squirmed, fighting at the irresistible arms that pinned her.

"Stop it, you little fool," a voice murmured, so low that though it was right at her ear she could barely hear it.

The injunction startled Anne into immobility.

House walls, close together, made a long, straight-sided tunnel of darkness that ended in a vertical slit of street-lamp luminescence. One side of that slit, low down, was not quite straight. Staring, Anne made out the outline of a man's chest, legs. A pale spot was a clenched hand with a pointing, too-long finger. *Not a finger.* The blued barrel of an automatic!

Anne's breath caught in her throat. If she had run on, if she had not been stopped by this unknown, she would have plunged blindly out, would have been shot down….

"That's Bulldog Ryan. Takes a smarter crook than you to outguess him."

"I'm not a…" she started to say, against the hushing palm—and stopped. That was exactly what she was. A crook.

"Listen," he was still talking, "There's a little window in the foundation of this house. You can reach the cellar through it, and there's another window opposite that will let you out on the side-street Your roadster is two blocks away, at Oak and Elm. Next time don't leave it so near your job. And make sure of your getaway before you start work."

Anne could make out his outlines vaguely, now. Something familiar about the poise of that head, something familiar about that voice, low as it was.

"You?" she managed to murmur past the gagging hand. "What are you going to—?"

"Watch."

He was gone suddenly. He was a shadow merged with the shadow of the house-wall. Even knowing he was there Anne could not see him or hear him. And then, with the abruptness of an amateur movie, a black figure appeared in the light-slit at the alley mouth. Its one hand slashed down at Ryan's gun, closed on the barrel and twisted it downward. In the same instant the other, fisted, darted upward. Bone thudded against bone, a lax body dropped. The mysterious stranger darted away.

A grunt behind her, the scrabbling of thick shoe tips against fence-boards, shocked Anne out of her momentary stupor. She got through the small window into furnace-warmth of a basement in the last possible moment before the climbing cop's eyes came up over the fence-top. Running across the basement, climbing through the other window so fortuitously open, slipping to the corner of Oak and Elm Streets, she carried a vision with her. Street lamp glimmer had shown her a mouth, in that eye-blink in which Bulldog Ryan had been slugged down. Only a mouth, but at the corner of it there had been a puckered, heart-shaped scar.

LANEVILLE'S BREAKFAST tables were agog, the next morning, with the screaming headlines that reported the burglary at the home of John Simpson. But at the Tavern on Bolton Turnpike preparations went on as usual for the coming night's business.

Not quite as usual. There was the matter of a new dishwasher to be hired.

"I never did trust that Rooshian with his great beard," Faith complained to a tired-eyed Anne. "A young man like him carryin' a mattress around on his chin."

"He—" Anne seemed to slough her weariness. "He left us. Faith. Who was he? Where did he live?"

"In some rat-hole other side of the railroad tracks, I'll be bound."

Anne looked up. The door had opened and a stocky, derby hatted man had come in—a man with a pinched, pointed visage and colorless eyes that peered with no expression at all from between drooped, lashless lids. An olive bruise disfigured his sharp chin.

He pointed that chin at Anne, and stopped stock still.

"Good morning," the girl ventured. "You're Mr. Ryan, aren't you? I remember you—up on Lane Hill when my car was stopped."

"Yeah," Bulldog's toneless accents replied. "That's me."

"Is there something I can do for you?" Icy fingers were tightening around Anne's heart, but her lips were smiling.

"Yeah. Mebbe there is. I been sorta thinking about that night. About the tracks in the snow. You was wearin' rubber-soled sport shoes, wasn't you? With one heel just a little worn on the sides?"

"I—perhaps I was. But I don't understand. Why should what I wore then be of any importance?" She managed still to keep her smile, but blind panic was running through her veins.

"Mebbe it ain't. I can't see myself how it could be, but I got orders to check on all the small-size rubber-soled shoes I know about. Y'see, there was marks of them kind of shoes on the wall of Mr. Simpson's house this morning. Let's see them."

"Surely." There wasn't anything else she could say. If he searched her room he would find them, and search it he would if she refused. There was a dumb, heavy persistence about him, that made her certain of that. "Faith, this gentleman has a peculiar desire to inspect my sport shoes. The last time I wore them was driving home from college. Do you happen to know where they are?"

The old woman turned from wielding a dust cloth. "Them yellow shoes with the tassels, Miss Anne? Why, I gave them to the Salvation Army with your father's things before we moved over here. I thought, being as how you was in mourning, you wouldn't have no more use for them and some poor woman might as well have them."

Ryan's look moved to Faith's face. She met his eyes with her bleared old ones, her faded orbs that mirrored honesty and frankness if ever eyes did. A hush invaded the Tavern— then it was Ryan's eyes that shifted and fell away.

"Well," he shrugged. "I guess they ain't no use tryin' to trace them, if that's the case. They might be anywhere's now." He walked to the door, turned there. "Happen to know what they call me on the force, Miss Marsh?" he asked heavily. "Bulldog Ryan. That's because once I get my teeth into a case I never let go."

The door closed behind him. Anne whipped around, started back toward the kitchen.

"Where you going?" Faith queried, coming close to the girl and speaking low. "If it's to look for them shoes, you won't find them. I saw that fellow out back talkin' to the kitchen boys before you got up, and I thought it a good idea to grind them up in the meat grinder with a lot of soup bones and send them out with the rest of the garbage. You see, they had fresh mud on them that didn't come from anywhere around here."

ABOUT A week later, the editor of the *Courier* was the recipient of a draft for ten thousand dollars, signed by the cashier of one of New York's largest banks. The payee of the draft was the Laneville General Hospital, whose quota of the vanished Community Chest would have been, curiously enough, exactly that sum. Bulldog Ryan went to the trouble of making a trip to New York to inquire as to the anonymous donor, but, naturally enough, the busy tellers of a Wall Street institution could remember nothing about what to them was a not unusual transaction.

DEATH WEARS A MASK

WITH THE FIERCE, BURNING LIPS OF HER UNKNOWN CHAMPION PRESSED HUNGRILY UPON HER OWN, ANNE MARSH KNEW THAT SHE WAS NOT QUITE ALONE IN HER DESPERATE, DANGEROUS BATTLE AGAINST HER RUTHLESS ENEMIES. BUT THOUGH SHE FELT HER MYSTERIOUS HELPER WAS NEAR, SHE KNEW DEATH WAS EVEN CLOSER—THAT NIGHT WHEN SHE DELIBERATELY WALKED INTO THE DEVIL'S WAITING TRAP!

ANNE MARSH'S pallid fingers plucked nervously at gay chintz window curtains. She was a small, forlorn figure in mourning that the drapes' gaudy coloring made more somber by contrast, and her eyes were the desolate grey of the endless drizzle into which they stared.

Behind Anne, flower-decked tables nestled in dim, empty booths offering privacy for whispered confidences. Behind her there was the friendly warmth of The Tavern on Bolton Turnpike. But the silent girl felt only the dreary chill of the spring rain, saw only of the drenched bushes lining the road whose boughs dripped slow drops like her own unshed tears.... Anne's hand tightened abruptly on the curtain and her lips were suddenly icy!

Those bushes had stirred, momentarily, with a movement that was not of the wind! Something alive was beneath them. Anne strained her terrified gaze to make out a vague, crouching form through the young leaves. Someone hid there, watching the Tavern—watching her!

It was nothing, she tried to tell herself.

Lane Hill's wooded height loomed mist-veiled and ominous above The Tavern. The highway was bleakly empty, its concrete a wet-black ribbon curving to cross the bridge over Waley's Creek and fray out beyond it into the streets of the city that once had revered Webster Marsh,

her father, and now reviled his memory. A brooding dread steeped the scene, a sense of peril irresistibly closing in.

Reason with herself as she might, Anne Marsh could not shrug off the feeling of eyes upon her, of cold, colorless eyes beneath lashless lids waiting for the one careless error that would mean prison for her.

Prison! This slip of a girl, whose close-cropped, tawny curls lent boyish allure to her tiny-featured, wistful face, was a hunted thief!

She was a thief who stole from thieves. She was an outlaw, while those on whom she preyed were smugly masked with respectability, their booty secured to them by the very law she flouted. Coming home from college for Christmas week, Anne Marsh had found her father a

"It's the bat—the bat!" screeched a voice.

suicide. He had, it seemed, embezzled charity funs entrusted to him, had been unable to face the disgrace of discovery.... Her world had crashed about her.

And then she had found a hidden letter. She learned how Webster Marsh had been lured into his betrayal of trust by a group of seeming friends, how they had wrecked the great utility company he had built up and had seized it with the very money of which, quite legally, they had robbed him.

They had murdered him surely as though their own hands had poisoned his drink, but they were safe from prosecution and punishment. They were respected, envied, while Webster Marsh lay in an unhonored grave, and Laneville's needy starved.

Penniless, ostracized, friendless but for Faith Parker, her aged and loyal servant, Anne had determined to take back from the schemers their booty, to return it to the poverty-stricken whom they had despoiled. Evicted from her home, she had opened The Tavern, with old Faith's aid.

Already its dim-lit, murmursome quiet had beguiled John Simpson, banker, into unwary speech by which he had been ten thousand dollars poorer before morning and the Laneville General Hospital that much richer. No one suspected Anne Marsh of being the cat-burglar who had narrowly escaped capture—

No one except the detective whose relentless pursuit of his prey had earned him the name of Bulldog Ryan. Was it he who hid out there in the bushes? Had he discovered the secret exit cunningly devised so that Anne might prowl the midnight while apparently innocently asleep in a bedroom she apparently could not leave unobserved?

"Miss Anne!" The girl swung around to Faith's chiding, querulous call. "Ain't you going to fix the deposit for the bank? We ought to get it out o' here. There was a garage-man murdered by hold-ups yesterday, other side of Lane Hill!"

"You—you frightened me," Anne gasped. She started toward her desk in front of the door to the kitchen.

"Frightened you!" Tiny, birdlike eyes peered anxiously out of a pinched face wrinkled and yellow as old parchment, "Miss Anne, there's trouble!"

"No, Faith. No. Only I—Ohhh!" Anne whirled to a thud at the entrance.

A man held on to the knob of the closed doors as if his weakness demanded support. Frayed trouser cuffs dripped moisture over broken shoes and a leaf that had dropped from him made a spot of vivid green on the floor. The girl contrived speech. "What do you want?"

His face was gaunt, wolfish with a week's dark stubble.

"Food," he croaked. "Something to eat."

"Go around to the back door," Faith snapped.

"Faith!" There was sharp rebuke in Anne's exclamation. "He's hungry." Then she was addressing the man and her tone was gentle, pitying. "Sit down there, in one of the booths. We'll have hot soup for you in a minute, and meat. Hurry, Faith."

Wordlessly the man shuffled to a cubicle, disappeared within it. Faith flounced out. Anne went around the desk to the chair where nightly she sat, greeting Laneville's elite with her shy, withdrawn smile. The old woman came back in with a tray of steaming dishes, went out again. The girl was scarcely conscious of her. She was reading, for the hundredth time, a newspaper clipping that lay under the desk's glass top.

It was an extract from an editorial the Laneville Courier had printed the morning of her father's funeral: *"As long as the naked are unclothed,"* it said, *"and the hungry unfed, the soul of Webster Marsh will have no peace."* Anne sighed, wrenched her gaze from the clipping, reached into a drawer for a bankbook and a thick sheaf of greenbacks.

Her knee touched a switch, by accident, moved it. Sounds whispered from under the desk, the rub of fabric against wood, the champ of chewing jaws. They came from a low-tuned speaker hidden there. The Tavern's offer of discreet privacy was only apparent! Every booth concealed an eavesdropping microphone. Adroitly arranged in the restaurant's clever decorations were mirrors revealing to Anne what went on at every table. Instinctively she glanced up into one.

THE MAN might be ravenous but there was incongruous breeding in the way he ate. Within the shapeless bulk of his shabby coat his frame seemed curiously lithe, vibrant. The hand with which he reached for a knife was clean.

On the cloth beside that knife was something Faith had not placed there. *A revolver,* huge and black and wicked!

The girl was devastatingly conscious of the closed kitchen door, of the absence of movement behind it. Faith must have gone down into the cellar for preserves with which to fill her pies and sent her assistant out on the back porch to peel potatoes. For minutes Anne would be alone here with the man—and the gun.

Her hand closed on the pile of currency. If she could hide it....

The roar of a motor outside diminished and stopped. Brakes squealed. Through curtained door-glass Anne saw a vague figure approaching. Relieved breath hissed between her teeth. Accident had brought her rescue. With others in the place he wouldn't dare....

The door opened. The newcomer was inside and the outer chill seemed to have come in with him. He was stark still for a moment against the vivid curtain, hands thrust deep into pockets of the rain-dusted black coat in whose turned-up collar his chin and mouth were buried. A broad hat brim shadowed the rest of his face, but Anne sensed that his glance was fastened on the money she clutched.

The silence in the room was a tense, threatening hush.

The man stalked toward her with the noiseless prowl of a panther. A muffled command reached her.

"Keep mum, or you'll get it in the belly."

His right hand was out of its pocket, was fisting a flat, savage automatic. If she screamed, Faith would rush in….

Curiously Anne felt no fear. Only fierce anger at the seeming waif who had played on her charity to spy upon her and had somehow signaled his accomplice when the coast was clear.

"Hand it over." The bandit's weapon pointed at her face. "Quick."

She pushed the money across the desk. Her eyes flicked to the telephone, flicked away. The fellow's left hand snatched the bills from her—and the knuckles of his gun-hand whitened with sudden pressure. He was going to shoot.

Fingers clamped on the fellow's wrist, forcing it down. Orange-red flare jetted into the floor. An explosion sounded in Anne's ear-drums, followed by the sickening crunch of smashed bone. The bandit folded, thudded down, and the hungry man was before her in his place, revolver clubbed in his hand.

His eyes, a glowing blue, fastened on her face and there was hunger in them, but not for food.

"I'll call the police."

The thought in her mind came out in spoken words. She reached for the instrument, her gaze still glued to that stubbled countenance.

Her reaching hand closed on another hand that was folded over the cradled telephone.

"You little fool!" His tones were no longer hoarse. "You don't want the cops messing in here." She had heard that voice before, somewhere! "You don't want to give Bulldog Ryan a chance to poke around and ask questions."

Anne's heart thumped against caging ribs.

"You… you're…."

Trapped the night of her first foray, those very accents had whispered warning to her out of the dark, had showed her the way of escape. Vanishing into the night from which he had mysteriously appeared, their owner had left her only the memory of a tiny, heart-shaped scar at the corner of a firm mouth and a dull, unacknowledged pain in her breast.

"Who are you?"

She was around from behind the desk. Oblivious of the tang of gun-smoke in the air, of the slumped, inert heap at her feet, her fingers dug into a shabbily clothed arm.

"Who are you?"

"Call me Peter." The arm jerked from her grasp—and was around her waist, was sweeping her close against a hard-muscled body. "Call me Peter—my dear."

Bristles rasped her chin and avid lips crushed against hers. They were ablaze. An answering fire leaped within her.

And then Anne was flung back against the edge of a booth wall.

"Damn!" the man blurted. "I forgot I have no right."

He stooped swiftly and straightened as swiftly, the thug across his shoulder, "I'll take care of this." Bleak bitterness underlay his tone. "Forget about it—and about me."

He swung around, plunged away.

"Peter!" cried Anne. The door slammed between them. The girl thrust shaking hands against the wall behind her. Her trembling legs refused her commands. The whir of an auto-starter was muffled by the closed door. The bandit's car surged away.

"Miss Anne!" Faith burst in, the tip of her long, thin nose twitching like a rabbit's. "What happened? I heard something drop, up here, but my arms was full of glass jars."

"Oh! I dropped something on the floor. It—I picked it up."

"Pretty loud drop," the old woman sniffed. She moved away, going into the booth out of which Peter had pounced with the lethal, silent swiftness of a tiger springing from its lair. "Your tramp's gone, I see."

"Yes." Anne's tone was flat, dreary. "He's gone."

"But he'll be back." Faith reappeared, loaded with dishes. "He'll be back for more."

"Do you think so, Faith? Do you really think so?"

There was brooding wistfulness in Anne's voice.

CHAPTER TWO
THE GREY BAT HITS

PALATE TICKLING aroma of Faith Parker's cookery; shaded candle-light mellow on gleaming cloths; a soft murmur of quiet talk; this was The Tavern at night. This, and the dreamy-eyed girl in black at her desk near the kitchen door, watchful that all went well and yet somehow withdrawn, aloof. As if, though her post was too far from even the nearest booth for the conversation there to be audible to her, she were listening, always listening.

Anne Marsh *was* listening, to low-toned voices coming from the speaker under her desk. A pair of young lovers whispered confidences. Anne's hand moved covertly, and the tag-end of a bawdy tale evoked snickers from a quartette just come from a church's vestry meeting. The switch tapped another connection.

"… going as an Indian Rajah. I'm having our costumes sent from New York. Yours is marvelous, and when you put the Martyr's Tear in your turban."

"When I what?" the man spluttered. "You're insane, Alice. I paid a fortune for that ruby."

A stolen fortune, Anne thought. Donald Reynolds' name was on her list. But she must keep listening. This sounded like….

"Please do not he difficult, Donald."

In the mirror reflecting that particular booth Anne's swift glance saw a sable wrap carelessly thrown back from sharpened shoulders exposed by a too youthful evening dress; saw a face whose time-graven lines rouge and powder could not mask.

"Nearly everyone invited deals with you, and you know as well as I that a stockbroker must impress his clients with his own wealth."

"You're right, dear." Reynolds shifted uncomfortably in his chair. "You are always right." He pursed thick, sensuous lips judicially. "But—"

He paused as a waitress passed, turning to caress her young curves with a covert glance. The eyes in his ferret-like face were predatory, and bluish pouches of dissipation showed beneath them. His hair was too sparse to conceal the fact that his head was egg-shaped.

"But what?" Alice Reynolds snapped, jabbing a fork into a crisply brown soufflé as if she would like to stab it into her husband's neck. "What's on your mind?"

"An affair like that, a big masquerade, thieves may get in. Everyone will be masked till midnight. It would be easy...."

"Nonsense! Pearl Brooks told us at bridge today that she is arranging every precaution. There will be a police squad to patrol the grounds and detectives to mingle with the guests inside. No one will be admitted except by card."

"Which might be lost or stolen."

"Every arrival will be identified in rooms off the foyer, the ladies by Pearl's secretary, the gentlemen by Henry's."

"We'll have to take the ruby out of the vault before three and have it home all afternoon."

"We shall not. John Simpson has arranged to have men at the bank all evening so that everyone going can pick up his jewels on his way to Brooks'. Since he was robbed John has grown very cagy. I want no more argument about it, Donald. You are wearing the ruby tomorrow night, and I will defy any thief to steal it from you."

"Very well, Al."

An approaching waitress forced Anne Marsh to switch off the voices. She made change mechanically, a glitter of excitement in her veiled eyes. A challenge had been flung at her. Dared she accept it?

TWENTY HOURS later, The Tavern's kitchen was filled with the spicy fragrance of Faith Parker's baking, with the hot, delicious aroma of roasting meats and simmering stews. A white-capped assistant cook peered into a huge pot, stirred it tentatively with a two-foot long spoon. A swart-visaged, simian-armed dishwasher made clatter in a corner.

Faith came out of the single-roomed lean-to that was the living quarters of the restaurant's owners. A pert, black-eyed minx who was fastening a tiny white apron around a trim waist turned.

"I hope Miss Marsh is feeling better," Hannah Walsh said. "Tony tells me she's been laid up all day."

"A little," Faith replied. "She wanted to get up but I told her to stay in bed. We won't he busy tonight with everybody going to the masquerade. You won't have any trouble taking care of the desk, Tony! You're putting too much mace in that sauce. How often have I told you a half a pinch is enough?"

"Excusa me, please. I listen how littla boss iss."

The kitchen resumed its customary bustle. The door through which Faith had entered was of inch-thick wood solidly set into its jamb, and the noises would not disturb the ailing girl. It was the only exit from the bedroom. There was a window in there, of course, but it was covered with iron bars and from directly beneath it a gully-side dropped twenty sheer feet to the bushes along Waley's Creek.

Moon-glow made that window a pale, gridded oblong in a dark wall. It filtered into the room, sought out an empty bed, seeped across the floor and was jogged by a black, square hole. There was a furtive scrape of wood on wood, the hole became rectangular, became a narrow slit, was gone. The floor was solid once more. The room was empty and there was no sign of how its occupant had left it.

The dank odor of underground earth closed around Anne Marsh, She felt along rough, splintery boards beside the ladder down which she had climbed, touched a button.

A small windowless room sprang into existence in the yellow light of a single unshaded bulb.

Anne's lips twitched with pain at the sight of a time-darkened work-bench, its scarred top cluttered with tools. Manual craft had been Webster Marsh's hobby and he had taught it to her. They had spent many happy hours together at this very bench. Every gouge in its surface held a memory.

There were wood shavings on the secret shop's earthen floor, and metal filings. Tonight there was other, more feminine debris. Bits of mouse-grey silk, tangled snippings of thread, a crumpled pattern cut from newspaper. On a rickety chair a shapeless pile of lustrous fabric that was one result of Anne's day long labors.

The girl's simple frock slipped to her feet. Grimy light stroked skin luminous with the faint, rosy sheen of a pink pearl. Fabric rustled as Anne picked up that which was on the chair, sat down....

She stood up, stretched out her arms, which became the voluminous, fluttering wings of a bat! But no bat ever had a body so seductively curved as that to which the grey silk clung.

A grey, tight helmet covered her curls, let down a mask to hide the small oval of her face. A closet yielded a long, light coat, mannishly cut; a checked and visored cap. She was no longer a bat, she was a slender, swaggering boy. The light clicked out. A panel whispered in the darkness. The bushes along Waley's Creek threshed to a gust of wind, or to a slight form pushing through them.

PATROLMAN FALLON leaned his back against the door of Henry Brooks' garage and gazed heavy-lidded at the back of the big house from which music thumped. It was swell jazz, he thought. They was havin' a swell time in there, with never a thought for a cop who was doin' double tour so they could show off their jools. Hell! If it wasn't for the skipper sayin' if anything happened the whole detail would be fined a week's pay, he'd go inside the garage an' take a snooze in a car. The midnight to eight he'd done last night, and he'd had to go to the dentist in the morning. He'd had about two hours' sleep….

What was that?

His hand jerked to his gun-holster and he was suddenly wide-awake, twisting to a stealthy scrape around the corner of the garage. There it was again. Someone was pushin' through the hedge.

A thin arm slid around Fallon from behind, tightened to clamp his gun-wrist against his side. Something wet slapped over his face, wet and sick-sweet smelling. He wrenched his arm free, spun around, clawing with his other arm at the soaked cloth that was blinding and choking him. He couldn't get it off. He was weak—the dark whirled around him. He whirled down into it.

Anne Marsh knelt to the sodden, prostrate form of the patrolman and unfastened the hook behind his neck with which she had clamped the ether-drenched pad to his head. It took all her small strength to tug him into the shadow of the hedge. She reached in under it, pulled out a block of wood, reeled in a long cord that trailed from it.

By pulling on the other end of that cord she had made the sounds that had diverted Fallon's attention for the instant she had needed to slip up on him. Now it served to bind his wrists and his ankles, to fasten a gag in his mouth, and to tie him to the strong roots of the boxwood.

Light splotched the space between her and the house. If anyone should look out of one of those lighted windows…. Breath caught in Anne's throat, but no bat's flight could have been more silent than her swift dart to the gloom that lay along the mansion's foundation wall. She quivered, crouching there, her soul in her ears.

Muted, far-off applause greeted the final, blared chord of "Rhythm in My Nursery Rhymes." A wine-cork popped in the pantry over her head. There was no shout of alarm, no sound of rushing footfalls.

There was a low window somewhere along here, leading to the basement. She had spotted it from the murk of the narrow alley between two houses backing on the Brooks' property where for an hour she had been hidden, searching for a weak point in the defenses she must penetrate.

Anne crawled a foot or two, found the window. A bit of thin metal pried open the catch and she slid through. She was inside the house!

Yellow glow from a furnace dimly lighted the cavernous cellar. A skeleton staircase rose out of the murk to a door which muted a shrill, excited laugh. Saxophones howled "Wahoo, I'm a buckaroo," and the shuffle of dancing feet drew Anne to the front end of the cellar. The ball room was just above, and that was all she needed to know. She recalled Mona Brooks' debut in that very ballroom, recalled a befuddled Cornell senior importunate in a palm curtained niche. That had been—right above here.

There were pockets in the wings of Anne's bat costume. They yielded a brace and a long, thin bit. She climbed atop a dusty trunk, set the spiral auger against the basement ceiling, an inch from the wall. Bits of plaster showered down, then tiny, curlings of wood. A star of white light in the basement ceiling.

A clock, somewhere, struck eleven. Anne, her preparations completed, listened against the door at the head of the basement stairs. There was no sound near it. She jerked it open, stepped out under the slant of another staircase, closed it. Turned… and thumped into the back of a tonsured monk!

"Hey, wash idee!" The brown-robed friar reeled around, forgetting to take his arms from around a Cleopatra whose only apparent covering was a mask and a network of coruscating gems. "Wash idee bumpin' into me? Can't y'shee I'm busy, young feller?"

"Young lady, you mean." The Egyptian queen laughed blurredly. "You're drunk. Can't see she's girl?"

"He'sh boy. *You're* drunk!"

Anne slipped away from the befuddled couple, smiling secret satisfaction. The folds of her wings, with her arms down, effectually concealed her sex. If either of the two secretaries who had checked the arrivals were to spy her, each would think the grey bat had passed the other's inspection.

The ballroom was a kaleidoscopic swirl of scarlet Satans and frothy ballet-dancers, of piebald Harlequins and nautch girls displaying immense stretches of nut-stained skin. A laurel-wreathed, portly Caesar chuckled at the giggles of a choread whose costume of balloons was slowly disappearing under the attack of his cigarette tip. A cadaverous Death was anything but macabre as he pursued a screaming Mae West with voluptuous hips. The spirituous ministrations of a corps of perspiring waiters behind a long buffet-table and the anonymity of masks cooperated to release primitive impulses from the inhibitions of a small city's prudishness.

The grey bat flitted through the rout, in it, yet unobtrusively not of it. She paid a visit to a small alcove at the farther end of the hall from the stamping, howling blackamoor orchestra. Almost at once she came out again from behind its screening palms. She was ready now for the Rajah.

There he was, sidling along the wall, the frail stem of a three-quarter filled wine-glass in his unsteady hand. The jewel was a spot of flashing, splendid color on the white swathing of his turban. The Martyr's Tear! It was large as a Malaga grape, but it was tear-shaped. It was a clot of frozen light, scarlet as new-spilled blood.

Anne gasped at the sheer beauty of it but under its shield of grey silk her mouth was grim. Whoever had named the ruby had visioned some Oriental Messiah weeping bloody tears for the sufferings of his downtrodden people. The man who wore it now had robbed the downtrodden of his own race.

She slid between a staggering knight in tin armor and a mincing Minnie Mouse.

"Oooh!" She reached for Reynolds' glass. "Wine! And I'm so thirsty. Gimme."

He avoided her snatching fingers with fumbling dexterity. "No," he said, with besotted gravity. "Wan' it myself."

"Oh, please." Anne extended her arms in entreaty. Her wings fluttered open, revealing to the Rajah alone the seductive slimness of her tempting form. "Pretty please. I'd do anything for a drink. Except push into the mob around the buffet-table."

"Anything?" His eyes were mask-hidden, but Anne knew just what they were doing. She had studied him to good purpose in the mirror at the Tavern. "Would you give me a kiss?"

"Of course." She came closer to him, so that the warmth of her body could reach him. He swayed, but underneath the cover of her fluttering wings his fingers touched her.

Her flesh crept under the greedy hand, but she let it stay there. "Of course I'll give you a kiss."

It was he who recoiled, as she knew he would, and looked furtively around. "What's the matter, Rajah?" she cooed. "What are you afraid of?"

"My—my wife. She'll see!"

Low laughter gurgled from her.

"Look." She pointed to the alcove. "There's no one in there."

Reynolds almost knocked over a palm-tub in his awkward haste.

The bat was close behind him.

"The wine," she demanded.

"The kiss first, m'dear." He managed to set the glass down on a small table without spilling more than half of its contents. "No tickee, no washee." He pawed at her. "Come on—. Oh, now look what you did!"

A flirt of Anne's hand had knocked the turban from his head. It rolled against the wall. Both stooped for it, collided. Anne snatched at a cord-end that came out of a hole in the floor, jerked it.

Darkness smashed down on the ballroom as the master-switch in the basement pulled out of its clips. Darkness, and a sudden silence that spattered into ribald cheers. In the alcove Donald Reynolds grunted:

"Where are you? Bat, where are you?"

And then his voice crescendoed to a high, shrill scream.

"My ruby. My ruby. It's gone!"

CHAPTER THREE
THE BULLDOG BARKS

BLACK WOULD have been a darker splotch in the blackness, but the bat's grey was the color of invisibility. Anne could not be seen as she flitted sound-lessly toward the ballroom entrance, beyond which stairs led down to the basement and to the rear of the house she had made sure would be unguarded. She filtered, an unsighted wraith, through a howling, screaming mob of merrymakers who made merry no longer. She was almost free of them....

"All right, men," a voice said, toneless and calm yet somehow clearly audible above the turmoil.

Abruptly the darkness was crisscrossed by spears of white light. The flashlight beams struck the big main door into glaring brilliance, sprayed with light a black-cloaked friar straddle-legged in its very center, an automatic in his hand. There was another, smaller door to one side. Anne whirled to it.

That too was lighted, guarded.

"It was a bat," Reynolds' squeal jabbered out of the murk. "A grey bat, stole my ruby."

"Look for a grey bat, men," the unexcited voice intoned. Bulldog Ryan's voice! The flashlights shifted, probing the crowd, searching it for a bat who was a thief.

A hand snatched at Anne. She pulled away from it, pulled away from the shout of "Here she is!" that beat flatly against other shouts. She ducked under a scything flash that blinded the man who had seen her, and through a surge of the bewildered crowd that carried him away.

Behind the momentary protection of a velour curtain shrouding a high window embrasure she found a temporary hiding place.

She glanced frantically out through the pane. Two uniformed patrolmen stared inquiringly at the darkened house, their guns fisted. No use trying if the window was locked.

"Keep quiet, everybody. If you'll keep quiet we'll have the thief in no time. Nobody can get out of this room."

Anne's small mouth quirked in a grim smile. She wasn't caught yet. She ripped hurriedly at stitches around her shoulders that gave as they had been designed to give. The bat wings came away, leaving her white arms bare. The wings were double layers of silk her flying fingers separated, and the surfaces that had been together were lustrously white. Hooks snapped into eyes, and a white, sleeveless robe rippled straight down from her shoulders.

Grey stockings stripped down, went into a hidden pocket with grey cap and mask, and grey slippers. Jeweled sandals came out, a cap of strung, pearly beads, a white domino. Anne Marsh knotted a silver, tasseled girdle about her waist and stepped out from her improvised dressing room no longer a bat but a white-cloaked, bare-armed and barelegged damsel from some medieval castle.

So short a time had been required for the metamorphosis that the clamor still burred, subsiding into silence at the detective's last command.

Anne saw now that the men with the flashlights were all dressed, as the one who had barred her intended exit had been, in the black monk's robes. They were pushing through the throng to the windows, hemming her in. The lights came on, dazzling her.

"I'm talking to the thief, now." Anne's vision cleared. Bulldog Ryan was in the center of the huge chamber, addressing the throng. "You hear me. You've changed your costume but that isn't going to help you any." He had not gotten rid of his masquerade, and he stood there stocky, weighty as the leaden lump at the pit of her stomach; his sharp chin thrust forward; his lashless eyes slitted. "You can't get away. You might as well give yourself up."

His voice thudded into the listening silence. He waited, his colorless gaze drifting over the varicolored crowd. It came to Anne, hesitated, A dark flood of terror surged through her blood. His look passed on, but her throat was still constricted on the confession that almost had found utterance.

"Yeah," Ryan said at last, heavily. "I didn't think you would. But it won't do you no good keeping quiet. It just makes it that we've got to search everybody in this room."

"The hell you say!" a man growled, and a woman protested, shrilly: "It's an outrage. I won't permit myself to be pawed by anyone."

The room murmured with the usual rebellion of good citizens when asked to submit a personal inconvenience in the cause of law-enforcement, but in Anne's brain despair was a turgid fog. The Martyr's Tear was on her. It was sure to be found. She should have gotten rid of it—but that would have been an acknowledgment of defeat. This was the misstep for which Ryan had waited, the fatal error.

"Mr. Ryan."

The individual in the red robe of an English judge was tall, cadaverous. The hatchet-edged profile of Fulton Zander, attorney to Laneville's wealthy, projected from his flowing, white-powdered wig.

"Perhaps it will be unnecessary to inflict on these good people the indignity of a search. May I suggest that the invitees are all known to our hosts. If you request the assemblage to unmask, any interloper will be discovered and will undoubtedly be the guilty person."

That was worse. That was far worse. She would have no chance to get rid of the ruby.

"All right, folks. You heard what Mr. Zander said. Take off your masks."

THERE WAS no way out! Hesitation would only hasten her discovery. Anne lifted shaking fingers to her domino—and froze as a voice rang out from the other end of the room.

"Try and make me."

She whirled to the clear, bell-like challenge. An archer in forest green darted to the musicians' dais, his slender, youthful frame lithely graceful, a long feather jauntily streaming from his emerald hat. He snatched the bass drum from its rest, spun again.

"Stop him!" Ryan bellowed above shrieks, screams, yells. "Nab him!"

His gun was out but he dared not shoot into the swirling crowd. He was plunging through them.

The archer leaped toward the nearest window. People scattered before him, hurrying out of range of the gat that the detective at that window was jerking up. A pulse throbbed in Anne's temple. The policeman couldn't miss. He had a clear shot at the youth in green. The drum couldn't stop lead.

But it could hurtle from the hands that held it and smash down on the detective's head. Its sheepskin head could split to engulf him. A green streak flashed past him, vanished through the velour curtains beyond. They muffled the splintering crash of glass as they bellied to the push of inrushing air. Sounds of a hoarse shout and the jolting shots fired by the cops came from outside. An abortive scream rasped Anne's throat.

The yelling mob surged toward windows that opened to let the other black-cloaked detectives out. The door guards were running across the floor. Anne Marsh was suddenly alone in the center of the ballroom, ignored, and there was no one between her and the inner passage.

No one to see her dash out to it; through the narrow corridor; down the wooden stairs into the basement.

In whimpering haste she grabbed up her coat and cap from where she had hidden them in a coal bin, donned them. Black stockings and shoes from the cache made her a boy again. She was at the little window that had first given her entrance, was peering out through it, was listening intently. There was no more firing from the front of the house. There was a distance-deadened clamor. Back here there was only a muffled grunting from the direction of the garage—from Patrolman Fallon, struggling against his bonds.

Anne climbed out, ran across the grassy backyard and slid through the gap between the hedge and the garage wall through which she had come. Then once more she was a silent, furtive shadow drifting across another backyard, through a dark alley. She was a slim, belated youth walking hurriedly, not too hurriedly, along a sleeping street.

There was a sob in her throat, grief and wonder in her brain. They had caught him, they must have caught him— or killed him. Why had he created the diversion that had saved her, at so great a sacrifice? Why had he once again come to her aid? Once again! For briefly her mysterious savior's green mask had fluttered aside from his mouth, and there at its corner she had glimpsed a tiny, heart-shaped scar.

She turned a corner, walked another long block. It was by his advice, given that other night of crime and alarm and escape, that she had parked her roadster so far away. Around this next corner. She turned it—and jumped back, choking a cry of alarm. She shrank, trembling and terrified, against the too feeble shield of someone's picket fence.

An instant later and she would have gone on, would have stepped into her car—and into Bulldog Ryan's clutching hands!

In that instant she had glimpsed him, his stocky form unmistakable even in the gloom, slipping into the car, crouching down to hide behind its dashboard to hide and wait for her. He was waiting there for her now!

A wail, melancholy in the distant, rose to a shriek, died away. The siren of a police radio car! Another echoed it from a different direction. They were calling to each other, howling hunting dogs in a city jungle. They were hunting for her.

She hadn't blindfolded the policeman she had gagged and bound. He had seen her making her getaway. By this time he had been found and had told his story.

Scores of blocks stretched between her and Waley's Creek—scores of blocks that the hunters prowled. Walking them, she would be sure to be stopped and searched. Beneath her coat was still the tight grey silk of the bat, and in its tiny pocket there was still the Martyr's Tear.

CHAPTER FOUR

FLIGHT

ANNE MARSH cowered in the flimsy conceal-ment of the stockade's barred shadow. Ryan's uncanny instinct had enabled him to forestall her every move, had brought him here, a squat nemesis, to snatch from her the safety she thought at last within her grasp.

Footfalls thudded against the dark. Another policeman! No. Swift-running, they were yet too light, too stealthy. Who then? Anne bent low, peered through the palings.

The runner was coming from the other end of the block in which her roadster was parked, the direction from which Ryan must have come. He was a vague, misty figure. He came into the cone of light from a street-lamp, passed out of it. Came on, swift, lithe, purposeful.

A great cry of thanksgiving pulsed in Anne's breast— and a scream of warning. His coat had flapped open as he loped through the light, and beneath it green silk had flashed. It was Peter! Alive! Free! Running straight toward the ambush where Bulldog Ryan waited:

Her larynx choked on the scream and then its was too late for warning. He had reached the roadster—and stopped! Turned to it. Flung his hand out to the handle of its door!

But he didn't turn it, didn't jerk it toward him. Using it as a lever, spurning the running-board with a foot-touch feather light, he leaped upward, vaulted the low half-door. Anne heard the impact of hard heels on human flesh, the sharper impact of fisted bone on fleshy bone—heard the soughing grunt of breath from lungs whose ribs had been driven in upon them!

The heaving mass in the car's seat disintegrated and a head pushed up above the windshield—a blunt-jawed head cocked sidewise with the arrogant swagger of a bantam about to crow his victory to the rising sun.

The girl didn't know she had moved till her foot was on the running-board he had spurned, her hand on the door-handle he had not twisted.

"Peter," she panted. "Oh, Peter!"

"Get in here and get the motor started while I get rid of this."

His command was brusque, low-toned. He lurched out of the other side, lugging a limp, flaccid bundle out of it. Anne slid under the wheel, keyed the ignition, stepped on the starter. The motor whirled as Peter passed around in front of the car and deposited his burden on the sidewalk. Then he was seated alongside of her and they were leaping away from the curb.

"Left at the next corner," he muttered. "Step on it. Right at the next."

She obeyed, was glad to obey. Was glad to surrender herself to his guidance.

"Peter," she said. "How did you get away? I thought you were killed!"

"Straight ahead for three blocks and then right again. Ikey Feinstein, the watchmaker in Bolton, is a fence. Take an old watch into him, its hands set at ten minutes past nine. He'll ask you where you bought it. Answer 'across the river.' He'll take you into his backroom and offer you about a quarter what the ruby's worth. Tell him the Owl says he's to give you double whatever it is, and he'll give it to you. Understand?"

"Yes."

They were twisting through narrow, tortuous streets now, the drab slums of Laneville. Anne felt as if she were dropping into a bottomless dark chasm. Peter was a crook! He couldn't know what he had just told her if he weren't a crook. He couldn't have known of the contemplated hold-up yesterday if he weren't one of the gang. She was a crook too, but—

"Right. Quick, girl! *Right.*"

She fought the wheel, slewing to the right. The car rocked off the street, was running down a lightless gully. It was a trough between a high railroad embankment on one side and the blind backs of warehouses on the other. She had to keep all her attention on driving, without lights as they were, or the bucking roadster would overturn.

"Just ahead the embankment is cut by a little bridge that makes a tunnel through which a brook flows. Watch for it and turn sharp left when you reach it. Duck. Your wheels will straddle the brook and you've got just enough head-room to get through. On the other side is a dirt road that will bring you into the Lane Hill woods. Run the roadster into the thicket. Leave it there and go downhill to The Tavern. You'll find the car in the cave where you hide it as soon as it's safe to take it there."

"Peter! You're not—"

"Left! *Left and duck,* DUCK!"

Anne dodged down, steering blindly through the pitch-darkness. When she came up again the seat beside her was empty. But the road was empty, too, that took her to where she could reach home in safety.

FAITH PARKER was kneading dough. The morning sun was unmerciful to the deep-graven lines of her sere skin. Her tiny eyes were red-rimmed, troubled, as they glanced at the door into the bedroom. She was alone. It was too early yet for the kitchen force to have turned up and Anne was still asleep.

"Faith!"

Anne wasn't asleep. She was coming out of that door, crisply slender in an earth-brown tailored suit, a brown felt hat pulled down over her tawny curls.

"Has the *Courier* come yet?"

"There."

The old woman jerked her head to the newspaper, on the table. Anne dropped a tiny package into her pocketbook, thrust it under her arm, snatched up the sheet. She scanned the headlines with feverish anxiety, the black headlines screaming the theft at the Brooks' masquerade. One in smaller type leaped out at her. POLICE OFFICIALS ASSERT ARREST OF ROBBER NEAR. Breath sighed from between her white lips. They hadn't caught him.

"Is the hunting season open yet?" Faith asked, spooning a blob of butter into her dough.

Anne looked up, her silken brow knitting. "Of course not. Why?"

"There's men in the Lane Hill woods with guns. They're all around here."

"Men. With guns."

"They looked like they didn't want to be seen. They looked like they're hidin' in there, waitin' for somethin' to happen."

Anne Marsh was rigid. The paper dropped from her nerveless fingers, the pocketbook slipped from under her arm, thumped on the floor. Sound of an opening door came from outside. The thud of ponderous footfalls. Anne bent to pick up her bag, found that Faith had forestalled her. The old woman handed the purse to her. Anne whirled to a toneless voice.

"Going somewhere?" Bulldog Ryan asked heavily. "Kinda early to be going out."

"I'm going marketing. Why? What's that to you?" Anne said steadily.

"I got a way of being curious, that's all." Ryan lurched forward. Before Anne could move, her pocketbook was in his grasp. "About what's in this, for instance."

He was fending her off with a pointed elbow, was digging into the purse. A handkerchief came out, a compact and lipstick. Coins. A market list.

And nothing else. Nothing else at all.

Faith turned her cake-dough into a round, tin pan, stepped to the range and opened the oven-door. She held her gnarled, fleshless hand within the black opening, closed the door again.

"What's the meaning of that?" Anne was white-faced.

"Nothing." Ryan threw the bag on the table where the newspaper had been, "I said I was just curious,"

The girl was bewildered. The ruby had been in there. She had just put it in there. What had become of it? But she managed a show of indignation.

"Maybe you'd like to search me too."

"Sure I'd like to. Matter of fact I got a matron out there in the car could do it. But I ain't got no right."

"Call her in. I'll give you the right."

Ryan turned, whistled. The woman who pounded in was clad in police blue, and except for the fact that her uniform was skirted and that her straggly, dirty-brown hair was twisted into a bun she might have been a patrolman as far as her appearance went. She went into the bedroom with Anne. After awhile the two came out again.

"Nothin' doin', Ryan," the policewoman croaked. "She's clean."

Faith was satisfied with the oven's heat at last, was sliding her panned dough into it.

"Next thing he'll be wantin' to tear the place apart," she sniffed, addressing no one in particular.

"No," the human bulldog grunted. "I ain't got no search-warrant and I wouldn't find nothing anyways. Then you'd be putting up a holler about police persecution and I'd draw a week's fine. I'll wait, I'm good at waiting. Come on, Maggie. We got important business. There's a lush roller been reported workin' the bus station."

They were gone. The slam of the door behind him whirled Faith around to the oven. She had the pan out, on the kneading board. She was digging into the hot dough with furious haste.

"Faith! What aye you doing?"

"Looking for this. Somebody might broke his teeth on it," She held a dough-encrusted little package out to Anne. "Like that fox-faced cop just broke his'n."

FROM THE Laneville *Courier,* dated a week after the events just related:

MYSTERIOUS DONATION

The Orphanage of the Sheltering Heart, 262 Elm Street, was the beneficiary of an unorthodox contribution this morning. It took the form of a paper parcel left some time last night in the cradle maintained in the vestibule of the institution for the unobserved abandonment of unwanted infants. When Super-intendent Veronica McGorty opened the parcel she found it to contain six thousand dollars in grimy bills of small denomination.

Police Detective Thomas W. Ryan evinced unusual interest in the donation, but was forced to admit there was no way of tracing it. Peculiarly enough, six thousand dollars is exactly the sum allocated to the Orphanage from the Community Chest funds embezzled by Webster Marsh.

BANDIT GIRL

ANNE MARSH, GIRL ROBIN
HOOD TO THE DOOMED AND
DISINHERITED, STAKES MORE
THAN HER OWN LIFE AND
FREEDOM IN THIS, HER MOST
BREATHLESSLY DARING VENTURE.
FOR THE MYSTERIOUS UNKNOWN
AIDE, WHO HAS SNARED HER
HEART, TAKES RISK FOR RISK
WITH HER—WHILE SHE, ALL
UNKNOWING, LEADS HIM ON INTO
DEADLY JEOPARDY!

LANE HILL was cool and quiet, fragrant with the spring splendor of azaleas bordering the long gash Bolton Turnpike made through its hushed woods. Anne Marsh, trim and slender and boyish in jacket and slacks of earth-brown corduroy, tossed back her cropped, tawny hair and breathed deep of the forest's winy tang.

The arboreal peace soothed the restlessness that had driven Anne to the long climb from where The Tavern nestled this side the bridge across Waley's Creek. From here the trees screened Laneville, the city that once had revered Webster Marsh and now execrated his memory. Here she could forget that she was a daughter of dishonor, her father dead by his own hand. She could forget that she was a secret thief, stealing from those whose machinations had caused that suicide, and restoring to Laneville's poor the charity funds of which they had been robbed by a smug, respected band of swindlers within the law. Here there was only the green, earthy woodland redolence, the mating songs of robins, the....

Anne twisted to a sudden, furtive threshing in the underbrush sloping down to her! It ceased almost as it began, but the girl stared fearfully into the leafy gloom, and into the grey depths of her eyes crept once more the

The farmer lad grabbed
the money bag.

outlaw's haunted, omnipresent dread of discovery and capture.

She could see nothing in the dank shadows to which the sun's rays could not penetrate. But she prickled with the eerie sensation of an unseen, inimical gaze upon her; and

the white hand pressed to her breast felt the frightened flutter of her heart, like that of a netted bird.

Reason fought with panic. That sound meant nothing, it insisted. A partridge leaping from its covert had made it, or a rabbit startled from its lair…. Even if it were Bulldog Ryan, the detective whose plodding, heavy persistence had more than once threatened her secret with exposure, her aimless stroll could not betray her to him. Let him watch her, if he wished, with his lashless, pale eyes.

But the woodland peace was shattered, Anne's hard-won moment of tranquillity ended. She turned, drearily, to return to the roadside restaurant that with aged, loyal Faith Parker, she had opened as a means of livelihood after Webster Marsh's creditors had taken her heritage. As a means of livelihood—and a mask for other, stealthier pursuits. Tonight, perhaps, she would trap another of her secret enemies in the snare that had already taken two of them.

To her left the hill dropped sheer from the road's curve. A patch in the highway fence was glaringly new. Anne halted. There, just there, she had seen a car hurtle through to destruction among the trees below, snow-whitened then. Its rusted corpse was still down there....

ABRUPTLY THE girl knew what it was that had drawn her here. This was where *he* had first come to her, the youth she knew only as "Peter." Here he had rescued her from the thugs who had met with death below, and then had fled from the siren of the police, leaving only the memory of a heart-shaped scar at the corner of a mouth gone suddenly bleak, and of a kiss that had burned, white flame, on her lips. Thrice, since then, when her need was greatest he had appeared to save her, and had vanished mysteriously as he had come. Lithe, and insouciant, and rapierlike in the quick flash of his movements, she knew of him only that his life, too, was outside the law—and that she could not get him out of her mind.

For months now a gang of bandits had been harassing Bolton Turnpike, striking swiftly, disappearing as swiftly. It was suspected that their hideout was somewhere in these woods, in one of the labyrinthine caves, perhaps, that honeycombed Lane Hill and made successful search impossible.... Was Peter one of them? *Was it he who had made that sound in the underbrush?*

Longing for him was again a slow fever in Anne's heart. "Peter!" She murmured his name as she peered into the rustling shadows whence she had heard that momentary threshing. "Peter!"

No answer came from the lush, vivid greenery, but increasingly the feeling pressed on the girl that someone was there. That someone was watching her.... On the road's dirt shoulder she glimpsed a single, blurred footprint, its toe pointing into the woods.

Anne parted the pink and white glory of the azaleas' screen. The footprint was repeated in the black loam beyond, twice. A toadstool was crushed into one of the marks, its wan color not yet tainted with the swift darkening of fungoid death. A vague path climbed deeper into the forest and the girl followed it, forgetting her fears, forgetting everything but the yearning that impelled her.

She must see him, talk to him. Words were forming in her mind. "Peter!" she would say, "You mustn't let the fact that you are a thief keep us apart. You know that I, too, am...." Something hard jabbed info her spine! A scream twisted Anne's throat, was muffled at her lips by a harsh palm that slapped bruisingly across them from behind!

"One yip out of yuh," a coarse voice growled, "an' I'll let yuh have it. It's a gat that's pokin' inter yuh."

Terror shot through the girl, and then was gone, leaving her icy, controlled. Her arms lifted above her head, signaling surrender. In her absence Ryan must have uncovered the concealed exit from The Tavern that furnished her with the alibis that had baffled him. Certain of his suspicions at last, he had followed and captured her. The game was up....

"Smart kid," the voice approved. "Keep on goin', straight ahead. An' don't try any tricks, I'd just as lief blast yuh as not."

ANNE SAID "all right," against the leathery, muffling palm, and it rasped away. She pushed through swishing tendrils into dank, fetid murk. Ponderous footfalls thudded close behind her, and she was afraid; horribly afraid. Ryan would not have ordered her further into the forest. He would have clicked manacles on her wrists and taken her down the road to the county jail. Her captor wasn't the detective. Who was he then? Who was he and where was he taking her?

A vertical wall confronted her, a high, vine-covered cliff. She halted, perforce, felt the gun pound again into her back.

"Go on," the gruff voice grunted.

"But—but I can't climb that. I...."

"I didn't say climb," the man chuckled hoarsely. "Go straight. T'rough them leaves."

Through...! Anne took a step forward, another. She *was* through the luxuriant vines, but there was no rocky precipice behind them. There was only impenetrable darkness, and a chill damp current of air, and a faint odor of wood smoke. She had entered a tunnel into the hill, its mouth screened by greenery that cut her off from the world....

"Stop!" The weapon was against her side. "Stop a minute." She sensed her captor pressing close against her. His hand was on her, was stroking the slim curves of her shrinking body, swiftly purposefully. Almost before she could recoil from that touch it was ended. "I guess yuh're clean. Get movin'."

He had only been frisking her for a weapon. But there was a new note in his voice, leering, lip-licking. It was not through any sense of decency that his search had ended so quickly.

Anne stumbled on the rough, uneven rock underfoot. Wet dripped on her forehead from the unseen roof, and the aroma of burning wood was steadily stronger. The man was right behind her, she couldn't get past him, and she could not see what was ahead. The tunnel floor pitched sharply downward.

"Turn ter th' right, keep turnin'."

The girl obeyed. The darkness reddened, glowed with flickering light. Her vision cleared and she saw that the light came from a small fire ahead. The passage widened, became a cave. A man was silhouetted against the fire. He whipped around.

"What the…!" His hand flashed under his coat, and magically there was an automatic in it, snouting at her.

"Hold it, Mike," the man behind her said. "I got her covered."

"You got—" Mike checked. His heavy featured, brutish face was suddenly a grim, furious mask. "Damn you, Stiffy. I told you I wasn't goin' to stand for you're foolin' with the dames. I…."

"Wait. Wait up. I wasn't foolin' none with this one. I picked her up in th' woods. She'd piked the path leadin' here an'—"

"Whyn't you conk her then?" The fire made Mike's shadow gigantic, seeming to fill the cave with it. "What'd you bring her in here for?" Anne made out boxes of food-stuffs piled against a wall, on the other side a tumbled mass that might be blankets. Between them another opening in the wall was vague in the shadow.

STIFFY'S FEET shuffled, behind her. "Well, she's a sweet piece of fluff an' I t'ought mebbe she'd listen t' reason. I t'ought mebbe...."

"You thought! With what? Listen you dope. The pickin's around here are too damn good for us to be takin' chances on any double-crossin' janes. This skirt's mouth's getting plugged with lead, right now." Mike's automatic lifted, the end of its muzzle a black eye of death staring at Anne.

"Just a minute." Somehow she was able to speak, calmly, steadily. "Has it occurred to you, Mr. Mike, that I am known to have climbed Lane Hill, and that if I do not return, a search for me will uncover your hiding place?"

The man hesitated. "Yuh see," Stiffy whined. "She's a smartie. She's an all-right moll an'...."

"No moll's all right. Maybe we'll have to scram, but she won't know about it." Mike's eyes narrowed, were tight slits through which gleamed the lust to kill. Into the brittle silence Anne knew was her last instant of life the burr of a distant auto motor came faintly, cut off.

"Wait, Mike!" Stiffy tried again. "Joe's got a right ter say what's what."

"The hell with Joe. If he sticks his two cents in this, I'll...."

"You'll what?" The quiet voice was somehow challenging. "What's this that I'm to keep my two cents out of?" The speaker was only a blacker shadow at the second entrance to the cave, but Anne's wrists throbbed with a sudden pulse.

Mike's lips pulled away from his teeth in a snarl, but as he turned he was cringing. "I didn't mean nothin' by that, Joe. It's just that this blasted goat, Stiffy, 's got me wingin' with this stunt he's pulled. Dat guy's skirt-crazy, an'...."

"And you're gun-goofy." Mike's simian frame no longer blocked the firelight. It reached the newcomer, illuminating his poised, lithe body; the clean, blunt line of his jaw; his firm mouth. Anne choked a cry of gladness....

The left corner of that mouth was puckered by a tiny, heart-shaped scar! Her peril was past. This was Peter. Once more he had mysteriously appeared to save her from apparently inescapable danger.

"Waddaye mean, gun-goofy?"

"The gat's all you can think about. I heard enough coming up the passage to know what the argument is. I agree with you that we can't take chances on keeping the girl here...."

"I'll keep mum about all this," Anne put in, anticipating what Peter was driving at. "You can trust me...."

"But there's another way of making sure of her silence," he went on, not looking at her. "A way that won't have the cops tearing this hill apart looking for her or for the one who put a bullet in her."

"The hell you say! Leave her alive and she'll talk."

"Yes." The monosyllable impacted on Anne's unbelieving ears. "But if her lead's bashed in by one of the falling stones the spring freshets have loosened from the face of the cliffs around here...."

Mike's chortle drowned the girl's moaned, "Peter!" She twisted to run. Hands clamped on her waist, her shoulders, flung her back into the cave.

CHAPTER TWO
BETRAYAL!

ANNE MARSH sprawled on the rocky floor, oblivious to the bruising shock of her fall because of the greater pain that twisted in her brain. Peter's face hung above her in the fire's lurid glare, a set, impassive mask. He wasn't looking at her. He had neither looked at her nor spoken to her since the moment he had entered. She was to him only a threat to his safety, to be disposed of as best he could devise.

"You're a smartie, Joe," Mike exclaimed. "One of them rocks near conked me yesterday just as I wuz goin', outta the upper tunnel."

"Exactly... Mike, I didn't take time to hide the car properly hearing the noise in here. You go down and fix that while Stiffy and I take care of her."

"Gees, you dope! Someone might see it...." Mike lurched past him into blackness. Peter jerked a hand at the girl.

"Pick her up and let's get moving," he ordered Stiffy. "We'll get this over with quick."

Anne's limbs were water-weak, so that Stiffy's cruel grip on her wrists, forcing them up behind her back till her shoulder sinews screamed with agony, was the only thing that held her erect. The trio stumbled out into the passage through which she had been brought, fumbled up the climb and around the curve. Ahead, the exit was a dimly green, jagged-edged arch.

"Hold her here a minute," Peter murmured. "While I go out and make sure the coast's clear. Come ahead when I whistle."

His slender form was silhouetted momentarily against the greenness. Leaves rustled and it was gone. Anne gulped the lump in her throat. "Listen," she whispered, "if you help get me out of this, I'll pay you a hundred dollars."

"Cripes!" Stiffy's hold tightened convulsively. "I can't. He'd skin me alive. He's a hellcat...."

A whistle, like the chirp of a wren, stopped him. "Here we go," the man grunted, and shoved Anne forward. The vines brushed her face. A fist lashed out, from the side, and something hard thudded on bone, behind her. Her arms were free. A heavy body pounded on earth. The girl twisted about, uncomprehending.

Stiffy was a flaccid heap on the ground, just outside the tunnel entrance. Peter was bending over him, was placing a fist-sized stone alongside the thug's bruised head. The youth straightened, his face alight with a twisted grin.

"My story is the rock fell and hit him as he came out," he snapped. "You broke away before I knew what was happening. I didn't dare shoot and I couldn't catch you...."

"Peter," Anne whimpered. "Oh, Peter." Her hands went out to him. "And I thought...."

"No time for that." He shoved her through the vines. "Run! That way, along the base of the cliff." He broke away from her, and, venting a single, hoarse shout, went threshing noisily through the underbrush, toward the highway. There was nothing for Anne to do but dart, silently as she could manage, in the direction he had indicated. Mike's shout answered Peter's from far below and the threshing redoubled. But the girl was angling safely away from the false pursuit.

When, after a wide detour, Anne finally reached the highway again only yards above The Tavern, there was fierce pain behind her shoulders, and a dull ache along her side where it had pounded down against hard rock. But she smiled happily, and her eyes shone with a radiance bright as the glint of the spring sunlight on the waters of Waley's Creek.

THE TAVERN on Bolton Turnpike was a place of whispers. At one flower-decked table nestling in the dim-lit privacy of a decorous booth a pair of lovers murmured endearments. At others a wife launched low-toned, barbed comments on her badgered husband's shortcomings, and a trio of heavy-jowled, paunchy business men plotted the discomfiture of a competitor. Soft-footed, deft waitresses quietly served Faith Parker's ambrosial food and flitted unobtrusively away.

The Tavern was a place of whispers. Anne Marsh, wist-ful-eyed, withdrawn, sat at her desk between kitchen and dining room and listened to those whispers, whose incaution the very atmosphere of the room was cunningly devised to encourage.

The space between Anne and even the nearest niche was too great for any normal ear to eavesdrop on the conversation there. It was from beneath the flat top of her work table that the whispers came. Inaudible except to her guarded listening, a speaker repeated what microphones hidden in each booth picked up. Concealed in the artful decorations, silvered glass mirrored for the girl the apparent privacy of each small cubicle. Faintly smiling, seemingly intent only on checking trays and making change, Anne Marsh spied endlessly on her unsuspecting patrons.

"… Don Reynolds in the club today," the speaker whispered. "He cringed like a whipped puppy when I looked at my watch and remarked it was time to go home for dinner. That wife of his isn't through nagging him yet about the way her ruby was stolen from him at the Brooks' masquerade."

The merest hint of a smile touched Anne's pale lips. Reynolds was on the list of her father's betrayers, and what a fence had paid her for the ruby in question had made up to the Orphanage of the Sheltering Heart the allotment it had lost from the Community Chest Webster Marsh was accused of embezzling. John Lawton, a fussy little merchant with a pointed, black vandyke and watery eyes, was also on that list. But there had been nothing in his talk tonight that she could use.

"It was cleverly done, chief." Lawton's companion, a tall, pince-nezed old-young man, responded. "The police haven't been able to find a single clue. I'm afraid we are none of us safe while that crook's loose."

"Nonsense!" The word was a blustering explosion. "It was Reynolds' own carelessness that victimized him. I'd like to see any criminal try to put one over on me… Here waitress," Lawton made an imperious gesture. "My check."

Anne's hand dropped surreptitiously into the kneehole of her desk and the whispers stopped. Her eyes narrowed. Lawton owned the big department store on Laneville's Station Plaza. Single-handed she could not hope to raid its bulky stock, but somehow he must be vulnerable. That very Napoleonic complex of his… look at the way he was strutting out past the lined booths, his short legs stiff with dignity, his chest out-thrust with pouter-pigeon dignity.

Lawton's sycophant checked, beside the last cubicle. His thin lips quirked briefly in a frosty smile to someone within it. Then he was out after his demigod.

ANNE FLIPPED her switch to tap that booth. "He saw you, Dick," a girl's voice quavered. "He'll tell Lawton and...."

"And what?" The youth with her could not quite conceal the quiver of worry underlying his attempted braggadoccio. "Even if the boss happens to eat in the same place, a fellow's got a right to celebrate a promotion hasn't he?"

"A promotion!" Her hand went out to him across the table. "Oh Dick!" Her frock was cheap, sleazy, her face pinched and pallid and tired, but her eyes shone. "Why didn't you tell me?"

"I was saving it till I took you home." He was blonde-haired, gawky in a shiny blue suit that fit him none too well. "Thought maybe you'd give me an extra kiss."

"What is it? What did they make you?"

"I've got old Forbes' job. Assistant to the cashier."

"Assistant... But Pop Forbes has had that job twenty years."

"That's just it. He was too old for it, with all the stickups that's happening around. You know the cashier's assistant takes the receipts to the bank after closing, don't you, Jen? Runs to six or seven grand, Dollar Day Thursdays, like tomorrow. A doddering old codger like him would be easy pickin's...."

"Dick!" There was consternation, a pulse of fear, in Jen's voice. "That's dangerous! I wish they hadn't...."

"Gee! Ain't that just like a woman! Instead of being glad...."

"But you might get hurt. I'd die if you got hurt."

"Hon!" The boy's tones were tender, thrilled. "Do you really go for me that way?"

"You know I do. Dick! Tell 'em you don't want that job. Tell 'em…."

"Aw now listen, Jen. Don't be like that. D'you want 'em to call me yellow? And besides, there ain't really nothing to be afraid of. Looka, Jen." Dick hitched forward, picked up a fork. "The boss has got a new routine worked out and it can't be beat. We rehearsed it and it's timed like clock-work. Here's the store," the fork impressed a line on the table cloth, "facing the depot across the Plaza. Next block, also facing west, is the Strand Movie. Then Apple Street comes through here to make the south side of the square. Along it there's the five-and-ten, the Berall's grocery, and here, at the southwest corner of Main Street and the Plaza, is the Bank. See?"

"Yeah." The two heads were close together, black hair inter-mingled with blonde. "I know all that."

"Now here, in the center of the Plaza, is the police booth, with two cops on duty. Tim Mara, the store detective, is going to be standing in the door of the store when I come out with the money bag chained to my wrist, right at six o'clock. The traffic light goes red, stopping everything. In front of the Bank their guard will be standing, and Mara and the guard and the cops will all have their gats out. I walk diagonally across the square, with all four men watching me every second of the time, and watching that no car moves and no one comes near me. In exactly one minute I'm across. A teller opens the bank door and it's all over."

"You'll—you'll be all alone."

"Sure I will. That's the honey part of the idea. If I had a bodyguard with me the two of us might be shot down, like those bank messengers in Bolton. This way I'm in full view of the guys protecting me all the time I'm in the open, and yet they're so far away from me that a gang would have to shoot up pretty near the whole town to cop the swag and get away with it. The scheme's fool-proof. No one's going to even make a try."

"Oh, I hope not. I hope not. But I'm afraid...."

"I tell you there isn't any danger. And even if there was a little, it's worth the chance. Jen.... I'm getting five dollars a week more. It's all going in a savings account, under the names of Richard Swayne *and* Jennie Galant. When that account's five hundred dollars...."

"When!" The girl's mouth twisted, bitterly. "Two years, Dick. In two years I think my feet will have dropped off, standing behind that glove counter...."

"Standing! There's a chair there...."

"Yeah. The law says there must be. But just let Lawton catch you using it.... I'm tired thinkin' about it, hon. Let's go home."

ANNE MARSH clicked off the switch. A pert waitress slapped a check, a greenback, down on the desk. The tawny-haired girl made change mechanically. Laneville's Station Plaza was a chessboard on the screen of her mind, and she was shifting pawns about on it. She knew every nook and corner of the environs. Somewhere in John Lawton's strategy there must be a weak point....

Her throat tightened, was suddenly dry. Glancing up, by habit, into one of the spying mirrors, she had met eyes, peering at her out of it; lashless, colorless eyes set in a sharp-featured, ferret-like countenance whose mouth was a thin, straight, cruel gash over a pointed chin. Bulldog Ryan had discovered that he could watch her in the glass she had set to watch others!

She hadn't seen him enter, but he might have slipped in with one of the chattering groups that had jammed the door at the height of the evening's business. He couldn't have seen anything to betray her, she assured herself. Nothing—except the reflector itself. Would he realize that if he could see her in it, she also could see him? That there were other mirrors set so that she could overlook every booth? Even if he did, would it mean anything to him? He was so shrewd....

The eyes fell away. She was needlessly alarmed. Perhaps he had not even noticed the mirror.... But the very fact of his being here was ominous. He was still hounding her, waiting implacably for the inevitable misstep that would deliver her into his hands.... His hand was fumbling under the tablecloth, under the table...!

A tight band constricted Anne's brow. The wires to the microphones were ordinarily concealed beyond risk of accidental discovery, but she had been working on a short this afternoon, had not had time properly to replace the filaments. Was it that table?... She could not remember! She could not....

CHAPTER THREE
CAMOUFLAGE!

ANNE MARSH thumbed a button on the desk-top. The kitchen door swung open and Faith Parker was at her side, white-aproned, bird-like eyes inquiring in her seamed, leathery face.

"Faith," Anne whispered. "Ryan's in number twelve booth and I've got to get him out of there right away."

The heat-reddened countenance did not change expression. "Number twelve? That's Hazel's. She's just getting his dessert. Coffee an' bread-pudding." She was gone, and at once was out again, a loaded tray in her gnarled, fleshless hand. As she reached the detective's cubicle his spatulate fingers were innocently toying with his cutlery.

Anne tapped her listening device into number twelve booth. "I brung this puddin' myself," Faith's querulous, thin voice said. " 'Cause it's a new recipe I'm tryin' an' you're the first one as has ordered it. Taste it an' tell me how you like it."

"Yeah?" Ryan grunted. "Didn't know there could be anything new about bread pudding." The old woman put a dish of creamy-yellow, shimmering meringue before him. "But it sure looks good." He picked up a spoon....

And somehow his arm collided with faith's hand, jolting the coffee-cup out of it! The black, steaming liquid cascaded over the table, over the detective.

"Woosh!" Ryan bellowed, leaping from his seat. "You clumsy old fool!" He grabbed his napkin, mopped frantically at the mess on his suit. "You damn near scalded me." His dancing rage was ludicrous.

Anne darted from her desk, choking back the hysterical laugh that bubbled in her throat. "O Gawd!" Faith Parker jabbered. "I don't know how I come to do that." Flutteringly she dabbed at the detective with her apron, hindering rather than helping him—and jostling him into the aisle. "I'm gettin' too old an' that's a fact."

"Oh Faith!" Anne panted, coming up. "How could you?... I'm terribly sorry Mr. Ryan. How can I apologize?"

"Look at this," Ryan yammered. "This is a brand new suit. I've only worn it three months. I...."

"We'll gladly pay for the cleaning. And won't you sit down over here and finish your supper. Faith, go fetch...."

"Hell with that," the policeman broke in. "I've got to get out of these clothes. Gimme my check an'...."

"There isn't any check, Mr. Ryan. There never is, for members of the force. And please don't forget to send me a bill for cleaning the suit."

Bulldog Ryan's countenance was suddenly bleak, his pallid eyes slitted, icy. "You'll get the bill all right," he muttered tunelessly. "For that an' for a couple other things that ain't settled between us yet. I'm good at collectin'. His gaze held Anne's and the chill in it was repeated in a ripple of queasy dread along her spine. "Yeah. I'm goin' now. But I'll be comin' back."

AIN'T YOU goin' to bed, Miss Anne?"

The girl turned from the barred window of the lean-to which housed the bedroom of The Tavern's owners. "No." Her grey eyes fastened broodingly on Faith Parker, scrawny and grotesque in a long flannel nightgown buttoned to her' leathery neck. "No sleep for me tonight."

"Miss Anne!" There was protest in the old woman's cracked tones. "You've got to stop these things you're doing. That man is bound to catch you.... I seen the woman's prison at Weatherby once. It was—it was...." A shudder completed her meaning.

"I've seen that prison too, Faith." The girl's voice was flat, intonationless. "But I've seen other things. The hovels in Slum Hollow. Where not only women and men but little children exist in filth and degradation worse than Weatherby ever knew. Starving little children, Faith, hungry for food and a chance to make something of themselves. And I've seen the mansions on East Drive, where the John Lawtons of Laneville eat cake and drink wine purchased with stolen money that was meant to buy bread and milk for the children of Slum Hollow. I can't stop." She choked on a sob. "I can't...."

"God help you, my dear." The aged woman clicked off the light to hide the lustre of tears in her own eyes.

"God won't help me," a wistful voice whispered in the dark. "God won't help a thief."

The Tavern on Bolton Highway held more secrets still than hidden microphones and spying mirrors. In the murk of that bedroom whose only apparent exit was a door into the kitchen there was a soft rasp of wood on wood. A narrow band of blacker black showed on the unlighted floor. It widened. An earthy odor breathed into the room. Light footfalls tapped stealthily, as if on a ladder. The floor was unbroken once more, and Faith Parker stared aching-eyed into otherwise untenanted darkness.

An unshaded bulb filled with garish light a windowless, subterranean chamber. Anne Marsh stepped down off the ladder, went across to a time-darkened workbench that bulked large at the room's center.

The girl's hands were deft, purposeful, clearing the bench's scarred top of its litter of tools, wood-shavings, wire-coils and bits of twisted metal. She was alone, but it seemed to her that another presence was beside her. She could almost see him, the kindly-eyed, grey-haired man who had taught her all she knew of manual craft, the man whose obituary the Laneville Courier had ended with words that still seared her memory. "As long as the naked are unclothed," they ran, "and the hungry unfed, the soul of Webster Marsh will have no peace."

"DOLLAR DAY" in Laneville was publicized throughout the surrounding farmland, and this Thursday, as usual, the Station Plaza was crowded with gawky, weather-beaten tillers of the soil and their faded women-folk. Paper pennants fluttered from long strings, making gay the drab facades of the store-buildings hemming in the square, and covering the three-story front of Lawton's Department store was a huge banner, emblazoned with a gigantic dollar sign.

The hands of the big clock over the entrance to the depot that closed in the west side of the square pointed to a quarter of six, and the excitement seemed to rise to fever heat. Lawton's invariably shut promptly on the hour, and then there would be no more bargains till next week....

A mud-spattered, rattletrap flivver racketed out of Main Street, shuddered to a stop at the north end of the railroad station. The palsy of its antique motor still shook it as the driver, a capped youth in denim jacket and overalls too big for his slight form, climbed out. He gaped open-mouthed around at the bustle, his features indistinguishable under a thick coat of road dust.

"Why don't yuh shut 'er off, bub?" one of the omnipresent loungers holding up the depot's front called. "Yuh're usin' up a lot of gas."

"Take me half 'n hour ter get her started agin," the farm lad answered. "An' I got ter get back hum quick ter milk th' caows. Ain't goin' ter be more 'n a minute anyhow. Jest gettin' some vittles over ter Berall's grocery." As if reminded of his mission he hurried away. The watchers saw him reach the other end of the station and scuttle across Main Street's traffic. Disappointed in their hope of another manifestation of bucolic ineptitude, they settled back to ogling giggling rustic maidens.

The boy from the country ambled past Simpson's Bank, gawked at the alley between the grocery and the scarlet windowed five-and-ten. Went into the bustling interior of Berall's.

The station clock moved inexorably on toward six. The Bank's bronzed portals opened briefly to emit a broad-shouldered, swart-jawed man in the grey of a special patrolman. He halted at the top of the three white steps. His hands rested lightly on the butt of the revolver holstered at his waist, and his brows knitted as he looked diagonally across at Lawton's.

A blue-clad city cop stood in front of a white-painted, octagonal booth in the center of the Plaza. He had his watch in one hand and the fingers of the other hovered near his cartridge belt. Within the little shack another policeman was poised at the lever that would cut out the automatic relay governing the flashing green and red of the traffic lights. A flip of a nearby switch would hold them all on red.

"That damn tin can's gettin' on my nerves," the busybody loafer muttered, "rattlin' like all hell. Ef it wuzn't too much trouble I'd shut off its damn ignition."

ABOVE HIM the clock burred, its striking machinery getting set to proclaim the hour. There was a bustle within the department store's entrance. A burly individual in civilians pushed out, cleared a space in front of it.

"*Bong!*" Six o'clock! As if struck with sudden paralysis by that deep-throated gong, all traffic in the plaza halted. "*Bong!*" Both policemen were in front of their booth now, their arms oddly prolonged by black, snouting revolvers. The bank guard tensed. The man in front of Lawton's had his gun out too as a blonde-haired youth pushed past him. "*Bong!*" Dick Swayne swaggered a bit, stepping off the sidewalk and angling between the halted lines of cars toward Simpson's. He was keenly conscious of the brown leather bag that was clenched in his right hand and fastened by a glittering steel chain to the manacle on his wrist.

"*Bong.*" Except for the clock gong, a curious hush had descended on Station Plaza. Even the pedestrians were stopped in their strides, were watching the one moving figure go past the police-booth, continue on. The silence was somehow brittle, expectant.

"*Bong.*" The farm lad pushed out of Berall's, bent beneath a fifty-pound sack of flour slung across his shoulder. He staggered along the sidewalk, suddenly realized what was going on and stopped stockstill, right in front of the bank steps.

"*Bong!*" Dick Swayne's heel hit the curb....

A sharp detonation was startlingly loud from the Plaza's far corner! A battered flivver there was wreathed in flames, was vomiting great billows of black smoke.

"Bomb!" someone shouted, and the policemen whirled to the sudden commotion, their guns snouting up.

The farmer lad's sack lurched down from his shoulder. Steel glinted momentarily. There was the sound of ripping cloth. The bag hit the sidewalk at Swayne's feet, exploded in a vast cloud of whiteness that blotted him and the overalled lad from sight. The Bank guard, plunging down off his steps, was choked, blinded, by a handful of flour flung into his face out of the seething fog. Gasping, spluttering, he heard footsteps patter past him.

Police whistles, shouts, the wailing of a siren made pandemonium. Suddenly a shrill, ear-piercing scream knifed through the tumult.

"The money. The bag's cut open. *The money's gone. It's gone!*"

CHAPTER SIX
DISASTER!

THE PLAZA was a veritable inferno of chaos, but Anne Marsh was momentarily alone far back in the narrow, debris-strewn alley between the grocery store and the five-and-ten-cent emporium. She ripped off the flour-blanched denim jeans, buried them deep in a case of rubbish with the cap that had protected her hair and the keen knife that had sliced open John Lawton's money-bag. From out of the same cache she pulled a damp rag which served to clean her face and hands of the dirt that disguised them and the flour that covered it. She made a quick dab at her shoes with the rag, threw it away.

The pocket under her skirt into which she had thrust her loot yielded a rolled-up hat of soft felt that expanded to jauntily crown her tawny curls. A small handbag came out of that hidden repository, furnished her with a vanity for the refurbishing of her lips and cheeks.

She was no longer a gawky rustic. She was a gray-suited, insouciant girl, flecks of secret mirth glinting in the depths of grey, innocent-seeming eyes. The metamorphosis had taken only an instant, a twinkle of time. If Lawton had rehearsed his scheme to safeguard his wealth, she too had rehearsed, many times, her own plot to confound him.

The brick wall of the alley-side was broken by the side-door through which the variety shop got rid of the debris Anne had utilized as a hiding-place and dressing room. The girl listened at the paint-peeled panel for a moment, smiled, manipulated a skeleton key in its lock. It opened.

She slid through into a cluttered backroom, went out, unhesitatingly, into the store proper.

Clerks, customers, were a close-packed crowd at the front of the long store, peering through its windows at the milling Plaza, struggling to get through the narrow door to take part in the excitement. The addition of one more to their numbers was utterly unnoticed. Once more a smile of covert satisfaction touched Anne's lips. The man she had robbed had set her an example of exact timing, of the utilization of crowd psychology. The little Napoleon himself had taught her how to defeat him.

She managed to worm out on the sidewalk. The Dollar Day crowd was closing in on Swayne and the guard, flour-covered and coughing, but otherwise none the worse for their experience. At the far corner of the depot the decrepit car was a blackened, smoldering wreck, its momentary blaze burned out... John Lawton, hatless, wild-eyed, his vandyke the opposite of trim, was running across the Plaza. One of his saleswomen scurried ahead of him, black-haired, pinch-faced.

"Dick!" Jennie Galant was crying. "Dick! Are you all right? Are you...."

A tiny muscle twitched in Anne's cheek and her eyes were thoughtful as she turned away. She would have to do something about those two, but first she must take advantage of the confusion to make good her escape. If she hurried she could catch the six-twenty bus on East Drive.

THE TRAFFIC light was still red where Apple Street came into the Plaza. The halted cars were almost all empty, their occupants gone to make part of the crowd behind her. So much the better, no one would spot her going away....

"Just a minute, Miss Anne Marsh." A stocky, glowering individual popped out, almost magically, from between a truck and a sedan. "What's your rush?"

Bulldog Ryan was planted, straddle-legged, in front of her, his pointed chin thrust almost in her face, his lidless eyes thin, colorless slits.

Anne gasped, got control of herself. "And what business is that of yours?" she said icily. "Seems to me you can do a lot more good back there looking for the robber than…."

"Oh yeah?" The detective interrupted. "So you think I ought to be looking for the stick-up artist. Maybe that's what I'm doing. Maybe I don't have to look any further."

"I don't understand you."

"You get me, all right. You ain't got any alibi for this job, like you had for them others. You can't say you wasn't in the Plaza when it happened."

Anne drew herself up to the fullest extent of her small height, her little nose tilted haughtily. "Of course I was. So were hundreds of other people. Are you going to arrest them all on suspicion?"

"Nope. I ain't even arrestin' you. I'm just askin' you to come to the station-house with me, nice and peaceable, an' let the matron search you. Of course, if you don't, I can pull you in for spittin' on the sidewalk. The commissioner was just raisin' hell with us for not enforcin' the sanitary ordinances."

The girl shrugged. "I take it violators of sanitary ordinances are subjected to the indignity of being searched?"

"An' bein' fingerprinted. An' being listed on the blotter. An' if they resist an officer, that just makes it worse. How about it?"

"All right. I'll go with you." There wasn't anything else for her to do. The bulldog had his teeth in her throat, and he was only aching tor an excuse to sink them. He'd have that excuse, full measure, when the matron found that bundle of banknotes.

"Come along. I got my car right here. An' don't try any tricks. I'm quick on the draw an' I ain't got no superstitions about knockin' a skirt over bein' bad luck."

The green-painted two-seater that had been hidden by the truck maneuvered back and forth across Apple Street to make the turn towards the police station. Behind, another motor roared. Anne glimpsed a closed coupé slithering into motion, its driver tired apparently of waiting for permission to cross the Plaza. Ryan straightened, jerked at his gear lever.

The other car came up fast from behind. The detective grunted an exclamation. Anne and he were thrown forward by a grinding jolt as the coupé smashed into the green car's rear. Two sets of brakes squealed.

"Here's where one crazy driver gets his lumps," Ryan gritted. "But first…."

Almost before Anne knew what was happening a handcuff had clicked on her wrist, the manacle at the other end of its short chain on the rim of the steering wheel. Then the policeman was out on the sidewalk, was pounding stiff-legged back to the car that had rammed him.

The girl twisted, saw him reach the coupé's door, saw him jerk it open. A blackjack flicked out at the end of an arm flailing swift as the strike of a reptile, split Ryan's derby, thudded sickenly on his skull. He went down on the asphalt collapsing like a gutted meal-sack.

A LITHE, slender form leaped out of the coupé. Anne's heart thumped against its caging ribs at sight of a familiar, bantamlike toss of a triumphant head, at sight of a grinning mouth whose left corner was marked by a puckered, heart-shaped scar.

"Peter," she exclaimed as the youth stepped upon the running-board beside her. "I might have known it was you…. But you can't help me this time. Look." She lifted her manacled wrist. "It would take hours to file through this."

Peter's smile vanished. Wrath whitened his face. "The dog," he rasped, his blue eyes bleak, dangerous. "I wish I'd hit harder."

"You didn't kill him then. I'm glad you didn't kill him."

The man's mouth twitched. "Forget it. Listen. What's he got on you?"

"Nothing yet, but he will have plenty as soon as I'm searched. I've got the money." She had no doubt he knew all about what had happened, though how was a mystery deep as the problem of his identity itself.

Amazingly he chuckled. "That's all right then. Give it to me. Hurry, before he comes to. And tell me what you want done with it."

Anne told him, hurriedly, while unquestioningly she extricated the pile of bills from their hiding place and thrust it into his hands. "You'll be okay now," Peter whispered. "Just keep your chin up. Like this." His fingers tipped her face up toward his. His lips were hot, clinging, on hers, and then he had leaped away, was back in his car, was surging away, going like a bat out of hell.

"Peter," the girl moaned. "Oh Peter."

Ryan stirred, rolled over, lifted to hands and knees. He shook his head to clear it, came erect.

"Are you all right?" Anne called.

The detective came slowly back to her. "Yeah. No thanks to your friend, though."

"My friend!" She looked wide-eyed, injured. "I never even saw the man. He hit you and then he was gone before I could even get a glimpse of what he looked like."

"I guess not. An' you wouldn't have no idea of what his license number was either, would you?"

"I was so surprised by what happened that I didn't think of looking at it until it was too late.... But your head must be splitting. Don't you think we had better hurry to the station so you can do something for it?"

Ryan was fumbling in his pocket. "I think I better." He brought out a small key, fitted it into place in the handcuff lock. "I think I better get my head examined to see if it's *all* bone." The manacle came free with a clink. "Come on, get out."

"Get.... But really, Mr. Ryan. You were so anxious to have me go with you just a moment ago. Don't tell me you've changed your mind."

"Yeah. If that's what you call what I've changed. I'm not wastin' the matron's time lookin' for somethin' that ain't there no more. Get out."

Anne shrugged. "I think you're very inhospitable." She scrambled to the ground. "I've heard of girls having to walk home, but I thought they got a ride first."

"Listen, young lady." The ferret-like face was ominous. "It's me that got the ride this time. But it won't be always. Some time I'm going to get the answer to a lot of things I want to know about. Don't you forget it. I'm going to get the answer to all of them."

"Yes?" The girl arched her pencilled brows. "As for example?"

"For example why I got coffee spilled on me last night. That wasn't no more an accident than what just happened. Now beat it. You've got just about time to make the six-forty bus."

THERE WASN'T any expression in Faith Parker's nut-cracker face as Anne came into the Tavern. None, that is, unless one saw the sudden flare of relief and joy in her eyes.

But all she said was, " 'Bout time you got back. I can't look after the front if you expect me to do any cookin'. That wop cook put too much garlic in the duck while I was talking to the young man what was askin' about where you was."

"The young man! Faith! Faith dear. Who was he?"

"I dunno. He came in here and when I come out he asked where you was an' I told him you'd gone to Laneville, to the Station Plaza."

"You told him...! Oh, Faith, how did you come to do that? You never...."

"Why?" The crinkling of the yellowed, parchment like skin might have been meant for a smile. "Didn't you want me to tell him?"

TWO ITEMS from the Laneville Courier are of interest in connection with the foregoing account of the third episode in the saga of Anne Marsh's adventures. The first is as follows:

SETTLEMENT RECEIVES DONATION

The Settlement House on Railroad Street, in the section popularly known as Slum Hollow, was yesterday notified by the Mid-Atlantic Charity Foundation that Six Thousand Dollars had been allotted to it for work among boys and girls under the age of ten. A draft for that amount accompanied the notification.

Strangely enough, the Foundation is not listed in any social-work directory, and the Chase National Bank, on which the draft was drawn, disclaims any other knowledge of the organization except that the check was purchased there by some person previously unknown to them.

The second, appearing some two weeks later:

LANEVILLE GIRL LOTTERY WINNER

Miss Jeanne Galant, 18, of 2246 Oak Terrace, this city, received One Thousand Dollars by special messenger this morning. This messenger explained that the money had been won by Miss Galant in a drawing of the Chihuahua Sweepstakes, an obscure Mexican lottery.

When interviewed, the lucky miss tossed her pretty head and said: "I've bought lots of lottery tickets, but it's funny I can't remember anything about this one. The money's going to come in handy though, because now I can get married even though my sweetheart got fired three weeks ago and only just got another job."

Miss Galant's fiancé is Richard Swayne, 22, of 2249 Oak Terrace, who, it will be remembered, was involved in the robbery of etc. etc.

The Settlement House had been a prospective beneficiary of the fund Anne Marsh's father was accused of misappropriating—but Miss Jeanne Galant's name had not appeared on that list. Miss Galant was the beneficiary of the warmth that had come to dwell in the heart of Anne Marsh—a warmth born of a stranger's kiss and the freemasonry of love!

PHANTOM HIGHJACKER

IT WAS NOTHING TO ANNE MARSH'S ENEMIES THAT SHE STOLE ONLY TO GIVE LIFE AND HOPE TO THE DOOMED AND DISINHERITED. RUTHLESSLY THEY PLOTTED HER RUIN. GLOATINGLY THEY WATCHED HER WALK STRAIGHT INTO THEIR TRAP— AND SHE NEVER GUESSED THAT DEATH AND DISASTER LAY IN AMBUSH, WAITING FOR HER WITH DREADFUL PATIENCE....

"**B**ULLDOG" RYAN, ace detective of Laneville's police force, froze suddenly, the muscles of
his stocky frame tense. His pale, lashless eyes peered into
the dark alley that came up from Laneville's freight yards
and opened into Main Street. The sound came again, the
furtive footfall that had caught Ryan's ear. The sleuth faded
into the stygian murk of a store doorway, and Main Street
was empty again, silent under a brooding, moonless sky.

The wan light of a distant street lamp glittered on the
great plate glass windows of Fred Harris's Auto Agency,
but was too weak to penetrate the areaway mouth on the
other side of which Ryan hid. The shambling steps were
nearer, more distinct. The alley shadow seemed to grow,
projecting itself out to the sidewalk. A slender, slouched
figure appeared, stood looking vaguely about.

The lad's cap was pulled low, so that nothing showed of
his face except the small chin. He was collarless, and his
frayed jacket hung loosely, evidently a much bigger man's
cast-off. His trouser bottoms were fringed, his shoes
broken. The detective relaxed. This was only a vagrant who
had ridden the rods into town. He'd have to pick him up,
but....

Something held Ryan motionless, stiffening the sinews
across his shoulders. The young tramp's fingers had plucked

nervously at the hem of his coat, momentarily tautening
its front against his body. The threadbare cloth had folded
to rounded, nubile curves. No boy had curves like that. And
no tramp was ever so lithe, so quiveringly vigilant!

The mist sprayed from the flivver's radiator....

The sleuth's thin lips tightened to a straight, cruel line gashing his pointed, ferret's visage…. The youth darted back into the alley.

"Got you!" Ryan murmured, inaudibly. "No slick alibis this time, young lady." His fingers stole to his waist, closed on a gun-butt. With slow, infinite caution he slid along the front of the store whose doorway had been his covert. In his colorless pupils, slitted now, there was the gleam of the relentless stalker who sees his prey within his grasp, after a long and baffling hunt. Something of lurking regret, too,

"Go ahead with what you're up to and I'll take you red-handed."

ANNE MARSH crouched against the brick wall of Harris's Auto Agency, far back in the alley. Her careful reconnaissance had revealed a sleeping, deserted city. She was certain that she was unobserved, but some shuddering sixth sense within her warned her of imminent peril. Eyes seemed fastened upon her, glaring inimical, hostile out of the lightlessness.

Stealing up from the Freight Yards she had had that same sensation, an apparently reasonless feeling that someone moved in the shadows, dogging her footsteps, melting into invisibility when she whirled and stabbed a terrified gaze into the darkness....

This wouldn't do. If she didn't get busy the careful timing she had planned would be disrupted. In five minutes the patrolman would be thumping along Main Street, pounding his beat. She must be in, and out, and away before he came.

Anne's slender, white fingers touched the roughness of the wall. Mortar crumbled, silted out under her probing touch with a whispered hiss. The acid with which, last night, she had painted the jointures between the bricks had done its work. She lifted one baked clay block out, another. A gap grew in the wall, blacker against its black. The last brick came away. The hole was large enough for her to squirm through.

Frederick Harris had wired all entrances to his place against burglars, but he had not thought it necessary to wire the walls. The girl's red lips twitched with a humorless grin and she knelt, poking her head into the opening she had made. Her shoulders caught, started to slide through.

Suddenly a foot thudded behind her. Rough fingers dug into her arm and something hard jabbed her side. "Come out o' there," Ryan's toneless voice said. "Come on out. I've got you for breaking and entering, and you can't beat that rap."

Anne's veins ran cold with terror. She gasped, was abruptly strengthless. Ryan's grip hauled her back. She found her feet, straightened.

The detective's sharp chin thrust at her, his eyes cold and merciless as the gun snouting at her. "Yeah," he said heavily. "This is the end o' the game for you."

"Please mister," she chattered, clinging to her disguise. It was inane, pointless. If he didn't know who she was now he soon would, when they started to search her at the police station. "I didn't mean nothin'. I wuz comin' up from the yards an' I seen this hole…."

"Quit it," Ryan growled. "I saw you…."

A black-sleeved arm slid around his neck, choking him off. Fingers gripped his gun-hand, wrenched the automatic from it. Anne was aware that a man had leaped out of the shadows, had pounced catlike on her captor, that a fierce, voiceless struggle had exploded there before her.

Voiceless but not silent. Gusted breathing, the thump of bodies against the narrow walls, were terribly loud in the stillness. Anne was free but she did not run. Hand to heaving chest she watched that savage combat, a soundless scream rasping her throat.

Far away a heavy footfall thudded. Another. Then they were coming faster, running. A shrill whistle split Laneville's drowsy quiet.

"The policeman on the beat!" cried Anne. "He's heard. He's coming."

"All right." The heaving mass in front of her separated. One part of it remained in the ground, inert, terribly still. The other was a lithe, insouciant silhouette against the grey glimmer of the alley mouth. "Come on."

Anne Marsh was running, running through the rough, cluttered wilderness of Main Street's backyards. The other ran beside her, cloaked with mystery by the darkness, and behind them the police whistle shrieked its shrill alarm. The girl was panting, gasping for breath. Fear clawed at her out of the shadows; but an odd, eager joy pounded in her temples.

"Peter," she gasped. "It is you, Peter?"

"Where's your getaway," the man grunted. "Which way?"

"In the culvert under the tracks, at the edge of Slum Hollow. Here...." She stopped. "But Peter, how did you know I needed you?"

"I'll always know, my dear." His arms were around her, pulling her fiercely to him. "Because *I* need *you* so myself. Always." His lips were crushed against hers, and a white fire blazed about them, consuming.... He was gone, vanished into the darkness without a sound!

"Peter," Anne whispered....

A siren howled, coursing down Main Street. The girl sobbed. Her fingers grabbed at her buttons. The boy's clothing peeled from her, was sunk in a tarry pool beside the waiting roadster. Anne Marsh was a girl again, black-frocked, crowned by tawny, close curls. She scrambled into the car. Its starter burred, it lurched into motion. In two minutes of furious driving through furtive back streets, Anne was out of the city, safely escaped.

IN THE alley alongside Fred Harris's Auto Agency Bull-dog Ryan groaned, rolled over. His eyes opened and he saw a blunt-jawed face hanging over him, grizzled in the glare of a flashlight.

"Did you get them, Fallon?" he blurted.

"Naw. They wasn't nobody but you when I got here. Who wuz it? The same guy what turned off Simpson an' Reynolds, and copped the Lawton payroll?"

"Yeah." Ryan shoved hands against broken concrete, shoved himself up to a sitting posture. "The same guy." His jaw set, and there was in his countenance the dumb, heavy, relentless persistence of the brute after whom he was named. "I'll get that guy yet. Even if I got tuh do some framin'."

CHAPTER TWO
HUMAN QUARRY

"WHAT TIME did you come in last night, Miss Anne?" Faith Parker's voice was querulous as her seamed old face. "I was a-scared somethin' had happened." Her white-aproned frame was scrawny, misshapen from years of toil. But in her tiny, bird-like eyes the deep, abiding love glowed that had bidden her cling to a wan-faced, orphaned girl when all she held dear had crushed about Anne Marsh's head to leave her friendless and alone in an inimical world.

"Something almost happened." Anne was pallid, pathetic in the deep black of mourning for a father who had been kind, and tender and understanding. "But it didn't."

Faith sighed. "We're makin' money here. Everyone thet is some one in Laneville comes here at night, an' pays fer the same kind o' meals I cooked all them years fer you an' your Dad. We could be comfortable an' peaceful. But you ain't satisfied." She sniffed. "Well, it ain't no use o' my warnin' you an' pleadin' with you to stop these things you're doin'."

"No, Faith dear. It's no use at all. Not as long as they are still hungry, down there in Slum Hollow." Anne's eyes fell to a yellowing newspaper clipping pinned under the plate-glass covering of the desk where nightly she sat as mistress of The Tavern on Bolton Turnpike.

That clipping came from the editorial page of the Laneville *Courier,* the morning after Webster Marsh's funeral, but it was such an obituary as seldom has been printed. *"As long as the naked are unclothed,"* the cruel arraignment ended, *"and the hungry unfed, the soul of Webster Marsh will have no peace."*

He had been wealthy, Anne's father, trusted and well-beloved. Then, one Christmas season, he had killed himself with his own hand. And it was discovered that he had embezzled the funds of the Community Chest of which he had been treasurer, that he was bankrupt... and a thief.

Only Anne knew that Webster Marsh had been robbed, swindled, by a group of Laneville's most eminent citizens. Her father was dead, and his memory execrated by those helpless ones whom the city's charitable institutions were unable to aid because they were impoverished. What those really responsible had done, had been done within the law. They could not be punished by the law.

Not by the law. But the tawny-haired young girl had found a way to punish crime with crime. Anne Marsh became a thief, and the proceeds of her theft found a way to the coffers of the very charities her victims had despoiled....

Anne abruptly ceased her somber musing and became rigid, listening tensely. Sharp sound had suddenly thudded into the dim quiet of The Tavern—sound the sound was flat and ominous.

"A backfire," Faith muttered. "Some car back-firing."

"No." Blood had drained from the girl's lips. "It came from the rear. East road is too far away to hear a backfire. It was a shot in the woods."

"Mebbe it was a shot then. Some hunter...."

"The hunting season won't open for months.... There's another!" Anne went through the door behind her desk, across the big kitchen, peered out of a window into the green obscurity of Lane Hill that loomed dark and fore-bidding. "Maybe it's the police. Maybe they're shooting at...."

She caught herself, so that Faith, close as she was, did not hear the name that quivered on her lips.

Across the deep gully that cut off the tongue of land on which The Tavern was built, close-growing bushes rustled furtively. A distant shout echoed, pulling Anne's wide-eyed look far up the mountainside. Blue flickered in the green-ery. Vanished.

Peter! the voice inside the girl's breast moaned. Was it Peter who was being shot at by the police—who was being hunted down like a wild beast? Were they hounding the youth who had saved her last night? More than once, when she had been seemingly hopelessly trapped by Bulldog Ryan, he had dashed to her aid out of the forest, and always he had mysteriously disappeared into it again when she needed him no longer. She suspected Peter of being one of the bandit gang who hid in Lane Hill's caverns and harried the countryside; but there was a daredevil glint in his blue eyes that Anne could not forget, and a puckered heart-shaped scar at the corner of a mouth whose kisses burned on her lips, white flame she could not rub away.

"They're coming down," Faith muttered. "A couple more minutes and they'll have him caught. If he tries to git across the turnpike they'll see him an' shoot him."

"No," Anne whimpered. She was through the open door, was kneeling at the edge of the bank that dropped vertically, lushly vine-clad, down into the gully. "Up here! Quick. They can't see you if you hurry."

A RENEWED rustle in the foliage below answered her. She glimpsed a dark form sliding through the leaves, starting a climb up the gully-side. "I'm going back into the kitchen," she called, "to watch for your best chance to get across the yard. Come running when I whistle."

From within the doorway she stared up the hill. The cops appeared briefly, two blue-clad dolls in whose hands lethal steel took the sun and glinted. Then they were invisible again in some fold of the tree-clad height.

The girl's lips puckered in a whistle. A lithe form came over the brink of the drop, dashed toward her. Crouched low so that she could not see its face, it had brushed past her into sanctuary. She closed the door, quickly but soundlessly, turned....

"Gee, miss," the fugitive chattered, cowering and dough-visaged in the center of Faith's spotless kitchen. "D-dey'd a had me if it wasn't fer you."

He wasn't Peter! He was a slender, gangling youth, but he wasn't Peter.

"Miss Anne," the aged spinstress exclaimed, "are you gone clean crazy?" She tarted for the open window.

A clawed, shaking hand caught her arm. "D-don't do dat. Please don't do dat. It was me foist job. I ain't had nuttin' to eat fer a week—an' I copped a car. Dey caught me up dere on East Road. Dey've got de heap back. It won't do no good to send me away fer twenny years."

"Let me go, you thief." Faith wrenched away. "I'm going to...."

"Faith!" Anne's cry was a whiplash, halting her. "Wait. You forget that I too am a...." She caught herself. "Think what twenty years in jail will do to him. We can't—give him up."

"Gawd'll bless yuh, lady," the quivering youth blurted. "It wuz me foist try, so help me. Me foist...."

"They'll be here in a minute, Miss Anne. They'll find him here. If he tries to get away now, back or front, they'll see him, and then we'll be in trouble."

"Wait, Faith. Maybe... Did they get a good look at you? Would they know you?"

"No'm. Dey wuz chasin' me, an' I wuz pullin' away when de car give out o' gas. I jumped out an' got into the woods before they started wingin' lead at me. Dat's howcome...."

"Come over here in the corner." She got hold of him, dragged him to a big sink. She ripped a voluminous apron from a nail. "Get this around you and start washing those pots. Run the hot water so there will be plenty of steam. Lucky thing Tony, our regular dishwasher, 'phoned he'd be late today."

"Here they are, Miss Anne." Faith interjected. "They're pokin' in the bushes. One of them is lookin' up here an' sayin' somethin'. He's climbin' up."

The girl whipped around. "You've got a soup pot on the stove. Make believe you've been tending it all the time. I've been making out this marketing list." She slid into a chair at a knife-scarred table, snatched up a pencil, pulled a paper toward her. "And we've neither of us seen...." A heavy foot crunched on cinders, outside the door, "…think three barrels of potatoes are enough, Faith? They may cost more next week—"

The door slammed open to reveal a florid-faced patrolman, revolver in hand. "What…!" Anne half-screamed, jumping up. "What's the matter?"

"Matter enough. Where's the guy that ducked in here?"

THE GIRL was round-eyed with surprise. "Ducked… Why, what do you mean? No one has been in here this morning but the three of us."

The cop's stare probed the big kitchen. "We chased him down the hill. We could see Waley's Creek an' the pike all the time, an' he didn't go across either of them. This is the only place he could of went."

"But we surely would have seen anyone coming in through this door, and it's the only entrance except the one out in front." Anne shoved open the door in the partition, revealing rows of booths within which flower-decorated tables were nestled. "Do you want to look around out there?"

The man in blue scratched his head. "Guess I'd better. But I'll swear we'd of seen him if he went 'round that way." He started moving across the kitchen… and halted as the front door opened. "Bulldog!" he exclaimed. "Bulldog Ryan!"

The detective walked heavily down the aisle, his sharp face still, expressionless as a sphinx's. "What's goin' on here?" he asked, tonelessly. "What's up, Fallon?"

Anne flashed a terrified glance to Faith. They might fool a flatfoot, but never Ryan….

"We wuz chasin' a car-snatcher, Ryan," the patrolman said. "He picked one up outside Harris's place an' passed us on East Road a minute before the radio call went out. We thought it wuz a good chanct to spot that hot short shop out towards Surton we've been tryin' to locate fer months, so we wuz lettin' the bloke pull away. But he run out of gas, an' hopped into the woods. We thought mebbe he got in here, somehow, but the dame says no."

Ryan's pale eyes flickered around the kitchen, found the fake dishwasher-passed on. "Hell," he said heavily. "He ducked into one them caves Lane Hill is full of. Most likely he's one of that gang hides out in them woods and knows every inch of the ground."

"Funny they should be takin' to snatchin' cars," the cop mumbled. "They're stick-up artists."

"Yeah. There's a lot o' funny things goes on around here. But there ain't no use standin' here gabbin'. You'd better get back to the road with your side-kick, before Harris's wagon gets picked up by someone else."

The policeman clumped out. A thin smile edged Bulldog's lips. "Cops is dumb," he murmured. "Ain't they?" And then he had turned, was going silently out through the restaurant. He paused at the door. "Too damn dumb." He was gone.

"Gawd!" the waif blurted. "Yer did that swell, miss. You didn't even lie ter him."

"Sh," Faith hissed. "Maybe they're listenin'."

"No." Anne turned from the window. "They've given up. They're climbing back up the hill."

The older woman's nose-tip twitched, rabbit-like. "Funny thet Ryan give up so easy. 'Tain't like him. I smell somethin' rotten...."

"Nonsense. You're just naturally suspicious.... The boy's hungry, Faith."

"I got some cold turkey in the ice-box. And some deep-dish apple pie."

"Gosh!" It was a sob, almost. "Apple pie!" The young car-thief came away from the sink, wiping his hands on the apron in which Anne had enfolded him. "Oh, golly!"

"Get it, Faith." Anne turned to the youth. "What's a hot short shop?"

BEADY, BRIGHT eyes sought her face. "What's it to you, lady?"

"I'd like to know."

"It's a fence fer snatched cars. Dat's hot shorts, see?"

"A fence?"

"Jees, don't you know nuttin'?… Boy! Let me at that grub."

Faith had come in with a heaping plate of white meat, had doused it with hot gravy from a pot on the stove and planked it on the table. The fellow grabbed a chair, began wolfing the food.

Pity brooded in Anne's grey eyes, pity and an almost personal pain. The look of shrewdness on the youth's face might so easily have been keen intelligence, if he had ever had a chance for proper guidance. The Settlement House in Frog Hollow had had to abandon an ambitious plan for vocational guidance because of lack of the funds it would have had if….

"Blokes what buys stolen goods is called fences," The lad spoke with a full mouth. "W'en dey deal in hot shorts dey pays de snatcher for 'em, an' den dey goes ter woik on 'em. New paint. New numbers everywhere. If dey's got t'ree or four dey rips 'em apart an' puts 'em together again mixed up, like a j-jig-saw puzzle. Dem guys woik quicker'n de factory dat turns 'em out. Dey kin take a car Hank Ford hisself's been drivin' fer years, an' overnight he nor nobody else could tell it from Noah's Ark. But dey pays best fer new ones."

"Here's some coffee." Faith shoved a cup of steaming brew across the table. "Seems to me you know an awful lot about that, young man, for it's being the first time you stole a car."

The youth looked up. "Hell," he shrugged. "De bloke wised me to de whole game."

"What bloke?" Anne breathed.

"De one what sat nex' to me on a park bench, and soft-soaped me inter takin' a try at it. He gimme a ignition key, an' he tells me jest how ter cop de heap, an' where ter take it. I got de map he drored in me pocket right now." He motioned to the side of his threadbare jacket. "Dere's easy coin in dat racket."

"Not so easy," the tawny-haired girl said softly. "Being outside the law is never easy. You're afraid. You're always afraid of being caught. Every stranger you meet may be the one to tap you on the shoulder and say, 'You're wanted.' There are eyes watching you all the time—watching you and waiting for you to make a mistake. Sooner or later you're bound to make that mistake. And then—then the grey walls of prison close around you, and you see the sky only with steel bars across it, and you—you drag out weary days in a living tomb. Don't keep on. You were lucky this time; you won't be so lucky the next. Don't do it again."

The lad spread grimy hands. "Yer right, lady. De law's sure ter git yuh. But—yuh eats in clink. An' dere's a roof over yer head w'en it rains. An' dere's steam heat in winter. Dat's more dan dey've got in de parks."

"Here." Anne snatched up her pocket-book from the table. "Here's—fifty dollars. That will feed you and keep you warm for a long time, long enough to be able to get a job. Conditions are getting better...."

"Jee no, lady. Yuh done ernough fer me, already. I can't take it."

"But you must." She came close to him, put the money in the side-pocket of his jacket. "There. You haven't taken it. I've given it to you."

"T'anks." He was on his feet. "T'anks fer everyt'ing." His face worked with some obscure emotion. He wheeled around, plunged blindly out through the restaurant.

"You fool," Faith sniffed. "Fallin' for them lies. He's a hardened criminal or I miss my guess. You've just gone and thrown away fifty dollars.

"No." Anne Marsh was smiling, but her small featured face was bleak, and there was no humor in her eyes. "No, Faith. I got something back for it. Something that will be worth a lot more."

And she held out a frayed, grimy piece of paper on which pencil lines made a smudged map.

CHAPTER THREE
SPILLED SALT
IS BAD LUCK

THERE WAS something in the dim-lit, murmur-some quiet of The Tavern that set its nightly patrons at their ease, so that their inhibitions were lulled and they talked freely. For one thing, they were so sure of not being overheard. The booth-sides rose almost to the ceiling. The trim waitresses who served Faith Parker's ambrosial food did not hover over the tables. And the desk at which Anne Marsh sat to check trays, and make change, and smile with shy sweetness at each entrant, was beyond earshot of even the nearest cubicle.

Strange then, that she should be always listening. As if a voice whispered to her that no one else could hear. Was it the voice of Webster Marsh, perhaps, the widowed father to whom she had been so close, and whose memory was still a poignant ache in her bosom?

No. These were no phantasmal whispers that hissed almost inaudibly from beneath Anne's desk. A speaker was hidden there, and artfully concealed wires ran from it to invisible microphones secreted in every niche. Mirrors, unobtrusive in the ceiling, reflected every last movement within the booths. Nothing that was said, nothing that was done within The Tavern, was secret to its wistful-faced owner. Impoverished, outcast for the sin of her father, the eating place at the bridge over Waley's Creek had given her a living. But it served another, furtive purpose too.

There was a list in Anne Marsh's mind, a list of six men who had killed Webster Marsh as surely as if they had held the poison cup to his lips. One by one, the whispers to which she had listened had betrayed three of those men to her.

She was listening to a fourth now, Frederick Harris, whose agency for an automobile in the highest price class had made him wealthy. "…business so damn good I can't get enough jobs shipped from the factory." Shaded light glinted on a shiny, hairless pate as Harris lifted a forkful of Lobster Newburg to his lips. "So I made a cash dicker with a Baltimore agency for five limousines. They'll be here about two a.m. By ten tomorrow I'll have thirty thousand in the till, ten of it profit. That's turnover for you."

Fulton Zander nibbled at a graham cracker soggy with the milk in which he had dunked it. "You must have a pull with the railroad to get them out of the freight yards so quickly."

"Railroad, hell! They're coming by truck. Blocked up on a low-slung steel chassis and one of them perched right on top of the driver's cab. Cheaper and quicker."

"Have to make a long detour, won't they, to get around Lane Hill?"

"Nope. They're coming through Bolton and right over the climb. Those monsters have plenty of power, Fulton. Road's kind of narrow but there won't be any traffic that hour, and a kid can handle them. Only thing that worried me was the bridge out here and I checked that with the Highway Department this morning. I wasn't taking any chances with twenty grand of my coin."

"It'll hold up?"

"They guarantee it.... Say, isn't it about time you swapped part of those whopping legal fees I pay you for a seven-seater limousine...?"

But Anne's hand had moved minutely under the desk-top and the whispers shut off. Unconsciously her eyes narrowed, while a predatory gleam stole into them. Somewhere south a twenty-thousand dollar prize was lumbering through the darkness. But how, single-handed, could she hope to capture it? It was now after ten. She had so little time....

"Hannah," she called to the pert head-waitress. "Take the desk, please. I'm very tired, we were open till almost four last night. I can hardly keep my eyes open."

Faith Parker's face was red from the heat of the stove over which she presided as the girl came into the now bustling kitchen. "Miss Anne!" she exclaimed. "Anything wrong?"

Anne smiled, drearily. "No, Faith dear. That investment I made this morning is already showing such good results that I'm celebrating by going to bed early."

The older woman came across to her, her lips twitching. "Miss Anne," she whispered, tremulously. "I just spilled some salt an' when I went to throw it over my left shoulder Tony bumped against me so it hit him instead. Thet's bad luck."

"Nonsense." The girl tossed back her close crop of tawny curls. "It's people, and not things, that bring us bad luck. Goodnight, Faith."

SOUP DRIPPED unnoticed to the immaculate floor from the ladle Faith Parker held as she watched the lithe, slender figure go through the door in the side-wall of the kitchen beyond which was the single-roomed leanto that constituted the living quarters of the owners of The Tavern on Bolton Turnpike. That was the only door to that room, and its steel-barred window looked out over a sheer drop into the gully behind. The assistant cooks, Tony the dishwasher, the waitresses coming constantly in and out, would be sure to see her if Anne Marsh left The Tavern that night.

Light from a setting moon, sifting in through the window, laid a flat, gridded oblong of pale luminance on the floor. Anne sighed, crossing to the aperture. Her slim fingers tugged at first one, then another, of the bars.

Behind her there was a grating sound, the rasp of wood on wood. A dank, earthy aroma mingled with the warm redolence of the summer night. As the girl swung around, another oblong showed in the floor's level plain. This one was black, and the grave-like odor seemed to come out of it.

Thirty seconds later the floor was once more unbroken. But the room was utterly empty.

Beneath it, however, there was movement in another room, one of which the assistant cooks, Tony the dishwasher, and the waitresses knew nothing. Yellow light clicked on, beat against earthen, window-less walls, cascaded down on a scarred, age-darkened work bench, all that was left of the old Marsh mansion. All that was left of the happy hours when a lithe, gay-eyed girl and a kindly-faced man had worked side by side at countless ingenious gadgets that had no real use but to nurture a comradeship between father and daughter that the grave itself had not availed to destroy.

Anne spread a Geological Survey map of the surrounding country on the bench. Her finger found Bolton, found where Bolton Turnpike started its curve through the wavering contour-lines of Lane Hill. A thin tracing left it there, to indicate a by-path, little better than a trail that circled the height and crossed East Road, the highway between Laneville and Surton. A half-mile beyond that crossing, off the by-road, a tiny square nestling in the diagrammed forest was labelled, "Farmhouse. Abandoned."

Perhaps it *was* an abandoned farmhouse. But on the pencil-smudged map for which Anne had substituted fifty dollars, not many hours before, it had been marked with black X. And there had been the scrawled words, 'Toot horn. Long—short—long.'

A RUMBLE, like long unending thunder, growled through the after-midnight dark that lay on Bolton Turnpike like a pall. Eight ponderous wheels made that sound, revolving under something that was like a primeval monster lurching through a prehistoric jungle. Impossible, it seemed, that mere man could control the black beast, could swing it dexterously around curves picked out of the darkness by its two fiery eyes. But the behemoth was man-made, and it was driven by a very sleepy man who wished that the snores of the helper slumped alongside him were not quite so rasping.

"Wake up, yuh hog." Tom Conlon grunted, driving an overalled elbow into the snorer's ribs. "Wake up."

"Huh!" Micky Hara gargled. "Huh. Wazzat?"

"Take a gander at the road map. Ain't that the stiff climb the boss was croakin' about, ahead there?"

"Yeah. Lane Hill. Guy at the Coffee Pot in Bolton was tellin' me there's a gang o' stick-up guys hangs out in them woods. Gee! Maybe they'll high-jack us, huh?"

"Not so long as Tom Conlon's got two fists an' a gat I'd like to see 'em try it."

"Listen, bo. Does we get the highball, you pipe down wid yer firsts *and* yer gun. They're killers, them…. Hey! What's that ahead? What…?"

Conlon's fist pounded the middle of the steering wheel in front of him, and raucous horn-blare flung itself against Lane Hill's loom. "Some damn farmer's flivver," he grunted. "It's flopping all over the road."

The mud-smeared rattletrap coughed into the headlight beam, tossing from side to side of the pike, seeming to rear, almost, as horses reared at the sight of a 'gas-buggy' when the century was not yet in its teens. The piping, shrill voice that came from it heightened the impression.

"Whoa," it squealed. "Whoa, Betsy. Drat ye. Whoa." The battered two-seater slewed sidewise, snorted, and was suddenly quiet.

Conlon jarred back his brake-lever. "Hey," he yelled. "Pull over. I can't get past yuh."

"Jees!" Micky gulped. "It's a dame. An' what a dame!"

There wasn't any glass in the flivver's windshield frame, so they could see her clearly. A black, lacy bonnet perched high on straggling, grey hair and a high-boned collar held the wrinkled, blear-eyed face stiffly erect. She sat straight as a ramrod, and her mittened hands had a death-grip on the wheel, as she goggled at the dungareed men in the cab of the car-truck.

"Pull over, gram'ma," Conlon yelled again. "T'ink I got all night tuh wait on yuh?"

"I can't," the apparition in the rattletrap piped. "The tarnation thing's stalled again, and I got tuh have someun crank her."

"Oh Gawd," Tom groaned. "Get out an' give the handle a whirl, Micky. Th' quicker it's done th' sooner we'll get goin'."

"Jees. I didn't t'ink they was any of them hand-organs left." Hara unfolded his raw-boned length, shambled the twenty feet of dusty concrete toward the Model T. "Some boat yuh got here. What keeps it runnin'? Two prayers an' a gol durn?"

"Prayin' would make yuh run a lot better, young man," the woman's nasal twang responded. "But Si puts somethin' in the gasoline that makes Betsy climb these hills like a colt."

Micky sniffed, bending to get hold of the rusty crank handle. "Yeh," he grunted. "It stinks like a hospital." He yanked the angled bar. The flivver shook with his efforts, spat a mist of what seemed like wet dust about him. "Phew. It kind of chokes yuh." He twirled the crank again....

His knees buckled under him. "Chokes-chokes—" he gurgled, thumped to the ground. He lay there, a dark heap....

"Hey!" Conlon bellowed. "What's goin' on?" He heaved from his seat, ran to his fallen helper. "What struck him?" He reached Hara, sniffed, and twisted, his ham-like fist jerking to his hip pocket. Ether! You...."

THE WET mist sprayed again from the flivver's radiator, and the ancient farm-woman's hand came up over the dashboard. A curiously thick-barreled tube in it jetted pungent spray at the lurching driver. Abruptly he thumped down alongside his companion, the revolver he had pulled out spinning, useless, away into the darkness of the ditch. The odor of ether hung sickly-sweet above him.

Anne Marsh leaped from her seat, pumped another spray of the volatile anesthetic into the faces of her victims. Under its grease paint her small face quivered.

The girl stooped over the prostrate men. Their pulses throbbed strongly underneath her probing fingertips. She twisted, ran back to the rear seat of the flivver, returned with blankets, ropes, in her arms. Exerting all her strength she managed to get the blankets around Conlon and Hara, making them cocoons warm against the night's chill— gagged and lashed bundles helpless when consciousness should return.

Anne rolled the unwieldy bodies into the ditch, where they would be safe from some possible late-faring vehicle. She jerked bonnet, and grey wig and Faith's old black shirt-waist from her, made a little pile of them in the opposite ditch, touched a match to them. A quick flare of flame showed them to have been impregnated with some inflammable substance, but though almost immediately they were ashes, the girl had already swabbed the paint from her face, had pulled a cap low over her tawny curls and slid into a thick lumber jacket that effectively concealed the seductive curves of her budding womanhood. Wearing frayed, shabby trousers, she was now a slender, lithe boy, very like the lad of the morning's adventure.

The battered car, reconditioned and hidden away months ago against some possible use, plunged into the thicket. It would be found there, but it would not be traced to her.

Meantime the flivver no longer blocked Bolton Pike nor the tree and darkness-concealed entrance to the by-road that seven miles away crossed the highway to Surton. Five minutes from the time Tom Conlon had grabbed at his brake, that brake was released and twenty-thousand dollars worth of black-gleaming limousines lurched east to circle Lane Hill and lumber toward the supposedly abandoned farmhouse....

The stygian woods closing in on her seemed to resent the thunderous invasion of the leviathan she guided. Anne shivered a little. What sort of persons awaited her? The excitement that till now had buoyed her up ebbed away, and she was a lonely, frightened girl, oppressed by a sensation of impending disaster.

Spilled salt. "That's bad luck," Faith Parker's whisper sounded in her ears. "Thet's awful bad luck."

CHAPTER FOUR
THE TRAP

THE HAND of the night reached down from the last gentle slope of Lane Hill, to cloak with impenetrable shadow a rambling, paintless farmhouse that shrugged into the clustered, murmursome trees as if ashamed of its squalor. No light showed from its gloomy bulk, and the forest heard only the rustle of a vagrant breeze in its own foliage, and the rap, rap, rap of a loose shingle on the sway-backed roof.

But within the drab walls there was the rasp of fabric against fabric, and the sound of a hoarse breathing. "Hell," a man muttered. "Must be damn near dawn."

"Yeah," another voice, heavy but low-toned, responded. "But I ain't goin' to have to wait much longer."

"What time is it?"

A match sputtered, blossomed into a minute, dancing flame. The light struck a face out of the darkness, a pinched, sharp-chinned face whose pale eyes were lashless and glittering with the excitement of a ferret whose prey is almost within its grasp. "Ten past one," a thin-lipped mouth muttered. "We'll know damned soon." The match flame flickered out.

"D'yuh think it'll work, Ryan? D'you think she's copped the truck? An' if she did, will she come here wid it?"

"Didn't she swipe the map from the kid's pocket? Didn't she quit the desk soon as Harris and Zander pulled their talk? She'll get here. And won't there be a surprise waitin' for her when she toots that horn an' she sees Bulldog Ryan comin'…. Hush! I think I hear somethin'!"

Silence clamped down once more. But now, underneath that silence, far-off sound lay. Distant sound, as of a long, muted, rumble of thunder.

"Smart," the heavy voice murmured. "Smart as the devil, that girl. But Fulton Zander is smarter." Somehow there was an evasive note of regret in the slow, heavy tones….

TERROR RODE with Anne in the great, lumbering truck, in the seat where Micky Hara had snored. Tree limbs were gaunt arms reaching out to stop her, every black pool just beyond read of her plunging lights was an ominous shadow-shape, crouching to leap upon her....

One of these shadows did not disappear as the headlight cone reached and passed it! It was a man, statuesque in the road, a man black-coated, black masked. The light glinted from blued metal of revolver, snouting pointblank at her. Anne gasped, slammed on the brakes.

The sudden silence hurt her ear drums. "What do you want?" she cried.

"All right." Someone was in the seat alongside her, another black-shrouded form that had materialized, eerily, from the forest. "All right, guy. You're highjacked. Get out and keep your mouth buttoned and you won't get hurt. Otherwise...." Something hard bored into the girl's side, and sharp click of a cocked pistol-hammer punctuated the gruff command. "What's it going to be?"

"Out, of course." With the actual appearance of danger Anne was again cool, collected. "What else?" She jumped down into the underbrush. Her ankle turned, she sprawled....

She came up again with an automatic in her hand. "Up!" she exclaimed. "Put 'em up!" The weapon swung from the man in the road to the one in the cab. "Drop your guns or I'll shoot."

The two weapons thumped, as one. Black-gloved hands lifted over black-masked heads. "I'm not giving up so easily!" the disguised girl said triumphantly.

The fellow she had first seen growled, "Think yuh kin put it over on us? What're yuh goin' to do now?"

"I—" the girl gulped. Her captives were too widely separated for her to make sure of either of them. If she moved to tie up one, the other....

A form jostled against her back. Cruel, twisting fingers clamped on her wrists, twisted the automatic out of it. Anne screamed, tried to whirl. Brutal arms held her, helpless....

"Now yuh get yours, Mr. Smartie." The man in the road was running up, his recovered revolver bluely threatening. "A lead pill in yer belly 'll cure yuh o' tryin' any more tricks...."

"But he isn't going to be cured." The other man came out of the truck cab, lithely, landing cat-like on the balls of his feet, crouched and ready for action. "Freeze, both of you, or you'll feel lead yourselves."

The actors in the melodrama were rigid, in a brittle silence. "Yuh gone nuts, Joe?" the one behind Anne grunted. "Lettin' the punk get away wid it?"

"No," Joe husked. "I'm not nuts. I'm the only one here with any sense. We've got to get this load moving quick; there's a lot of work to be done on it before morning. We haven't got time to get rid of any corpses and if a plugged body is found in the woods here we'll have to scamper out of the county. The punk has got to keep his mouth shut, and he will. Won't you, youngster?"

"Yes." Anne breathed. "Yes. I'm licked and I know it. Let me go and you won't have any trouble, or ever see me again."

"Well, maybe yeh're right." The pinioning arms were suddenly loose. "Git!" a voice bawled in her ears and a thick sole thudded against the seat of Anne's frayed pants, lifting her into threshing woods darkness. "Git!"

THE GIRL fought through brambles, angling over a spur of Lane Hill toward Waley's Creek and The Tavern.

She was sobbing with frustration, with a sense of outrage. And then, quite suddenly, she was no longer sobbing.

A visual memory had popped into her mind. Something that she had not noted in the flurry of that final quick turning of the tables, but which came back to her now. As the man they called Joe had leaped out into the road his mask had fluttered, momentarily, and exposed the corner of his mouth. There had been a scar there, a puckered, heart-shaped scar....

"Hell, Ryan!" A muttered exclamation once more broke the waiting silence of the farmhouse trap. "She's bogged down or somethin'. The sound of the truck's stopped."

"Wait. Maybe it's just a shoulder of the hill cutting off the noise. Yeah. That's what it was. Hear it? She's comin'. She's comin' fast. Get ready."

Rasp of fabric on fabric. Heavy breathing in the darkness. Then, "Gees. That noise ain't comin' no nearer. It's—it's gettin' further away."

"Hell!" Ryan's expletive was rage-filled. "She's turned off on East Road, towards Surton. She's goin' to the real hot short joint, the one the auto squad's been tryin' to locate for six months. Come on! We can track that rumble far enough back so we can't be spotted!"

Two vague forms burst out of a propped-up back door that had been used only once for a generation, ran through slicing bushes to a hidden car. Headlights flared. A starter burred....

Nothing happened. The motor did not catch, did not turn over.

Bulldog Ryan pulled in a deep, hissing breath. "Cut it out, Fallon," he said heavily. "Get that smell. Gasoline. I don't have to look to see that all the gas that was in our tank is siphoned out on the ground. An' there ain't no fillin' station for two miles."

ANNE MARSH came out of the kitchen the next morning, moving wearily. Her eyes were red with sleeplessness and worry, and the wistful smile was gone from her lips.

A rasping at the door pulled her frightened gaze to it. A shadow moved furtively outside the curtain-draped pane—a slender lithe shadow that bent, and straightened, and blurred, retreating.

The girl broke into a run, snatched open the door. "Peter!" she cried, "Peter!" flinging her high voice after a car that spurted toward the up-curve of Bolton Highway, and the slope of Lane Hill. She was running in that dust-cloud, her eyes on the head of its driver, a head cocked sidewise with jaunty, taunting triumph. A hand waved to her just as the forest greenness closed behind the vanishing auto.

A sob lumped in Anne's throat. "He needn't—he needn't have come back to crow over me," she murmured. "I hate him. I hate him!" She turned back, drearily returning to The Tavern.

A long, bulky white envelope lay just inside the threshold. Had he thrust it under the door? Was that what he had come for?

Anne held it in her hand, as she stumbled toward her desk. She slumped into the chair as if her legs were abruptly too weak to support her. After a while she picked up a letter-opener, slit the envelope.

Oblongs of green paper sifted out onto the desk-top. Crackling oblongs of paper from which numerals stared up at her. $1000. There were ten of the papers and each of them was a thousand dollar Federal Reserve Note!

The squeal of grating hinges pulled her wide-eyed stare from them. The front door was opening. A squat form thrust in. Bulldog Ryan thumped stiff-legged toward Anne. His pale eyes lit on the money strewn over the desk. Their lashless lids slitted, and red signal lights flickered in them.

"Where did *them* come from?" his heavy, toneless voice queried.

There was sly mockery in the girl's smile. "Business was very good last night. Or so I am told. I went to bed early."

Ryan's thin lips twitched. "If you took in that much here in one night or a month o' nights, I'm a ring-tailed baboon."

Anne shrugged. "You really don't expect me to argue the point with you, do you, Mr. Ryan?" she murmured sweetly.

White spots of wrath showed either side of the cop's pinched nostrils. "Maybe you wouldn't. Maybe you've made a monkey out o' me again. But I'm a monkey that can figure. As for instance, five twelve-cylinder limousines at hot short prices is worth about ten thousand dollars. You wouldn't happen to have just ten grand there, would you?"

"What a strange coincidence! That's exactly how much it is. I'm so glad you came in, Mr. Ryan. I've decided to make a donation of this to the Settlement House in Slum Hollow, for their crime prevention work, and if you take me down there in your car I won't be afraid of being—what is the word?—*highjacked.*"

THE BENEVOLENT BLACKMAILER

ANNE MARSH WAS NO STRANGER
TO DANGER AND DEATH. IN
HER DARING, LONE-HANDED
BATTLE AGAINST THE SINISTER
FORCES WHICH HAD KILLED AND
DISCREDITED HER FATHER SHE
HAD COME FACE TO FACE WITH
THE GRIM HARVESTER MANY
TIMES, AND HAD NEVER FALTERED.
BUT WHEN, ATTEMPTING THE
MOST DANGEROUS EXPLOIT OF
HER CAREER, SHE FELL BENEATH
THE THREAT OF THE MAD-
HOUSE ON THE HILL, SHE HAD
THE SOUL-CHILLING FEAR THAT
HER COURAGEOUS CAMPAIGN ON
BEHALF OF THE DOOMED AND
DISINHERITED WAS DESTINED TO
END IN BLACK TRAGEDY....

ANNE MARSH, standing in the doorway of The Tavern on Bolton Turnpike, was lithe as a young birch. Her simple frock was molded to the vibrant, frank curves of budding womanhood. Her soft lips were tender with wistful sweetness, her small chin clean-cut, determined. A faint blush of ruddy health underlay the satin smoothness of her skin, and the early morning sun glinted tawny in her close-cut crop of unruly curls.

But tragedy brooded within the grey depths of her eyes, and her slim frame was taut with omnipresent fear.

"It's a shame, that's what it is," a querulous voice broke into her reverie, "makin' the old Marsh place into a nuthouse right under our noses." Faith Parker's age-dried body was scrawny within the black silk, high-collared dress she wore, and a rusted bonnet perched weirdly atop her scant grey locks. "Wouldn't of been so bad if they was a decent family come to live there."

The girl's mouth twisted with a bitterness too poignant for her youth. "Decent…" she whispered. "Two decent people lived there once. The father killed himself because he could not face dishonor. The daughter is—a thief."

"Miss Anne!" The exclamation was not so much shocked as pitying. "You mustn't say that. I—"

"Say it or not, Faith dear, I am just that." A sob choked the low voice. "A thief. An outlaw."

The fingers that tightened on Anne's arm were fleshless, calloused by long and loving service. "Outlaw you are, and proud you should be of bein' outside the law that calls them honest men who swindled Webster Marsh of the charity money with which he was trusted, and murdered him as sure as though they forced the poison through his lips." There was a strange, fierce intensity in the words, and unac-

customed eloquence. "Thief you are, and proud you should be that you steal from thieves to return their loot to the starvin' ones they robbed. *I* tell you that, and 'twas at my knees you, a motherless tot, learned what truth is, and honor."

A little muscle twitched in the girl's downy cheek. "Don't tell it to me. Tell it to the world. Tell it to the detective who—who—" Her speech broke into a choked gasp, and the fear in her eyes flared into the reflection of a creeping, dark fire. A long quiver ran through her.

"Child!" Faith gathered Anne into her skinny arms, nestling her head against the spinster's flat breast beneath which beat the devotion of a faithful old heart. "Child, the load is too heavy for you to bear."

"Bulldog Ryan," Anne sobbed into the threadbare silk of the familiar bosom. "I see him all the time, his lashless, colorless eyes, his pointed face that shows no expression at all. I dream about him. Closing in—always closing in. Dumb, dogged, persistent. Terrible as the blind, merciless law whose hound he is." She shuddered. "Sooner or later he'll get me...."

"Not if you give it up," the thin old tones crooned. "He suspects you, but he has no proof. If you stop now he will never have any. You must give up this mad scheme of yours. We could be so happy if you did. The Tavern is doing well. We could be comfortable, and safe...."

"Safe! How good that sounds. Not to be afraid any more...."

"You *will* stop then!" Sudden hope throbbed in the old servant's voice. "I'll work my fingers to the bone...."

"*No!*" White, tapering hands thrust Anne out of Faith's embrace. "Not till I have finished." She was a straight, slender figure of white flame in the sunlight, and there was no longer any weakness in her. "Not till the last of them has paid for what he has done. I have taken care of four; but Fulton Zander is left, and Doctor Wayne...."

"Miss Anne!"

"You'll be late with your marketing, Faith." The girl's tones were hard now, almost brutal. "Go!" She jerked a pointing finger to the small roadster that stood waiting in the road.

A grey pallor filmed the old woman's face. Her wrinkled lips trembled—clamped shut on whatever it was she had been about to say. She shambled to the car, climbed wearily into it. A starter burred, gears clashed. Then the road was empty, and Anne Marsh was alone.

THE TOWERING loom of Lane Hill, out of whose woods the highway's pale ribbon curved to pass The Tavern and, dipping, crossed the stream on whose high bank it stood; was a blazing autumnal glory, but the girl saw none of the beauty. Her long-lashed lids were slitted, her ruby lips a tight, straight line. Her hands knotted into hard little fists.

The rattle of the roadster had faded into silence when Anne turned. Her brooding gaze slid across the small concrete bridge over Waley's Creek to a tall hedge that bordered the road beyond it. From her slight eminence she could see over the hedge, could see the velvety lawn and the gabled house of red brick it guarded. The ivy clad structure was still stately, still dignified, though its windows were striped now by the gleam of newly installed iron bars and its precincts fenced by high, close-strung barbed wire. It was still home to Anne, though a sheriff's gavel had pounded an auction block to expunge forever the name of Marsh from the deeds of ownership.

Over the pillared portico gilt letters glittered on a black sign-board. She read them once again:

LANEVILLE SANITARIUM FOR MENTAL CASES
Dr. Thomas Wayne
Director and Proprietor

Anne smiled. There was something hard, almost feral, about that smile. And her eyes were utterly without humor.

"Dr. Thomas Wayne," she murmured. "I wonder...."

The squeal of an upthrown window sash pulled her startled look to the rearmost corner of the big house. A pallid oval blotched the black oblong of an aperture just beneath the slate-shingled eave of a gable, became a face framed in streaming hair, a face twisted, distorted. Its eyes were two splotches of black soot....

A bare arm flung out between two bars and something white fluttered from abruptly spread fingers. It darted high on an ascending current of air. The face jerked out of sight. A scream shrilled from the window, utter terror in its piercing keen... *Then it was cut short by the thud of a fist on flesh!*

The window thumped shut. Someone shouted, unintelligibly, within the house. Wind, swirling from off the hillside, carried the bit of paper higher, in darting, swallowlike flight.

A door slammed open in the red brick façade, and a hulking, brute-faced man in a green uniform hurtled out of it. He lunged down the flat steps, pounded across the lawn. Anne leaped into a run that carried her around The Tavern's corner, angling toward the creek's bank.

The wind was gone as the girl reached the brink of a sheer drop to the shallow stream's nearer border. The paper dropped straight downward. The man was beneath it, was waiting to grasp it.

Something in his pose, in the avidity of his upstraining arm, his clawed fingers, gave the kiting fragment a queer importance. Why, the question flitted through Anne's brain, should he be so eager to retrieve a lunatic's scribbling? Was it because he feared that *she* should read what was written upon it? Excitement tightened her throat.

He had it! No! At the final instant a new gust puffed the white flake upward again, out of his reach. It went high, spiraling so that it was now over the enclosure, now over the creek along whose other edge the fence ran. Then it was skidding down again, on a long, erratic course that made it impossible to know where it would reach the earth.

The girl went over the bank's lip, slid down its almost sheer wall in a slither of loam and rolling stones. A slime-covered rock almost threw her headlong into the water. She kept her feet, lurched across the creek, and was stopped by the barbed wire.

"Keep away," the man shouted. "Keep—"

The paper struck the topmost strand of the fence, spun breathlessly, slipped off, *outside*. Anne snatched it from midair, twisted away. Iron-hard fingers clutched her shoulder, hauled her back.

"Gimme it," a coarse voice growled in her ear. Sharp, cruel points jabbed through her soaked garment, jabbed into her side. But her arm was stretched straight out, the paper beyond the uniformed thug's reach. "Gimme it."

Pain rayed through Anne's body. "No," she moaned, digging heels into sodden, crumbling earth, fighting with her small futile strength to wrest loose. "No." She succeeded only in tearing the barbs through her flesh, in redoubling her agony.

The savage grip on her shoulder dug in excruciatingly. "Help!" Anne screamed. "Faith! *Help!*"

Then she remembered, desperately, that Faith was gone, that the Tavern's workers had not yet arrived. The Turnpike was deserted. She might scream till her lungs burst.

"ALL RIGHT. If you won't…" Hot breath, noisome, gusted on her neck. Her head twisted to a purpling, enraged face; to piggish thick-lidded eyes red with evil intent. A snarl pulled cracked lips back from rotted teeth. A black, slim something flailed upward in the guard's free fist. A blackjack! It arched down, lashing at her skull…. Something cracked, somewhere. Anne sprawled into the creek, startlingly free of the brutal grip that had held and tortured her. Through an explosion of water she saw the blackjack plop to the ground, saw the thug reeling, fingers clutching a reddened, limp wrist; pain, amazement, making his ape's face almost ludicrous. Then she was on her feet, was somehow on the stream's other side, scrambling through a thicket of bushes and up the gully wall. Projecting roots and precariously held rocks made steps for her desperate climb.

It was not till she had scurried across the small back yard above to the shelter of the restaurant's kitchen, not till she had locked front door and rear, that Anne thought to ponder how she had been saved. A shot—it could only have been by a rifle-shot from the hill. But who had fired it?

She leaned against the sill of the kitchen window, a pool glowing at her feet on Faith Parker's immaculate floor. She stared up at the red and yellow and orange height.

A lithe, insouciant figure showed momentarily between two shaggy tree trunks, high up. Vanished. And Anne knew who it was that once more had rescued her from apparently inescapable peril.

She breathed his name. "Peter." That was almost all she knew of him. Only that he had told her to call him that, and that he hid in the lonely hills where also skulked a bandit gang that terrorized the countryside. That there was a little, heart-shaped scar at the corner of his mouth and that his lips had been hotly sweet, crushing hers.

He too was an outlaw. Their common lot drew them together—and kept them always apart. For them there was only the agonizing bliss of swift kisses stolen in the dark, of danger-harried tiny seconds of happiness snatched in the very presence of danger....

"Joe!" The word came clearly to Anne through the half-open window. She twisted, looking across Waley's Creek. The guard, still holding his wrist, was stumbling toward the low, colonaded porch. His progress seemed strangely reluctant, and he appeared to cringe; fearful, for all his bulk, of the tall, painfully thin man who stood in the doorway.

Dr. Thomas Wayne, frock-coated, annoyingly dapper, was motionless, cloaked by a dreadful stillness. Not a muscle moved in his hollow-cheeked countenance. His mouth was a tight grim line; his lids drooped, concealing whatever expression there might have been in the eyes behind it. His long arms hung lax at his sides. But there was about him an aura of icy cruelty, of a cold anger somehow the more terrible because there was no outward sign of it.

"Gees boss," the guard whined, reaching the steps. "Gees. I...."

"Get inside!" That was all Wayne said. But Joe's florid countenance was suddenly ashen as he fumbled past the physician. "I only tried to get dat paper," he whimpered, "like yuh said..." The door shut silently, hiding the two from Anne.

The paper! It was in her hand, crumpled, wet. She spread it on the sill, discovered it to be triangular; letters of print along the slanting jagged edge showing it to have been torn from some wide-margined book.

There were other markings on it, brown, smudged, exhaling a faintly medicinal odor. Scrawled letters making blurred words that were hard to read. Anne studied them, a frown creasing her white brow and a pulse thumping in her wrist as she deciphered them.

"Help me," they said. "I swear I am not mad now, but I will be soon. He is driving me…" There was more, irretrievably washed away by the creek, and then… "for the love of God."

It was signed: "Katherine Stringer."

Katherine Stringer! Anne knew that name; all Laneville knew it. The soaring chimneys of the Stringer Mills belched smoke over Slum Hollow; mile-long freight trains carried their products to the ends of the earth. Kate Stringer never went near the mills. She lived in a mansion on East Drive and spent the dividends that flowed from the enterprise her dead husband had founded. Her brother lived there with her, on her niggardly bounty. He was a paunched, pompous parasite.

Kate Stringer, leader of society had been the first to draw away her skirts from the daughter of dishonor. When the hearse bearing Webster Marsh to his grave had passed her door, Anne had seen her cold, enameled face at the window of her mansion, had seen her shrug, and turn away….

Minutes ago the girl had seen that same face at another window, framed by streaming hair, distorted by terror. She had heard the thud of a fist on flesh….

The knob of the outer door rattled. There was a rap on its glass pane. Through the opening in the partition between kitchen and dining room Anne Marsh saw who it was that demanded admittance. Tall, thin, his completely bald scalp glistening, the sardonic, infinitely threatening figure of Dr. Thomas Wayne lifted a broadcloth covered arm and knocked again.

CHAPTER TWO
DARK WHISPERS

A GASP rasped in Anne Marsh's tight throat. Wayne had come for the paper. He had come for her, *to silence her!* He must know that she had read it, that she was aware of his secret—that there was a sane woman imprisoned in his asylum whom he intended to drive mad. He would go to any lengths to protect that secret.

Terror ran gelid through Anne's veins as Wayne rapped again. The sound was a sharp, insistent finality, as if it said, "The next time I'll break the glass, twist the key and come in. You can't keep me out. You can't fight me off. You are helpless. Alone."

Not quite alone! There was the telephone on the desk just outside the partition. The girl sprang for it, jerked the receiver from its hook, jammed it against her ear.

There was no sound in the hard, cold cylinder. No wire hum. It was dead. Of course! He would not have forgotten to cut the wire. He....

And then, faintly from outside, she heard the far-off mutter of an approaching motor Faith! If only it was Faith returning. Wayne would not dare.... She must talk to him, stall him....

She hurried through the dim coolness of the room, between the circumspect booths within which flower-decked tables waited for the bustle of the evening. She reached the door, twisted the key in its lock, opened it.

"Yes." Surprisingly her voice was low, calm. "What is it?"

"Miss Marsh!" The tall man made no effort to force his way in. "I want to apologize for my man's uncouth actions."

The unexpected words jolted Anne, jarred her as though she had been struck a physical blow. "He took my instructions much too literally. I am infinitely sorry."

His tone was suave, too suave to be sincere. But why were there words at all, and not action? The roadster's rattle was nearer, but it still sounded from the distant woods. Wayne still had time to....

"He is a brute!" Indignation was in the way Anne said that, but no hint of the fear that chilled her.

"Of course. Senseless. Unfortunately that is the only type we can secure as attendants in an institution for the insane." Wayne spread deprecating hands wide. "I've discharged him, but I'm certain his successor will be no better. I hope you understand, and will do nothing to embarrass me further. Let me pay for the dress I see has been ruined. And—if you are hurt...?"

"A little iodine will fix up the scratches from the barbed wire." There was a nightmarish quality to this exchange of amenities that were so civilized, while underneath the polite phrases pulsed a weird, savage undertone, an exchange of question and answer, of threat and defiance. He was offering a truce in exchange for silence.

Well, why not? She owed Katherine Stringer only hate. The woman was the leader of those who had treated Anne as a pariah, an outcast, for what even in the most far-fetched analysis could not have been the girl's fault. There was a certain terrible justice in her present plight. Why should Anne take any risk to save her from it?

"You relieve me." The physician's pallid lips quirked in a grimace that might be meant for a smile. "And now perhaps I can do the same for you. I can sense that you are upset by the paper that has caused this tempest in a teapot. My patient wrote that she is sane, did she not? She appealed for help in rescuing her from my dreadful clutches."

ANNE'S PUPILS dilated with astonishment. "Why— yes." Her amazement was not at his knowledge of the contents of the Stringer woman's desperate message, but at his daring to drag it into the open.

"Yes. Something to that effect."

"Naturally. It never fails. They always think themselves persecuted, falsely imprisoned. If I have seen one note like that I've seen a thousand. Usually we manage to intercept them."

The effrontery of the man! He was so sure that he had her terrorized, that she would not dare to....

"But sometimes one gets out, and then we have to assure some agitated layman that we are not kidnapers, or criminals. Luckily the laws of the state enable us to do that very easily. As in this case...." He broke off, reached into his inside breast pocket, brought out a crackling, folded paper. "We always can show our authority." A flip of his wrist opened out the document. He held it so that Anne could read it.

It was a printed form, blank spaces filled in by typewriting. "WARRANT OF COMMITMENT," in bold black letters, headed it.

The girl read: "Having been shown to our satisfaction.... Katherine Stringer... reasonable cause for deeming mentally incompetent... committed... Laneville Sanitarium...." There were two scrawled signatures over the printed words, "State Lunacy Commissioners." There was a red seal embossed in the lower corner, and the written notation, "Approved, Condon Foster, Judge of the Superior Court."

Hysteric laughter twisted in Anne Marsh's breast. A fool—what a fool she had been! Silly to have thought for a single moment that Thomas Wayne, M.D., President of the Bolton County Medical Association, member of the Board of Directors of the Union Light and Power Company, tycoon of Laneville Society, would hold a woman captive without warrant. Imbecilic to have feared him as a killer, to have been half-mad with fear him.

"I—I see," she managed. "I ought to apologize to you for...."

"Not at all." He put the warrant back into his pocket. "I think we fully understand each other now." Again that faint, humorless smile licked his lips. "Please don't forget to let me replace your dress." He bowed. Was it with courtesy or mockery? He strode off.

The roadster roared out of the woods. Faith Parker's satin-clad, stiffly erect shape at the wheel was a symbol of the naturalness, of the sanity, that had returned to Bolton Turnpike. Anne dodged back into The Tavern, hurrying to her room to repair the damages wrought by her adventure, so that she would not have to worry her old servant, her only friend, over it.

She had been a fool.... Wait! Why had the telephone wire been cut? Why was Wayne not complaining to the police about the man who had shot from the hills, wounding his employee? Surely if there were nothing wrong about Katherine Stringer's incarceration, the physician had no reason to conceal what had happened here this morning.

If there were nothing wrong....

DIM LIGHTS gleaming on spotless napery, the spicy, aromatic fragrance of Faith Parker's miraculous coffee; of her ambrosial food; soft-footed, smiling waitresses; quiet, hushed talk in booths that gave a feeling of discreet privacy to each group in the crowded room—this was The Tavern. All Laneville, all that mattered, made it their nightly rendezvous. Anne Marsh sat at her desk before the doorway in the kitchen. She was silent, wistful, her gaze veiled, withdrawn.

For almost a year she had sat here, watching, listening. Listening to almost inaudible voices that came, strangely enough, from beneath the desktop on which she checked bills and made change.

Within the cubicles where they sat, her patrons were unguarded in their talk. As long as they kept their tones low, they thought, they could not be overheard. The partitions were too high, too thick, the tables too wide apart. They did not know that hairlike wires led from each booth to a switchboard within reach of Anne's slim hand; that every single word they uttered could be repeated to her at her will by the whispering diaphragm concealed in the kneehole of her desk.

John Simpson wondered still how a midnight prowler had known exactly where his bedroom safe was hidden, and just when it would be richly stuffed. John Lawton had not yet solved the mystery of how every detail of his ingenious scheme to safeguard his bank messenger had been learned by the daring thief who single-handed had defeated it. Donald Reynolds and Fred Harris had never discovered how they had betrayed themselves to the secret nemesis who had lightened their pockets of the ill-gotten gains the law approved.

Only Fulton Zander and Wayne were left. But these two had not visited The Tavern for weeks. Anne was getting impatient, waiting for them. Perhaps she would have to resort to some other method....

A strident, high-pitched voice interrupted her thoughts, rising shrill and rasping out of a booth in the farthermost corner. "Purple pansies! They clash with my dress. Tell them to take them away at once."

Hannah Walsh, the pert, black-eyed head waitress, hurried in that direction. A male voice rumbled—and then Hannah reappeared, carrying a bowl of velvety, gorgeous flowers. The dancing-eyed minx winked as she passed her mistress, and murmured a scathing sentence.

"Zelda Angton making sure everybody'll see her new sugar daddy. She'll lead Henry Vance a merry dance."

Henry Vance! Katherine Stringer's brother! A pulse thumped in Anne's temple. Strange that he should be here, with his sister a closely guarded patient in the lunatic asylum just across the creek. Stranger still that Zelda Angton should accompany him. A notorious demimondaine, it took real money to support her in the style to which she had accustomed her protectors. What interest could she have in a man whose scant pocket money was miserly measured out?

There they were. Anne had missed their entrance, probably when she had stepped into the kitchen in response to a call from Faith. But she could see them now, in one of the ceiling mirrors that, apparently a part of the artful decorations, were yet skillfully arranged to give her a view of every inch of the place. Vance's black toupée was bent forward over the table, his massive shoulders hunched forward as if in an endeavor to get closer to his green-sheathed, voluptuous bosomed companion.

ANNE COULD see them—and she could hear them now, as her darting fingers moved the speaker-switch to its proper setting!

"There now, Zelda," his accents were the syrupy, fatuous ones of an infatuated oldster, "stop pouting. They're gone, like that." He snapped pudgy, dough-yellow fingers. "Just a word from you and—and you can have anything you want. Anything at all."

"Like having pansies taken away when I don't like them." Mascaraed eyelids were narrowed, speculative. "Sure. But how about putting orchids in their place? How about that sable wrap you've been talking about?" She was being crude. She did not have to be subtle with the enamoured satyr.

"I've promised it to you, and you'll get it, if you'll only have a little patience."

There was queer assuredness in his speech. From where did he draw it? Anne's brow puckered. Could it be that...?

"Patience!" The Angton woman's hands closed on the edge of the table, her scarlet nails digging in. "That's all you can say. How long do you expect to get away with it?"

"A week. Only a week more. I saw Zander today, and he told me that everything's set. The final papers will be signed in a week, and then I'll be boss of...."

"Hush!" The monosyllabic warning was sharp—frightened. "Don't say it." Zelda Angton's flabby chin, where art could not conceal time's ravages, quivered. "Don't talk about it, here or anywhere else."

Vance sank back in his chair. Whatever terror had made the siren momentarily forget her role seemed to have communicated itself to him. Anne could see his face, color-drained, yellow. His tongue licked pendulous lips.

"You're right," he whispered. "We must be careful. Careful. Zander said...."

"Shut up, you senile ass!" It was the hiss of an enraged eat. For an instant Anne thought Zelda would claw the man with her curved talons. Then she was smiling...."No, dear. I don't think I shall have any dessert." Hazel Jervis, their waitress, appeared in the open end of the booth. "My diet, you know. And we'd better be going. Little girl must get her beauty sleep."

The eavesdropper switched off her microphone. There would be nothing more of interest said in booth number twelve.

There was some connection between what she had just heard and what had happened this morning. Some dark, evil thread between them. They were bits, small bits of a jig-saw puzzle; too few, too small to give more than a hint of the completed picture.

Through the months the whispering voice of Anne's loud-speaker had brought her many such tantalizing fragments of other people's lives. She had listened to them and dismissed them—usually. But she could not dismiss these. They concerned, somehow, the two who remained of those responsible for Webster Marsh's disgrace and suicide, the two who thus far had evaded her vengeance.

Had she found their Achilles' heel, their vulnerable point, at last?

CHAPTER THREE
SHADOWS IN THE NIGHT

"**HENRY'S KICKIN'** up while his sister Kate's on her trip." Gossip-loving Hannah Welsh chuckled.

Anne Marsh looked up, her grey eyes round, innocent of anything but mild interest. "Is she away? I hadn't heard."

"You don't read the sassiety column in the *Courier* like I do. She's takin' that Mexico cruise they was advertisin' so much this year. She ought to be gettin' back in a week, she's been gone three already.

"Funny thing, though. She slipped off kind of secret this time. Usual thing when she goes away is a big delegation at the station, a cartload o' flowers an' everything. Me, I got a hunch maybe she's steppin' out herself. She ain't been a widow too long, an' she ain't too bad lookin', especially with her wad, for some guy to be buzzin' round her. Mame Joyce, in the beauty parlor, was sayin'."

The head-waitress' prattle was a meaningless babble falling on deaf ears. The real reason, then, for Mrs. Stringer's absence from her usual haunts had been carefully concealed. Anne was thinking. Her remarriage would in all likelihood exile Henry Vance to the outer cold of his poverty. Yet he was promising Zelda orchids, sables… in a week.…

The outlines of a dastardly plot grew firmer in her mind.

Fragments of forgotten knowledge floated out of the girl's subconscious. An article she had read somewhere, on the insanity laws of the state. No inquiry in open court was required to commit a suspected incompetent to an institution for observation. Only a hearing, easily kept secret, before two lunacy commissioners whose appointment was usually a reward for political services. Routine approval by a judge who never read the papers submitted for signature. Easily, too easily arranged.

True, after thirty days, the patient would receive a public hearing before the final adjudication was made and a guardian, usually the nearest relative, was appointed to take complete charge of his estate. For this he must be scientifically proven insane....

"I swear I am not mad now," words in brown tracing wavered before Anne's inner vision, *"but... he is driving me...."*

She recalled a scream, the thud of a fist on flesh.... Horror brushed her spine with a feathery chill. Then a fiery indignation seared her, burned to nothingness a resentment she had nursed through long, bitter months.

She whose once *seigne*, aristocratic countenance had peered from a barred window ravaged by terror and despair was a helpless woman caught in the machinations of heartless fiends. And those who plotted her destruction were the same as had encompassed the death of a kindly, well-meaning man by his own hand!

They had the law on their side. The law! *Long ago Anne Marsh had discovered how far apart were the law—and justice.*

"Hannah," she interrupted the girl who still rambled on, "I'm awfully tired. Will you please take over the desk for the rest of the evening?"

"Sure. You go lie down, dearie. You do look bad!"

Faith Parker, bustling about the busy kitchen in a white apron, a white cap that confined her straggling hair, checked her acidulous berating of an assistant cook who had stopped his stirring of a redolent sauce a half-minute too soon. A frown of anxiety deepened the wrinkles of her bird-like, leathery visage.

"Miss Anne!" she exclaimed. "What's wrong?"

"Nothing, Faith dear," the girl replied, crossing to the door that gave on the single room that was the living quarters of the couple who had made so great a success of The Tavern on Bolton Turnpike. "I've been up late every night for a week, and I've decided to go to bed early tonight."

Anne opened the portal, went through it. Cooks, dish-washers, waitresses, could swear, tomorrow, that they had seen her enter that room, that she had net left it again. They knew this was the only way in or out of it. They knew that its single window was barred, that below that window was a sheer drop of twenty feet to the bushes shrouding Waley's Creek.

BUT THE worry remained on Faith's face, and her gnarled old hands trembled a bit as they snatched the stir-ring spoon from the erring cook's grasp. Her lips moved, as if in silent prayer for the safety of one dearly beloved.

Anne Marsh did not bother to switch on the light in the bedroom. The heavens were overcast, and the chamber was dark as the inside of a tar barrel, but she went unstum-blingly across it to the window in its further wall.

Her slim hands closed on the iron bars. Momentarily she peered through them, staring wide-eyed at the dark, serrated bulk of the old Marsh House against the city's faint sky-glow. Her glance, clung to the triangular jot of the gable beneath which a woman lay, weltering in the agony of despair.

Something of that agony quivered over the fenced lawn, over the murmuring creek and the gully whose precipitous face fell sheer from beneath Anne's vantage point, and entered her soul. "For the love of God…" Katherine Stringer had written. "Help me."

There was only one way she could be helped. She must be produced in court, still sane, a week from now.

Till then the law said she must remain in that house of evil. Anyone who helped her escape from there, who harbored her, would be a criminal in the eyes of the law.

That bitter, mirthless smile contorted Anne's velvety young mouth once more. Her hands twisted the bars they held, moving the cold iron minutely in its sockets.

Somewhere behind her there was the hiss of wood rubbing softly against wood. A dank, earthy smell crept into the room.

Anne turned, moved with silent surety toward a widening strip of blackness that broke the floor's black plateau. She reached it. A second later the floor was solid once more….

And the bedroom was empty of any living being.

Beneath it a small, windowless chamber sprang into existence in a sudden yellow light released by a touch of Anne's finger on the button of a wall switch. She stepped off the lowermost rung of a wooden ladder, went with quiet purposefulness toward an age-patinaed workbench bulking in the center of the hard-packed, earthen floor.

Tools lay carelessly scattered among curled metal and wooden shavings on the gouged top of the bench, as though dropped by a worker who would soon return. Anne caught her breath, and pain darkened her eyes.

She never came in here without feeling the living, breathing presence of her father, as through the years he had guided her fumbling childish hands in the intricacies of manual craft while the comradeship between them grew till it was something infinitely precious. And then she would remember that he lay, disgraced, dishonored, in the little cemetery beyond the hills. She would remember the use to which she put the skill he had taught her.

For a long time there was no sound in the underground workroom but the scrape of keen edges on metal and wood, the rasp of rope fibres being twisted into a certain useful form. Then there was the rustle of silk garments being hurriedly discarded, the harsher hissing of rougher clothing hastily donned.

A slim, lithe, figure in the garb of a boy hung a bag to its belt. A finger touched the switch, and again-darkness invaded the secret, subterranean chamber. Once more there was the furtive whisper of wood surfaces sliding upon one another, this time not in the room's ceiling, but in its roughly boarded wall.

The bushes along Waley's Creek rustled to the passage of a slim form, closed again as if to keep the secret of the feminine Robin Hood who worked justice outside the law.

THE NIGHT was dark, but nowhere was it darker than in the space underneath the bridge that carried Bolton Turnpike over Waley's Creek. There, where the sun never penetrated, it was wet too, and very cold.

Queer, then, that a man should crouch there, huddled in discomfort. Queer that he should have crouched there, night after night, unsleeping, with lashless eyes scanning with untiring vigilance the night-shrouded purlieus of The Tavern where there was light, and warmth, and quiet comfort.

Bulldog Ryan shifted a bit, to ease the numbness of his prickling haunches. "Hell!" he muttered. "Mebbe I'm wrong. There ain't been a sign o' nothin'."

He fished a cigarette out of his pocket, lit it with a patented lighter that showed no flame to betray him. Faint glow from the tiny cylinder's end illumined his countenance; pinched, thin-lipped, ferret-like.

"No." Even in breathed soliloquy his voice was toneless, heavy with the animal quality of dogged persistence that had earned him his sobriquet. "You're stayin' right here, Tom Ryan, till she gives herself away. You've got it figured right. She must have some way o' comin' out o' the place through the back, when she goes on the prowl. An' you're goin' to be right here, so's you can tail her an' catch her red-handed. She's played with you long en—"

He broke off, freezing rigid. Not twenty yards from him a shadow drifted across the stream. He had noticed a line of stones there, had wondered whether anyone had ever crossed there, dry-shod....

The cigarette spark blinked out. Not one, hut two corporeal shadows stole silently through the darkness-shrouded night.

CHAPTER FOUR
RESCUE FROM HELL

A STRAND of barbed wire curled away from the fence along Waley's Creek. Its end, dipping in the water, had been cleanly cut by keen clippers.

Anne Marsh huddled against a brick façade that was red by day, but now was a black loom soaring high above her. Her fingers touched the shaggy roughness of a thick vine-stem, lovingly. It was an old friend. Every inequality of the ground she had just crossed, every blade of grass, it seemed, was part of her memories.

Nostalgia was a leaden weight in her bosom. This house was home. She had been born behind this wall. She had been happy here. Now she was about to enter it again—as a criminal, a thief by night.

She listened, taut, quivering. Behind her there was the ripple of the brook, the shrill, unending chorus of nocturnal insects. Over her the ivy rustled. From within the house, just above the threshold of hearing, she could distinguish hushed sounds; a snore, the creak of a restless bed; but nothing to show that anyone was awake within, except a muffled, unending sobbing directly above her. Up there was the gabled window where Katherine Stringer's pallid face had appeared....

This house was home no longer. From within its walls an aura of evil flowed. Suddenly Anne Marsh was afraid, her blood a gelid quiver in her veins.

What would they do to her if they caught her inside? What would Thomas Wayne do? Even Joe, his brute-faced, brute-thewed servitor, had cringed before his silent, slit-lidded stare....

"Go back!" Panic shrilled in her ears. "Go back! You owe Katherine Stringer nothing. Go back, you little fool!"

White, sharp teeth bit into a quivering underlip. Anne Marsh lifted, stifling a whimper of dreadful fear. She started climbing....

The vine trembled under her weight. Long ago it had trembled thus when on some girlish midnight escapade she had climbed it. It had held, that night. But there had been no bag slung to her waist, heavy with a queerly shaped thing of metal. That night her hands had not been clumsy with gauntleted gloves of thick rubber.

Relieved breath hissed faintly from between Anne's teeth as she found the vine took her weight and still clung to its ancient holds; as she found that her grip was sure and certain, despite the strange covering on her hands.

She passed the line of the first floor windows, of the second. Stopped suddenly, just beneath the sill of the one that was her goal. She clung there, a flat blotch of darkness against the dark wall.

At the level of her waist two thickly covered wires swung out of the darkness to where glass insulators fastened them to the corner of the building. One of Anne's gloved hands reached out, drew them in to her.

Her movements were deft, sure, as if they had been rehearsed. The linesman's clippers came out of her bag, stripped a bit of the insulation from each of the electric cables. Her hand brought out two other wires, their copper ends gleaming in some vagrant light beam as rubber-protected fingers twisted one about each of the bared spots on the power lines.

Anne renewed her climb, and two wires trailed behind her, coiling out of the receptacle she had filled in the secret room beneath The Tavern. Her knee found the sill of the window in the gable. As she remembered it, the ledge was wide enough to hold her and leave her hands free.

The sobbing was louder now, though still muffled by the shut pane, but between the woman whose soul-agony it voiced and the girl she had scorned, were three thumb-thick steel bars, fastened securely into the stone jamb of the aperture.

There was no way to force those bars from their sockets. But the small, flaming arc of an electric cutter could slice through them as a hot knife would through butter. Anne pulled black goggles over her eyes, pressed a switch on the small, grotesquely shaped apparatus she held....

In lashless eyes, far below, a spark of reluctant admiration flared in response to the tiny flare above. "The little devil," Bulldog Ryan grunted. "She's got what it takes, all right. She'll be inside in three minutes." Then his pointed visage was a steely mask once more.

He rose out of the shrubbery where he had been lying, watching his quarry. The long trail was ended at last. The prowler—there was no uncertainty in his mind as to who it was, though all he had seen of her was a flitting, veiled shape in the night—would find him waiting for her when the bars were cut away and she went through them into the room they guarded. *This* time there would be no escape for her, no alibi.

His squat, stocky body slithered soundlessly through the darkness. He rounded the asylum's corner, went up on the porch. His stubby, spatulate fingers tapped softly on the door within the columned porch.

"Wayne always keeps a guard right inside here," he muttered. "Hope he's got sense enough not to make any noise."

A bolt rasped inside, coming out of its sockets. The door moved inward.

"Joe!" the detective breathed. "It's the law. It's Tom Ryan. There's someone breakin' in, upstairs, an' we can cop him pretty if we don't scare him off."

"Got yeh!" The hoarse whisper vibrated from stygian darkness in which the speaker was a vague, barely perceptible presence.

"Come on in."

THE SMELL of hot metal was pungent in Anne's nostrils. The last bar came away. She caught it, twisted one of the wires around it, dropped cutter and bar below her.

The glowing end of the bar pendulumed to the twanging of the cables she had tapped, faded out.

The window went up easily. The sobbing inside cut off.

"It's all right," the girl hissed sharply.

"I've come to get you out of here." She slid through the opening, was within the room. She shoved the goggles up on her forehead, saw the faint, pale oblong of a tousled bed, a form stretched out on it.

Something awkward about that form, something unnaturally stiff. Closer, the girl saw that it was bound to the bed by wide straps of canvas webbing whose edges cut into plump, quivering flesh that had never known anything harsher than silk sheets and filmy, gossamer underclothing.

Anne slashed at the bonds with a knife drawn from the capacious receptacle at her waist, her eyes darting fearfully to the door that cut the wan glimmer of one wall. Some sixth sense warned her of imminent danger behind that door. Dread tightened an iron band about her temples.

"Listen," she whispered, "while you're letting the blood get in circulation again I'll be dropping a rope ladder out of the window. You go down it, duck across the lawn. Don't wait for me. You'll find a gap in the fence. Go across the creek, keep on straight through the bushes on the other side, straight toward the gully wall. There's a hole in it. Go through that. You'll find yourself in a room. Push the panel shut. I know how to open it from the outside. Understand?"

"Bless you. God bless...."

The bonds fell free, and the girl flung back to the window. The last of the contrivances she had fashioned on the old work-bench was a rope ladder. She fastened its steel hooks into the sill, let it unroll down the side of the house. Kate Stringer, beside her, gasped with hysteria.

"I can't climb down that," she whimpered hysterically. "I can't...."

"You will!" Anne lifted her knife. The goggles had dropped back over her eyes, and she was a gnomelike, fearsome thing to the woman who had been driven to the edge of madness by calculated ill-treatment. "Get down there. Hurry, or...."

Katherine rented a little scream, went over the sill. The hooks shook as Anne watched them, then they were still.

She lifted a foot to follow—"Hold it," someone said behind her. "Hold it just like that. And keep your hands away from your sides. I've got you covered." Then, as she obeyed. "Turn around. Slowly. I want to get a good look at you."

CHAPTER FIVE
DISASTER

ANNE MARSH'S skin was an icy, prickling sheath for her body. Fear curdled her brain, dried her throat, tightened clutching fingers on her fluttered heart.

The man in the doorway was wrapped in a terrible silence. Light falling on him sideways from some unseen hall lamp sketched Dr. Thomas Wayne in bizarre shadows so that his spare, tall form was somehow satanic. Not the blue-glinting automatic in his bony fist struck terror into the rigid girl, but the implication of the faint smile edging his fleshless lips, the drifting flecks of cruel light in his deep-socketed eyes.

They were taking in the empty bed, the burned away bars, the ladder-hooks gouging the sill behind her. They drifted over her quivering form, and Anne felt as though they were stripping her boy's clothing from her, as though they were searing her naked flesh.

"I see," he hissed. "I see what you've been up to. It was a mad thing to do, wasn't it. Insane."

Insane! What did he mean? *Why did he say just that— here in this madhouse?*

"An insane thing," the slow words dropped into the room's quivering silence. "Well, I know the right treatment for that. You couldn't have come to a better place."

"Stop it!" Anne whispered from cracked lips. "Cut the talk. Call the police! You've got me dead to rights. Call the police and turn me over to them."

She'd have a chance to tell the story when they came. She'd send them to find Kate Stringer, still sane....

"No." Why should light glittering on a bald head seem so sinister? "No. Not till you tell me where she's gone. I want her back."

"Never!"

That cold, humorless smile again. "I think you will change your mind. Yes. If you have a mind left to change." He looked at a table she had not noticed before. There was a brown bottle on it, a hypodermic syringe. "You seem to know something about what that can accomplish. Or perhaps you would like to find out.... Where is Katherine Stringer?"

Anne's lips made no sound, but she shook her head in refusal to answer.

"Very well." A thin membrane seemed to drop over Wayne's eyes, appallingly like that of a vulture's. "If I must convince you that you *must* answer..." He started into the room.

The girl swayed back. She was at the window. A twist, a sudden leap—death below would be preferable....

"A shot in the leg will stop that. I wouldn't try it if I were you."

Anne swayed back. Something uncanny about the way he read her mind. "You'll have to shoot me in the heart before you lay hands on me," she grated, defiantly. "You'll have to kill me...."

Wayne halted. "Very admirable," he chuckled dryly. "Perhaps you might get away with that if I were alone. But, fortunately, I have help." Then he was calling, aloud. "Fred. Come up here." He did not turn however, did not take his eyes from her. "Fred."

Somewhere below there was an answering call, and the thump of footfalls hurrying upstairs. Coming down a long hallway. A shadow fell across the doorway, then a man was lurching in.

"Yes, doctor," he said. "What—?"

He sprang. His hand flailed from behind Wayne, gripped the automatic, wrested it from his grip. His other arm was around the physician's neck, garroting him.

The doctor fought viciously, snarling, but unavailingly. Anne staring at the struggle, saw a bristling, unshaven face—*saw a puckered, heart-shaped scar at the corner of a twisting mouth....*

THOMAS WAYNE was spread-eagled on the bed where Katherine Stringer had lain a prisoner. He was helpless, bound with the very webbings of canvas with which he had strapped her there.

The man he had called Fred rose, panting. Anne got across the room to him, seized his hand. "Peter!" she exclaimed. "I...."

"How do you two think you're going to get away with this?" Wayne granted, his countenance a grey false-face of hate. "If you don't kill me I'll hound you to the ends of the earth.... You especially, Miss Anne Marsh. You didn't think that disguise could fool a trained physician, did you?"

The girl's hand was an icy lump in that of her lover. This was the end of the trail, then. She would have to give up The Tavern, give up her plans, and flee....

"I don't think you'll be telling anyone about Anne Marsh, or about anything else that's happened here tonight." Peter's voice was steady, calm. "Not after you know I have this." His hand went to his breast pocket, came out again. "When you I came up here I had a chance to get into your bedroom safe and get this letter. Recognize it?" He held it so that the physician could see it.

Anne managed to read enough of it to get its sense. It was from Henry Vance. It promised Wayne a quarter share in the Stringer Mills when the writer's sister was declared insane and Vance was placed in charge of the property. It ended with the phrase, "I am making this promise on your assurance that you will accomplish this by the time of the final hearing."

Wayne's lips were blue with fury. But he was still defiant. "That is no evidence against me in a court of law," he said. "What that ass wrote doesn't bind me."

"But it binds *him*, especially when the sister will appear to testify as to what was done to her here. And if you think Henry Vance won't spill his guts to save himself from jail, you're crazier than your patients. You're goose is cooked, Dr. Thomas Wayne."

The bound man blinked. Then he was speaking again. "You win," he muttered. "I should have known there was something wrong when you showed up so pat after I fired

Joe this morning and 'phoned for a man to take his place. I suppose you tapped my wires."

"Right."

"And you've got the goods on me. All right. How much will you take to burn that letter and keep your mouths shut?"

"Nothing," Peter blurted. "You—"

"Wait." Anne's eyes were aglow with excitement. "Wait Peter. Listen." She drew him aside, whispered to him.

The two came back to the bedside. "You're lucky," the young man said. "Miss Marsh has intervened for you. We're going to talk business with you."

"I thought she'd make you see sense! How much?"

"Not a red cent."

"But...."

"But a couple of signatures. One to a complete confession of the plot against Katherine Stringer. That's for security The other to a deed for this house and its grounds, a deed, Dr. Wayne, making it over to the Laneville Home for Orphans. You remember, don't you, that the institution's mortgage was foreclosed because the Community Chest funds were embezzled, last Christmas?"

BULLDOG RYAN rolled over, bruising his throbbing brain against its enclosing skull. The grey light of the false dawn showed him that he was on the portico of the Marsh house. With an effort, he remembered stepping through its door, hearing the swish of a blackjack in the darkness, feeling it crash against his scalp....

He pushed numbed palms against the porch floor, pushed himself to a sitting position. He was facing The Tavern. Two figures in its doorway were locked in each other's arms.

"Gees!" Ryan groaned. "That looks like two boys, kissin' each other." He rubbed the bump on his dome. "Or maybe I'm seein' things." He pushed shaking hands against the porch floor, pushed himself erect....

The kiss on Anne's lips was white-hot fire. Then Peter whirled away from her.

"Goodbye, sweetheart," he blurted. "Goodbye." And he was running up the road, plunging into the thicket where its lift over Lane Hill began.

"Peter," the girl moaned, looking after him. "Peter..." Then she was whirling to the crunch of a heavy footfall on gravel.

"Up early," Bulldog Ryan grunted. "Ain't you?"

The girl forced a trembling smile. "You seem to be also, Mr. Ryan."

"Yeah." His eyes were heavy-lidded, red-rimmed. "Yeah. I'm lookin' for a goat."

"A goat? Oh, Mr. Ryan! Whose?"

"Mine. It got lost a while back. Last spring, matter of fact. Somewhere around here. I been lookin' for it since. I thought I found it last night, but I was wrong. I'm goin' to find it though. I'm goin' to keep lookin' for it till I find it. An' when I do, it's goin' to be hell for the party that's got it."

"How interesting," Anne's eyes were round, innocent. "How very interesting." But somewhere in their grey depths there was an evasive glimmer of fear.

"Yeah. I thought you'd like to know. Well, I got to be going back to Laneville."

"You might do something for me, Mr. Ryan. Would you?"

"Sure. What is it?"

"If you happen to see Henry Vance, you might tell him his sister's coming home sooner than he expected. I'm sure he'll be enthralled to hear it."

THE PASSING OF ANNE MARSH

THROUGH DANGER AND EVER-PRESENT DEATH ANNE MARSH HAD FOUGHT TO MAKE RESTITUTION TO THE WRECKED AND RUINED VICTIMS OF THE CRIMINAL COMBINE WHICH HAD DRIVEN HER FATHER TO DEATH. AND NOW, AT THE MOMENT OF HER TRIUMPH, WHEN, AT LAST, SHE STOOD READY TO DELIVER HER MASTER STROKE—THE HAND OF HER RELENTLESS NEMESIS FELL IRREVOCABLY UPON HER SLENDER, SHRINKING SHOULDER....

"**I**T'S COMIN'** on to snow, Miss Anne," a thin querulous voice called. "It's goin' to be a white Christmas."

Faith Parker's work-gnarled fingers were red and ungainly against the gay-hued chintz curtain they held aside from a frost-edged window. Her eyes, peering through the glass, were tiny, birdlike in a countenance yellow and wrinkled as old parchment—sere and sharp-featured. Her flat-breasted, scrawny frame was enveloped by an immaculate white Hoover apron, and there clung to her the spicy redolence of the crisp roast meats, the savory gravies, the toothsome, mouth-melting pastries that made The Tavern on Bolton Turnpike the nightly rendezvous of Laneville's élite.

"It had snowed already the day I came home, just a year ago. There was snow and ice all the way from the college. Lane Hill was all white and the white on the dark boughs of the pines was very beautiful." Anne Marsh spoke as though to herself. She moved with an unconscious lovely grace between dim booths within which holly-decked tables nestled discreetly. Her garb was that of a slim, athletic boy, high-laced leather boots, whipcord breeches, plaid lumber jacket, visored wool cap, but she was utterly feminine. The thick wool of her mackinaw could not hide the tender curves of womanhood. Tight, tawny curls escaped from under the black cap to set off a wistful small face. Her lips, deeply red and velvet soft, were fashioned for caresses but incongruously were edged with pain. Her long-lashed grey eyes were destined for laughter but mirrored only a lurking, sleepless fear.

"Beautiful," Anne's low, throbbing voice repeated. "The icy air was like wine bubbling in my veins, and I was happy. I was coming home to Dad, Faith, to the man who had been father and mother to me as long as I could remember. For two weeks we were going to tramp together over the hills, and spend long evenings together in our workshop, happily contriving some clever, useless little gadget. I reached home, and…."

"Miss Anne! You mustn't…!"

"And found Dad dead by his own hand; his name, for years so venerated in the city he loved, a synonym for dishonor." The girl's mouth twitched with a suffering one so young should not have been called on to endure. "He had stolen the charity money entrusted to him to be distributed at Christmas."

"He did not steal it," the older woman denied fiercely. "He did not mean…."

"No, he did not mean to take it. Relying on the promises of a half-dozen of Laneville's leaders to replace it before it would have to be paid out, he had borrowed the Community Chest funds to save his Union Light and Power Company, to save the hundreds of small investors and the thousands of laborers who depended upon it for their living from disaster. But his false friends broke the promise they never intended to keep. The company failed, and they bought it in for a song, as they had planned. It was they who were the real thieves, but they stole within the law, safely and cleverly."

"It was that lawyer who told them how to do it Miss Anne. Fulton Zander. He's shrewd...."

"Shrewd and cunning as Satan. He and his clients are called honest men by the same law that says Webster Marsh was a thief. The same law that says I am a thief—It's right, Faith. I *am* a thief, an outlaw. A pariah...."

She checked. Clear and distinct, a cheer came in through the Tavern's walls, the shrill, piping outcry of many merry children.

"Listen," Faith Parker exclaimed. "Listen to them orphans. Would they be cheerin' like that if you hadn't got that home for them by blackmail, or would they be shiverin' in Slum Hollow, blue with cold and hunger?" She turned back to the window. "Look at them, Miss Anne. Come here and look at them."

THE GIRL came alongside of her. Outside, to the left, the wooded height of Lane Hill loomed against the sky's leaden vault; but to the right, across the concrete bridge over Waley's Creek, the highway dipped and she could see over the tall hedge that bordered the road.

Far back from the highway a gabled dwelling of time-darkened ivy-clad brick was stately and dignified as when anciently Joshua Marsh had built it to house his progeny of whom she was the last. Over the pillared portico a newly painted sign said, LANEVILLE CHILDRENS' HOME. On the velvet lawn sloping to the pike, winter had killed the plants and shrubbery, but it was a live and vibrant garden of human flowers. A throng of warmly clad, ruddy-cheeked youngsters darted about, screaming gleefully as

the dancing first snowflakes eluded their chubby little hands.

"Oh they *are* happy, Faith." A smile tugged at the corners of Anne's mouth and a little of the bitterness faded from her winsome face. "It was worth the price to give them that."

"Anne," he groaned, "get away from me—"

She grew sober again, remembering the night of dire peril out of which she had wrenched that home for the homeless. She had felt death's hot breath on her neck, that dreadful midnight, and almost the teeth of the law's bull-dog had sunk into her soft flesh. If it had not been for Peter....

Her glance came away from the gay scene and strained through the sudden thick veil of white crystals that with silent swiftness already obscured the mountain from which Bolton Turnpike curved.

He was somewhere up there, she thought, the youth who so many times had appeared out of his mysterious abode to save her from disaster and so many times had vanished again into that mystery, carrying her heart with him. Peter! She knew of him only that no matter what the odds against him his dark head was jauntily cocked and his blue eyes dauntless, that there was a heart-shaped little scar at the corner of his mouth....

And that his kisses had burned like white flame on her lips.

Her hands tightened, abruptly, on the sill. "Faith," she gasped. "Faith. There's someone..." Then she had whirled to the Tavern door, was out in the blinding swirl, was running up the road.

There it was, the form she had glimpsed through a momentary gap in the seething downfall. She had seen the man stagger, fall. Now he was crawling, like some dark beast, on hands and one knee in the highway. Crawling slowly, painfully, while behind him a scarlet stain trailed for a moment, melting the snowy film, and was almost instantly blotted out by a new coating of white.

"Peter," Anne whispered through frozen lips. "Peter. What's the matter? What...."

He kept crawling; as if he did not hear her; hitched himself along, slowly, painfully. The leg from which dribbled that gory thread dragged, a lifeless, useless thing, behind him.

"Peter." The girl bent to him, got shaking hands on his shoulders. "It's I. It's Anne. Don't you understand, it's Anne Marsh."

He stopped then, twisted his hanging head to look up at her. His lips were whiter than the flakes that settled on them and melted in the feathery vapor of his breath; his cheeks were sunken, quivering; his eyes were dark pits of agony.

"Anne," he groaned. "Get away from me. Go away. They mustn't find you—with me."

"You're hurt, Peter. Your leg's broken."

"Shot," he whispered. "I was almost—free. But a lucky bullet—" He coughed, the spasm seeming to rack every fibre of his lithe, slender body. "They know I came this way. You—leave me. They…" He pitched forward, fell inert, a still mound in the snow.

A sudden frigid gust flailed icy particles against Anne's cheek, but it was not the savage onslaught that lined her face with drab despair. Long ago she had surmised Peter to be one of the bandits who skulked in the No Man's Land of Lane Hill and descended from it in swift forays. The police had made many raids into that mountain fastness and had returned empty-handed, but they had routed Peter from his hiding place at last. They must be close on his trail. In minutes, in seconds, perhaps, they would overtake him.

If they found her with him—that's what he had been trying to say—she would be gathered into the net of the law. Bulldog Ryan, the plodding, indomitable detective who alone had suspected her own outlawry, would seize the chance to arrest her. Armed with a search warrant he would at least be enabled to probe The Tavern thoroughly, and he would find indubitable proof of her guilt.

"Peter," Anne groaned, going to her knees beside him. "Peter. Wake up. You've got to wake up!"

She shook him with frantic hands. Muted and incoherent through distance a shout reached her from far up the mountain. Another answered. It was nearer. The police! They were still far away, but they were coming fast?

"Peter!" Her palm spatted against his cheek, stingingly. "Wake up."

"Ugh," he grunted. "What?"

"Try and get up, Peter. Try hard." She had an arm under him, was trying to lift him. "If you can hop on your good leg I'll be a crutch for the other. Get up, Peter. Please get up."

HE WAS struggling. He was breathing hard, and his eyes were closed, but he was moving, trying to get his uninjured leg under him, thrusting at ground with his cold-blued hands. Anne threw all her small strength into the effort to aid him. She managed to slide her shoulder under his arm pit, to get his arm over her back. She heaved upward, pain tearing at her chest, tearing at her back, his weight like lead holding her down.

The rising wind howled eerily in the tree-tops she could no longer see. It wasn't the wind. It was the siren of a police car, wailing down the white slope. They dared not go too fast in this white sightlessness but they were coming surely, inexorably.

"That's it, Peter darling." Anne's voice was low, encouraging and very steady. "That's fine." She had one arm around his waist, her other hand clutched the wrist of his arm that was around her neck, and they were erect on their knees. "One more try and we'll make it. When I count three. Do you understand?"

The siren yowled.

The motion of his head was somehow grotesque, as though it were the head of a marionette manipulated by someone unskilled. But it was a nod.

"One…" The siren howl was nearer. "Two…" The hunters were coming faster than she had thought possible "*Three!*"

Peter's attempt to rise was pathetic in its feebleness, but he did make it. Anne found some unguessed-at reserve of strength in her aching thighs and with that slight aid they miraculously surged to their feet.

It was too late! They were only fifty-feet from the tavern's door, but the juggernaut must overtake them before they could possibly reach it!

CHAPTER TWO

TRAPPED

"RUN ANNE!" Peter muttered, thick-tongued. "You... can escape." He had regained a modicum of consciousness, but he was a lax, almost lifeless burden, leaning heavily upon her.

"No!" the girl sobbed. Like a grotesque, three-legged monster in the bleached darkness of the blizzard, the two lurched into the roadside bushes.

Snow-laden withes slapped at them, parted to let them through. Snow poured down, stifling the threshing of the brush, stifling Peter's moan of anguish. Anne, abruptly rigid, put her lips to his ear.

"Quiet, my dear," she whispered. "Be very quiet."

Through the white, almost solid pall the siren's scream was a long, menacing howl borne on the breast of deafening engine thunder that battered against the screening bushes—and roared away.

"They've gone past, Peter," Anne dared a murmur of throbbing triumph. "The snow covered the marks where you fell, as soon as we got off the road, and they didn't see it—"

Voices reached the trembling girl, deep-throated, rumbling. And then another made intelligible words, carrying more clearly through the snow-filled air because it was high-pitched and thin and querulous.

"No I ain't seen nobody come out of the woods." Faith Parker said. "I been standin' right here too, the past half-hour."

Once more the hoarse rumble. Once more Faith's reply. Was she talking so loudly on purpose, hoping to be over-heard?

"You better come inside if you're bound on waiting here. There's a fire an' I can heat up some coffee, an' you can watch the road from here while you're warming up."

The police were at the tavern, then, watching the road, waiting for their prey. They knew that although they had somehow passed him, he must come out of the woods on the highway. The steep ravine through which Waley's Creek ran, on whose lip the restaurant's kitchen door opened, would cut off his escape to the east. West of the road was a treacherous bog, not yet frozen sufficiently to be anything but a death trap for anyone who attempted it in this blinding storm. Death, just as sure would overtake the wounded man in the arctic cold of the mountain.

Yes, they could afford to wait there in warmth and comfort while their quarry chose between death or capture.

Anne Marsh's lids were slitted against the driving, icy blasts. She hugged Peter closer to her.

"Try to walk," she said. "Please try to walk."

Perhaps he heard her. Perhaps the movement of his flac-cid frame was sheer automatism. At any rate there was some response in him as Anne started off, some little aid to her own painful progress. Otherwise the task she set herself would have been a sheer impossibility.

As it was, every nerve, every cell of her slim young body quivered with exhaustion before she managed to gain the bottom of the creek's ravine and struggle along the narrow shelf of ground that was all that stretched between the ice-scummed water and the side of the gully through which it ran. They were twenty feet away from the tavern.

ANNE STUMBLED to her knees, let her burden slide flaccidly to the ground. For a long minute she remained like that, pulling deep breaths into her lungs.

After awhile she heaved erect again. And then she did a very queer thing. Facing the earthy wall, she tugged at an ice-encrusted root tendril, reached sidewise and pulled at another.

A section of the bank moved out toward her, as if it were a door on hinges. It *was* a door, the earth a mere covering for the boards revealed on its inner side.

With a last fierce effort Anne dragged Peter's motionless form into that space, and the door thudded shut.

Soft footsteps whispered in the dark. A switch clicked. A small windowless room sprang into existence in the yellow light of a single, unshaded bulb, a room that was earth-floored but walled and ceiled by rough, splintered boards. In the center was a time-darkened work bench which had belonged to Webster Marsh.

Every gouge in that old wood was poignant with memory for Anne Marsh, every stain on it spoke of a comradeship few fathers and daughters are ever privileged to know....

But Anne had no time for reminiscence now. Certain strange garments hung from a row of hooks screwed into one wall; disguises that had masked her in her raids on the despoilers of Laneville's poor. She took an armful, bent and deposited them on the floor and heaved the unconscious man onto the rough pallet.

His countenance was no longer blunt-jawed and competent. It was color-drained, and the laxness of fatigue and suffering made it the poignantly pathetic face of a sick boy. His lips moved.

"Anne," they muttered. "I love—" and twisted abruptly, writhing with a pain not physical. "No!" he moaned. "She's his daughter. She's a Marsh. You must hate her. Hate…."

"Hush, dear." The girl's cold hand rested on the sweat dewed brow. "Sleep."

He sighed, shrugged more closely into the pile on which he lay, was silent. There were tears in Anne's eyes as she threw off her soaked cap and jacket. What was it that lay between them? The first time she had seen him, up on the hillside where he had rescued her from a kidnap gang he had said something like that when he had discovered who she was.

"If I had known," he had said. "I wouldn't have…." But after that he had kissed her, had stopped to kiss her though the police were closing in on him.

Her deft hands unbuckled and tugged off the fur-lined galosh that was wet with something more viscid than thawing ice. Reddened, they rolled up the drenched trouser leg.

Anne shuddered at the scarlet mess the act revealed, but she got to her feet, darted across the room to the closet that contained first aid supplies.

Breath hissed from between her teeth in a gasp of relief as she bathed the blood away. The gash was ugly, but the bullet had only scraped the shin bone, paralyzing but not breaking it.

As she plastered down the end of that white swathing the tramp of heavy feet sounded dully overhead. A door slammed closed. Anne smiled wryly. The police had tired of waiting. They had gone.

She could get hot water now, put up the strengthening broth to heat that Peter would need so badly when he awakened.

She wiped her bloody hands with cotton waste, twisted to the wooden ladder that lifted from the dirt floor and ended against a seemingly solid ceiling. Her hand flashed to the switch as she passed and blackness smashed into the hidden room again.

Anne's feet whispered on the ladder treads. She reached the top of the ladder, fumbled. Her fingers found nailheads in a beam, pressed them in a certain order. Wood scraped on wood and pale luminance slitted the blackness above her. It grew slowly, became an aperture wide enough to let her through.

She went up into the bedroom she had shared with Faith since death and disgrace had taken her home from her and they had pooled their slender resources to build this tavern. She flung across the room to the single, iron-barred window, twisted at those bars. Behind her there was again the sound of scraping wood,

When she turned there was no longer any aperture in the floor. It was a level of wood, solid, unbroken.

This was not the tavern's only secret, not the only hidden thing that Bulldog Ryan would give his pension to unearth. That he suspected their existence Anne knew beyond doubt, but the courts demand more than vague suspicions before they issue a search warrant.

The hot breath of the huge range met her as she opened the door to the kitchen. She stepped out into that grateful warmth, pulled it shut behind her.

"Hello," a toneless voice said. "I see you decided to come back."

Anne twisted to the sound. The doorway framed the speaker; stocky, derby hat crowning his pinched, pointed visage, a mocking sneer twisting at his thin lips.

The police had gone, but Bulldog Ryan had remained behind.

CHAPTER THREE
WHISPERS OF DOOM

"**COME BACK?**" Anne Marsh managed to force through the clamping muscles of her throat. "I haven't been anywhere."

"Yeah." Ryan stood stolidly motionless on spread, thick legs, but the girl had an impression that he was advancing on her with that plodding, persistent pace with which he had come after her, always come after her for a fear-filled year. "I been right here the past half-hour an' you ain't gone out. It must be snowin' in your room there an' that's how you got your tootsies an' your pants wet."

The girl said nothing in reply. What was there to say?

"He's in there, huh," the heavy, expressionless voice began again. "Slippery Joe."

"I—I don't know what you're talking about."

"Yeah. I know you're dumb. I know you don't know nothing about Joe, just like you was asleep in there when some guy emptied ten grand outta John Simpson's safe. Somethin' funny about that room. I been wantin' to take a look at it for a long time an' now I'm goin' to."

He *was* moving now. His thick-soled shoes thudding purposefully toward her. "No," Anne whispered, spreading her arms wide. "You can't go in there." He wouldn't miss the marks her wet boots had made on the floor in there. Not Ryan. They would show him the hidden trapdoor and…. "You haven't got a warrant."

"No, I ain't got a warrant. I'm breakin' the law. But there ain't nobody here 'ceptin' you to see me do it, an' there won't nobody ask too many questions when I bring in the guy we been huntin' for a year. *Get outta my way!*"

Spatulate fingers lashed out at Anne, clamped on her shoulder. The kitchen whirled around her and the floor came up to hit her. Anne rose on hands and knees, stayed that way, heart pounding, a soundless scream twisting her lips as Ryan lumbered through the opened door, and vanished within.

It was over. With only one left of those from whom she had set out to exact vengeance and reparation, Ryan had run her down at last. When the tracks had shown him the trapdoor and he'd broken it open he'd go down through it to find not only Peter but also the disguises that would tie her inescapably to certain unsolved crimes.

"Hey!" he snapped. "How the hell did you get in here?"

"That, Mr. Bulldog Ryan, ain't the question."

It was Faith's acidulous voice that sounded in reply. "It's what you mean by breakin' into a lady's bedroom."

Anne didn't know how she regained her feet. But she was erect, and she was where she could see into the room, where she could see Ryan's broad, squat back and the old woman facing him, a kimona fluttering about her bony, angular form, her wrinkled countenance a mask of righteous indignation.

"Get out!"

"Wait." His head moved and the gasping girl knew that no inch of the chamber was escaping his scrutiny. "Wait. Now that I'm in here, I'm goin' to look around."

"Go ahead and look, if you think it's going to do you any good. Maybe it will. Maybe it's the first time you've been in a decent woman's room."

Anne's hand went to her breast. It was coming now. He would see the wet marks on the floor and....

There weren't any there! The boards were dry. The old woman had wiped them dry!

RYAN MOVED around the room with a clumsy diffidence. He came to the window that was latticed by iron bars. He tugged at the black rods, peered out into the white swirl of nothingness without. Then he turned.

"All right," he said heavily. "You two have put it over on me again. Maybe I fell asleep standin' in that kitchen doorway. Maybe the two of you walked in and out of this room and I didn't see you. Yeah. But I've got a hunch there's something queer about this room, and I'm going to find out what it is damn soon."

"What do you mean?" Anne couldn't stop the question, though all she wanted was for Ryan to get out of that room, out of the house.

"I mean that you've got about a week more to stay here. Union Light and Power's bringin' a high tension line in from Bolton along this road and they're goin' to condemn this property for the right of way. Fulton Zander's in court right this mornin', gettin' the papers approved. When their crews start tearin' down I'm goin' to be here, with bells on."

He thudded out into the kitchen and banged the outer door shut.

"Faith," Anne exclaimed. "You slipped out through the front door and around to the creek. I didn't know you knew about the secret entrance."

"I know about that and I know a lot more things. Includin' that we're through here. I'm glad of that. Maybe we'll go away from here now, and live a normal life where you'll be Anne Marsh and not Webster Marsh's daughter...."

"I'm still his daughter, Faith, still the daughter of dishonor. There's Fulton Zander left to deal with."

"You little fool— Here, where are you going?"

"To make some chicken broth. I...."

"I'll attend to that. You get some blankets and clean sheets and a pillow and take them down to your Peter. The idea," she sniffed, "of letting that poor hurt boy lay there on them filthy rags."

"You're an angel, Faith...." Anne's arms were around the stringy, dried-up little figure.

THE SNOW laid a blanket of soft white over the roofs of the mansions along East Drive, and edged the windows of the stores on Main Street with unintended beauty. Even Slum Hollow was crisp and white and clean in the sunset glow when the blizzard ended. And in the hovels of the very poor there was a little laughter, for there would be lots of jobs clearing the streets.

The shovelers started along Main Street at dusk and by ten they had reached the bridge over Waley's Creek where Bolton Turnpike came down off Lane Hill. They stopped there—because the state highway plows had opened the road to this point—and leaning on their long shovel handles squinted across the bridge at the windows of The Tavern, bright yellow oblongs in the night. That Marsh girl ran that joint didn't she? The daughter of that guy Webster

Marsh who swiped the Community Chest money last year and made everything so tough?

Yeah. We was pretty sore at him then, even though he bumped himself off, but what was the use keepin' a grudge? After all the charities around town been gettin' money all year in all kinds of funny ways, pretty near as much I guess as they woulda got if old Marsh hadn't done what he did. An' before that the ginks what worked fer his company were treated white, a lot better than this new gang's been doin', cuttin' wages an' not givin' no holidays with pay, an' so on—

Slim, somehow pathetic in the black of the mourning she still wore, Anne Marsh sat at her desk by the door between the dining room and kitchen and covertly read a yellowed clipping that had appeared in the Laneville Courier the morning after Christmas—a year ago.

> "As long as the naked are unclothed," it ended, "and the hungry unfed, the soul of Webster Marsh shall have no peace."

"Only a little more, Dad," the girl whispered. "There's only one more left who must pay for your rest, and then...."

And then, what? The tavern that had grown to mean home to her would be torn down by the first of the New Year. She would be homeless again, her mission accomplished. Where would she and Faith go? What would they do...?

Anne's thoughts abruptly ended. Another voice was whispering from under her desk. A ghostly, disembodied voice it was.

"It's so cosy here, Dickie," the voice said, "So nice to be alone with you here. It's always nice at the tavern but tonight the storm's kept people home, and it's like everything's just for us."

Anne's hand moved under the desktop to the switch that connected the tuned down loudspeaker there with the one occupied booth. That was another of the secrets of the tavern, the concealed wires by which she had been enabled to listen in on the conversations of her guests, relaxing and guarded by the seeming privacy the little cubicles afforded them. This was how she had learned the plans by which John Lawton had sought to safeguard his payroll money and had been enabled to circumvent them. This was how Dr. Thomas Wayne had betrayed himself....

"Guess we wouldn't be here either if the governor hadn't been called over to Fulton Zander's house so I could grab the car." Anne didn't switch off the talk. She did not make a habit of listening in on lovers' murmurings, but this....

"Gee! Won't he be sore?"

"Naw. He seemed all hipped up after that 'phone call. Said something about splitting a melon in cash.... Hell! Keep that quiet, Rhoda. I shouldn't have spilled it. He told me to keep mum about it. Reason why he wasn't using the boat was because this here meeting was so all-fired secret."

"Ooh, Dickie, that's positively thrilling. Tell me some more."

"But...."

"Oh you needn't be afraid I'll tell anybody. All the girls tell me their secrets and I never repeat them. Come on, I'll give you an extra kiss if you do."

"Well, to tell you the truth I don't know anything more except that it's the Union Light and Power bunch that's going to be there."

"Oh, it's business." Anne didn't have to glance up into the artfully concealed mirror that would have given her a view of Rhoda's face to know that she was pouting. "I thought it was something interesting."

"Maybe it's more interesting than you think. The governor cracked wise about a stickup making a rich haul if he got a notion to...."

THE VOICE clicked off as the kitchen door swung open behind Anne. A neatly dressed waitress came through, swinging supple hips....

"Mary," Anne said, stopping her, "who are the youngsters in booth ten?"

"The girl's some dizzy deb from East Drive."

"And the boy?"

"Him? He's Dickie Lawton."

"I didn't know John Lawton had a son."

"Gosh, where you been, Miss Marsh? Dickie made the winning touchdown for Yale in the Dartmouth game. He's All-American left halfback an' some sugar for the dames."

"Oh yes. I remember now. Look Hilda, tell Hazel Jervis I want her to take the desk. There isn't anything doing tonight and I think I'll go to bed early."

"Sure." The girl swung away with her tray. Anne arose and went through the rear door of the dining room.

The trapdoor scraped shut over Anne's head. She went down into the darkness of the secret room, tiptoed across its floor. Her hands found that which they sought in the blackness.

For a moment there was no sound except the soft whisper of breathing. Of *two* persons breathing. The girl had not turned on the light because Peter lay here asleep. Peter—her heart sang the name....

And then the song was a dirge as she recalled the muttering of his delirium. "She's his daughter. You must hate her. Hate...."

Hate! That was her heritage. But why must *he* hate her?

She stifled a sob. Fabric rustled in the darkness, rubbing against satin-smooth skin…. Anne whirled to a sudden footfall, was blinded by yellow light….

Her vision cleared. Peter was crouched against the wall, his hand on the light-switch. His clothing was wrinkled, but dry, his wounded leg straight again. The heart-shaped scar at the corner of his mouth was a white pucker. A small, flat automatic snouted from his fist.

"Up with 'em," he grunted. "Reach."

CHAPTER FOUR
CONSPIRATORS' CABAL

ANNE MARSH'S hands went over her head. "Peter!" she gasped. "What… What's the idea."

Astonishment peered from the youth's blue eyes. "It's— it's you. It's Anne." He pulled the gun dazedly across his forehead. "I heard someone in here, and I thought…."

"You'd been found out. But you saw me when the light came on. Why did you still…?" And then she laughed. "Oh, it's because I'm dressed as a boy." Laughed and blushed, remembering that she had made the change with him lying only a yard away, that her dress, her frothy undergarments, still lay at her feet.

His blue eyes laughed with her. "Dressed as a boy but too damned beautiful to be one. You couldn't fool anybody except a sleep-doped dummy like me. Look at your hair…."

"I'll fix that." Anne snatched a checked cap from the hook where the boy's clothing had hung, stuffed her hair into it. She bent, came up with a handful of black loam from the floor, rubbed it over her face. "How's this?"

She strode toward him, and she was a grimy-faced, shabby street urchin to the last small inch of her. "Watch yer car, mister?" she whined. "Only cost you a nickle."

"You're pretty good at that." Peter applauded.

"I ought to be. I've had enough practice. But that's enough fooling. Put out the light. I've got to get out of here."

"Out! Where—what…?"

"Put out that light." She stamped her foot. "Please. It's getting late."

The darkness smashed in again. Once more there was the scrape of wood on wood.

Anne climbed to the road. She was a small, lonely figure trotting toward the heart of the city.

Close-drawn window drapes muffled the scrape of the snow shovels that were clearing East Drive. "We're all here," Fulton Zander's acidulous tones remarked, "If everyone is sure he was not followed here we can get down to business."

"What's the idea of all the secrecy?" The question oozed greasily from John Simpson's thick lips. "You'd think we were running a stag, the way you had us sneak in here."

"That's just what my Alice thinks," Donald Reynolds, grey of hair but dissipated of ferret-like countenance twittered.

Zander's fleshless lips scarcely moved. "You'll be able to bribe your Alice with a new diamond for Christmas, Don," he murmured, "and as for you, Simpson, I imagine some of the big depositors in your bank would be interested in knowing you were here tonight; those who hold bonds of the Union Light and Power Company for example—when I move in court tomorrow for a receivership!"

"A receivership!" John Lawton, Laneville's department store owner, spluttered; "I thought we were making money."

"We have been," Zander replied. *"We* have been, but the books show the corporation has been running at a terrific loss. I told you a year ago that there was more to my plan than just getting hold of the outfit. You gave me authority to operate it in accordance with my ideas, and I've done so. I've been...."

"Milking the business. Good man!" Tall, completely bald, Dr. Thomas Wayne was too sardonic even to pretend ignorance of Zander's machinations as the others were doing. "Gentlemen!" He lifted a small glass, "I give you Fulton Zander, shrewdest lawyer in seven states."

"I don't like it," the last of the half-dozen seated around the table moaned.

"I think we're going too far. I'm sorry I ever threw in with you fellows, I've been sorry ever since—ever since Webster Marsh—killed himself." Fred Harris's neatly manicured hands tugged at his trim van dyke, trembling, and the tiny lights of hysteria jittered in his red-shot eyes. "I keep seeing him in my sleep, pointing a finger at me, accusing. I feel him looking at us now, listening...."

Outside the snow gleamed with an eerie, internal luminance, but along East Drive bomb-like flares waved the orange-red pennants of their flames to illumine the labors of the shovelers. The lurid glare deepened the shadow of a great fir in the Zander grounds so that it was a tar-hued, impenetrable mass lying against the sidewall of the house.

Within that shadow a black shape crouched silent and motionless and somehow feral. A gloved hand held a small round diaphragm against the wood and from this two slender, hollow rubber tubes curved to shell-like ears covered by hair that light would have revealed as tightly curled and tawny.

Fulton Zander's eyes moved to the dapper little man, blue lids folding vulture-like over their pale gaze. "Would you like to refuse your share, Harris, and let me split it up among the rest of us?"

"No. I'll be damned if I will. In for a calf, in for an ox."

"Then I shall proceed." The lawyer's smile was a humorless, vinegary twitch of pallid lips. "I shall not bore you with the manipulations by which it was accomplished, but, as I have already said, while the books of Union Light and Power show it to have run this year at a terrific loss, I have here, in this box, the round sum of fifty thousand dollars in cash. I am reserving ten thousand for myself and distributing eight thousand to each of you. A pretty little Christmas gift from the people of Laneville, gentlemen, I think you will agree."

"NOT BAD," Simpson rubbed pudgy hands. "Not bad," his buttery accents repeated.

"I take it you are satisfied," Zander murmured. One of his claws moved to his vest pocket, came out with a small key that it fitted into the cash box's lock, clicked over....

A dull detonation, the crash of splintering glass, sounded from somewhere outside the room, "What's that," Harris squealed. "What was that?"

The attorney's head jerked up and his beak pointed at the closed door. "An explosion. It sounded like an explosion somewhere at the back of the house."

"Damned right it was," Reynolds shoved himself up out of his seat. "Look. Look at that." His hand pointed to the threshold of the door. Something grey, slender, curled from under it, stretched a lazy tendril into the room. "That's smoke. The house is on fire."

Zander leaped to his feet, a moment behind the others because he took time to relock the money box and shove it under his arm. "Fire," he gasped. "There's no one back there. I gave the servants a night off. We've got to…."

He didn't need to finish. Wayne had flung the door open on swirling grey smoke, the others were crowding through it behind him. In that moment darkness smashed down on them, stygian, complete.

Someone shouted incoherently. Someone coughed. Then Fred Harris's cry was a thin squeal in the dark smoke-pall that flickered with a wavering, lurid glow. "The door is wedged."

"Good thing." Zander's voice was cool, collected. "If the bunch of you poured out that way it would be a dead give away. Go through the back, the way you came." Feet thudded, obeying.

In the deserted room a window scraped open, scraped closed again, the sound unnoticed.

Snow-glimmer came in through a smashed window, outlining the gleaming kitchen into which the rout burst. The smoke was fading, here, thinner with a strange swiftness.

"What's this?" Dr. Wayne exclaimed, pouncing on a round, black object that lay in the center of the kitchen floor. "Well, I'll be damned. A smoke pot."

He came up with it, and the others crowded around him. Someone struck flame from a cigarette lighter and astonished eyes widened, staring at that which he held.

It was one of the bomb-like road flares that lined East Drive. Its wick was wrapped around with a grease-smeared rag that still smouldered acridly!

194 THE COMPLETE CASES OF ANNE MARSH

"What the hell Zander?" Lawton grunted. "What kind of trick is this you're pulling on us?"

There was no answer.

"Hey, Zander!" The men peered at one another. There were only five of them. Their host was missing.

"Skipped!" Wayne snarled. "The—that's why he had the front door locked. He got us in here and skipped with the cash."

"You're nuts!" Reynolds, holding the lighter, protested. "Something's happened to him." He turned, shoved through the white-faced knot, went through the kitchen doorway into the narrow passageway from the front of the house. Then he spoke again, his ejaculation a throaty gasp. "Here he is!"

The others, crowding out behind him, saw Zander too. He was a crumpled, grotesquely awkward heap across the threshold of the room in which the interrupted meeting had been held. A blue bruise on his forehead told what it was that had stunned him.

The cash box was nowhere in sight.

CHAPTER FIVE
CAUGHT

ANNE MARSH'S little heels thudded into the soft ground where she had crouched, listening in on the men who had killed her father as surely as though they had held the poison cup to his lips. She huddled in the ebon shadow that had served her so well, and worked at the boy's jacket she wore, trying to button it over a black metal cash box that held fifty thousand dollars in untraceable cash.

The wide street was a river of eerie light dotted by the mufflered, overcoated forms of laborers. But to her right there was a thick hedge that drowned the radiance, and between her and that shelter there was only ten feet of open ground.

Her muscles tensed, as a sprinter's would, waiting for the starter's gun. Then she was off, a flitting shadow across the white snow blanket.

Strong arms clamped around her, pinning her arms to her side, holding her helpless. "Got you!" a toneless voice exclaimed. "Got you at last! And dead to rights."

Anne moaned, and slumped, knowing it was useless to struggle. Bulldog Ryan's pinched visage glimmered out of the darkness, his thin lips pulling away from his teeth in a grimace of gloating triumph.

"I figured the only way you could get in and out of that damn room of yours was if there was a tunnel through the bank underneath, and I camped out in the bushes across the creek, where I could keep watch. I followed you, and I let you have plenty of rope, and by jingo, you sure have hung yourself with it."

"All right," the girl said, her tones flat, dreary but very steady. "You've got me, and it's all over. Put the handcuffs on me and take me off to jail."

"I'll put the cuffs on you all right," the detective grunted, suiting the action to the word, "but we're not goin' to the station yet. We're goin' back there an' see just what it is you've been up to.

THE ELECTRIC light wires had been clipped outside the house, could not be repaired till a linesman was called, but someone had found candles and the room with the long table was illuminated once more. Fulton Zander was back in his chair, the bruise livid on his forehead.

"Look here, officer." The words slid from his thin, scarcely moving lips. "You've recovered my cash box and that satisfies me. This is the Christmas season and I'm disposed to be charitable. Let the boy go."

A twisted steel chain linked Anne's slender wrist to Ryan's burly one. "Let him go, is it?" The detective's eyes were slitted, dangerous. *"Him—"* His free hand jerked the cap from his prisoner's head and her hair sprang from confinement, a russet nimbus in the wavering candlelight. *"Her,* you mean. You don't know what you're askin'. This is Anne Marsh, gentlemen, the slipperiest crook that ever prowled Laneville. You ought to know it. There ain't one of you here she ain't rooked. I been pluggin' after her for a year an' I got her at last, an' you say let her go. Not if I have to pull you all in for compoundin' a felony."

"You can't do that," Zander snarled. "We'll swear you're lying. A cop's word against six of the most reputable men in Laneville! Which do you think a jury will believe?"

"I've got the cash box and I've got the tracks under the window. That's evidence enough to bear me out, and by God I'll put it over."

"Maybe you will," Simpson wheezed. "But if you try it, we'll break you. There's enough influence in this crowd to break a commissioner, let alone a flat-foot."

Ryan's big hand fisted at his side. "Break and be damned," he growled. "This wench goes behind the bars if I have to turn in my badge the next day."

Anne flung her head back. "You won't have to turn in your badge, Ryan. It's been a clean fight between us, an honest fight. Take me in to prison. I'll sign a confession. And I'll go on the witness stand and tell the world exactly why the directors of Union Light and Power were here, exactly why they're threatening you to keep the fact quiet that they were here."

"And that, gents, is the payoff," Ryan flung at them. "So long. I'll see you in court."

He turned, and there was a curious gentleness in that growl of his. "Come along, Miss Marsh. Come...."

"Not so fast!" A lithe, dark-haired figure confronted him in the doorway, a figure whose slender hand thrust the muzzle of a vicious little automatic point-blank at him. "Back up, Ryan. Let go of that chain and grab air. One peep out of any of you, one move, and I'll blast you!"

The detective's thick arms went ceiling-ward. Three voices tangled, each gasping a name.

"Slippery Joe," Ryan whispered.

"Peter!" Anne exclaimed.

And from Fulton Zander, his face livid as the bruise on his brow, gasped: "Peter Corbin!"

It was this last to which the intruder responded. "Yes, Zander. Peter Corbin." His mouth twitched, bitterly. "You didn't know I escaped from the steel-barred hell to which you sent me. You and your boss, Webster Marsh, framing me for sabotage—that you hired done on the Apple Street dynamo to drive the Company stocks down so you could buy it cheap."

"NO!" ANNE'S cry was a low throb, pain torn. "No, Peter. Dad never did anything like that. He couldn't."

"The hell he couldn't." The youth's laugh was icy. "He packed me away in the pen for twenty years, but I crushed out, and I've been skulking in the woods ever since. That's what Webster Marsh did to me. That's why I hate his memory, hate everyone who belongs to him."

"No," the girl moaned, and was across the room in a flash, was leaning over Zander. "Tell him. If there's any good in you at all, tell him Dad didn't do that terrible thing to him."

Her grey eyes held the lawyer's vulpine ones, and there was a breath-bated, tense silence in the room. Silence, utter stillness, the only motion that of the barrel of Peter's automatic flicking from one to another of the group.

"Tell him," Anne's tear-filled voice broke that silence. "You must!"

Zander's fleshless lips moved. "Marsh didn't know anything about it. I rigged the whole thing, and I bought in the stock."

The girl spun to the man she loved. "You heard that, Peter," she cried. "You heard him."

"I heard him." The grim lines of the youth's darkly handsome face broke, and it was boyishly appealing. "I heard him, my darling." And then it was stern again.

"There's a roll of wire in my pocket, Anne, cut into short lengths. Get it out and tie it around their ankles and their wrists. Their handkerchiefs will do for gags."

It was done. Peter and Anne were gone. The six directors who had stolen and milked and wrecked the Union Light and Power Company sat around their leader's long table, unable to move or speak.

In another chair sat Bulldog Ryan, gagged and bound like the rest. Peculiarly enough, there was the faint shadow of a smile on his face, as though he found some secret satisfaction even in defeat.

THE SCRAPING of snow shovels were almost inaudible now, as their wielders worked away from the Zander house. A candle guttered, went out. From an infinite distance the howl of the night express came deepthroated and melancholy into the room.

Bulldog Ryan stirred. His shoulders heaved. His wrists came free of the wires that clamped them. It could be seen now that he had used an old trick, swelling them as the girl lashed them, so that they had actually not been bound at all. He bent, unfastened his feet, rose and thumbed the gagging handkerchief from his mouth.

"I got an awful short memory," he grunted, "and I think you birds got the same. Nothin' happened here tonight. Nothin' at all. Only, I reckon you birds will want to be certain my memory stays bad—so supposin' you ante up about fifty grand for that Christmas Fund."

Starting to work on Fulton Zander's lashings, he sighed. "I'm puttin' in for retirement in the mornin'," he muttered. "I'm gettin' too soft to be on the cops." He paused. "And anyway, there won't be no fun in the job, with only common, ordinary crooks to chase."

Two extracts from the Laneville *Daily Courier* of Dec. 23rd, 1936. The first:

The COURIER'S CHRISTMAS FUND, that had not filled its quota this year, was put far over the top this morning by two anonymous contributions of fifty thousand dollars. One was delivered by Western Union Messenger. No information as to its source could be obtained except that the package in which the currency was wrapped was left at the depot office by two young men who dashed for the midnight express just as the gates were closing. The other fifty-thousand was found in the morning mail at the Fund's headquarters. There are absolutely no clues as to its source.

The second:

The popular Tavern on Bolton Turnpike closed its hospitable doors forever today. Miss Faith Parker, one of the co-owners, cashed the condemnation award and immediately left for parts unknown She refused to confirm or deny the rumor that she was to join Miss Anne Marsh, who, it will be remembered, is the daughter of the late Webster Marsh.

Bulldog Ryan sipped his breakfast coffee as he read the two items with his eyes that held a strange light. The tight-lipped mouth quirked faintly. "Hope the old gal don't have as much trouble findin' her as I did," he muttered.

THE HOUSE THAT TERROR BUILT

REMEMBER ANNE MARSH, THE GIRL ROBIN HOOD, AND HER MYSTERIOUS BENEFACTOR, PETER CORBIN? WE'VE PREVAILED UPON ARTHUR LEO ZAGAT TO TELL US THE ENSUING ADVENTURES OF THIS AMAZING COUPLE, NOW MARRIED. THEY BELIEVED IN JUSTICE AND THE LAW. BUT WHEN THE LAW BECAME A MOCKERY; WHEN INJUSTICE AND DEATH JOINED HANDS WITH THE POLICE IN A CARNIVAL OF TERROR.... WELL, READ THE STORY AND SEE FOR YOURSELF! THE FIRST OF A NEW SERIES ABOUT THIS LOVABLE YOUNG COUPLE!

CHAPTER ONE
THE MAN IN THE SNOW

VAULTED BY a sky of stainless blue, the air sparkled as though there still hung in it invisible crystals of the freshly fallen snow that folded, white and unmarked, over the summit of Savin Ridge. Halfway down the slope, the woods began, high enough that only smudges of smoke rising straight up into the stillness evidenced the town of Ailchester nestling in the valley below them, with its shops and its cottages and its sprawling, huge factory.

The boughs of the winter-denuded trees were a lacy mass of brilliant white and shining icicles, but beneath that glittering glory the trunks on the edge of the woods were gaunt and twisted and black with wet, and behind these was black darkness.

A crunch of footfalls splintered the hush of the hilltop. A clear, girlish laugh rang out. Two figures came over the crest and halted.

"Isn't it glorious?" exclaimed the girl who had laughed. "Everything is so bright and clean and new!" Ski pants and mackinaw could not hide her slim young grace. "All winter's ugliness is covered over, and when the snow melts the earth will be awakening to a new life. A *new* life, Peter, like the one we're beginning together."

Tight, tawny curls, escaping from under a knitted cap with a crimson tassel, clustered about the small oval of her face. They framed frost-reddened cheeks, pert little features. Her lips, velvet soft as the petal of a rose, were still parted with her laugh, but an odd, haunting wistfulness hovered about them and in the girl's grey eyes there was unforgotten pain.

"A new life, Anne," her companion breathed. He took her into the tight circle of his arm with a strange, almost desperate fierceness. "God help me to make it a happy one for you."

Within his garments' warm bulk, he was loose-coupled and lithe and jaunty. There was strength in his blunt-jawed, cleanly chiseled countenance, and tenderness, but there was also the brooding recollection of agony not long past.

Anne Corbin looked up into that face, and a little of the radiance faded from her own. "Peter," she murmured. "There was snow on Lane Hill, too, when we first met. Remember?"

"I remember, dear." As if he could ever forget! When the bank robbers had fled too near his own hide-out, and he, fearing that they would bring discovery, had driven them away with shouts and snowballs! Only to find that he had rescued a beautiful girl.

"Then you learned my name was Anne Marsh and you told me you hated me."

There was a little of bitterness in Corbin's slow smile. "I thought then that it was your father who had framed me into the prison from which I had escaped, and I hated him. I thought I hated you too, because you belonged to him."

"Poor Dad," the girl sighed.

Peter was silent. The man was dead now and what could not be forgiven, could be forgotten. It had happened just after he had met Anne. Suicide—when it was discovered that Anne's father had embezzled the charity funds he had been meant to administer. But it had been weakness more than criminal intent. Old Doctor Marsh never saw a penny of the funds he stole. He had been the dupe for a group of wealthy men who were safe from the law because nothing could ever be proved.

And Anne—his own Anne—had turned thief herself and had stolen back and returned to the poor every cent that had been taken! He spoke his thoughts out loud. "You were so clever and so brave…."

She did not need to ask him what he meant. It was still too fresh in their minds.

"No, Peter," she replied, her eyes grown somber. "Not brave. I was paralyzed with fright every minute, every move I made. And I wasn't really clever either. Bulldog Ryan, the detective, would have caught me a dozen times if it had not been for you. You were the one that was clever and brave. The thought of you, eternally hunted, wet and cold and hungry made the year one long nightmare for me."

A long shudder ran through her, and Peter held her tight to him to stop it. "The nightmare's all over, sweets. We have our own little home down there in Ailchester. On Monday, I start on my job in the factory office. Laneville's a thousand miles away, and no one will ever trace us here. We needn't be afraid of the police, sweetheart, ever again."

"Not ever, Peter?" She asked it in a wee small voice, the voice of a child waking from a bad dream and demanding to be comforted. "You're still an escaped prisoner, you know. You've never been pardoned."

"But Fulton Zander, the lawyer who was the chief schemer against your father, confessed to framing me and Bulldog Ryan heard him. We had to run from Laneville that night because of what you had done. But I have a notion that Ryan sympathized with you and covered you up, and some day, soon, I'll go back to clear myself. Ryan's testimony, and Zander's will do that. I— Hello!" He broke off, stiffening. "What's going on down there?"

A man had broken out of the woods, so far below that he seemed but a toy figure. He was running, but he was crouched over as he ran, as though pain tore at his entrails, and his course was a zig-zag, stumbling effort that took him along the edge of the forest, trailing a dark spoor through the white snow.

"He's hurt, Peter!" Anne exclaimed. "He's terribly hurt."

From among the trees out of which the man had burst came a threshing of underbrush and the pound of heavy footfalls. He pitched forward to his knees, pushed feebly against the ground in a pitiful effort to rise again. A shout

Her approach was soundless
as a phantom's....

came thinly up to Peter and Anne from the darkness of the woods. The fallen man twisted, his face, diminished by distance, a tiny circle, white almost as the snow. His arm jerked toward the trees.

"He threw something in there!" Peter grunted. "He…."

"Look!" Anne cut in. "There are the ones he's running from. Two of them."

They were coming out into the open. The pair paused for a moment, uncertain, and then they were running once more.

So intent on their chase that they had not once glanced up to the ridge crest and so did not know themselves observed, the two followed the track of their quarry. The latter was crawling; moving in queer small jerks as if he still had some mad hope of escape, though his pursuers bore down on him at a speed that would have overtaken him had he still been on his feet.

Sun glinted from metal that could be only a revolver one of the manhunters carried, but he did not fire it. There was no need to shoot. Their prey was a dark heap in the snow, twitching still as though he was trying to evade them.

They reached him. The three doll-like splotches merged into one that was formless. It swayed, grotesquely, while a hoarse mutter drifted up the hill through the stillness. Then the group split apart.

The hunted man dangled from the straight, stiff arm of one of his captors, his feet awkwardly bent under in the snow, his legs boneless, his body limp as a ventriloquist's dummy from whose cloth torso the sawdust has run out. The mate to the arm that lifted him crooked. It darted toward his lolling head.

THE HEAD jerked back. The sharp smack of fist on flesh reached the amazed couple on the hilltop. The wounded man started to drop, was straightened by another vicious blow from his tormentor, thudded down. The man with the gun kicked at the sprawling form....

"Damn!" Peter Corbin growled. "I can't stand here watching that." He jumped away from Ann and was plunging down the slope, his heels sending up little spurts of the powdery snow, his long legs scissoring.

"Peter!" the girl cried. "Peter! They'll shoot you!"

And then she was after him, was half-sliding, half-running down the long descent. *"Peter!"*

Without slowing, his head twisted and he gestured to her to stay back. A half-sentence from him reached her. "...out of this." Anne kept on, though the two below, much nearer now, had heard their shouts and were wheeling to them.

"What's going on!" she heard Peter cry, and gasped as the revolver came up to bear point-blank upon him.

It was easier to start running than to stop, and though Corbin's legs tried to brake him at the wordless threat of that gun, he slid downward in a flurry of the powdery white crystals till he was within two yards of the gun muzzle. Anne bumped into her husband as he halted, snatched at his arm to save herself from falling.

"You brutes," she sobbed, her eyes on the blue-jowled faces of the pair who stood above a pathetically crumpled heap in the snow.

"Yeah?" came from between thick lips. "Yeah?" The one who spoke was the shorter. His lumberman's jacket swathed a barrel-like torso propped on straddling, columnar legs and his eyes were the small, heavy-lidded eyes of a hog. "Get a look at this." His hand came out of his pocket and held up something that shone silvery in the light. "Get a good look at this, Miss Buttinsky."

The thing in his palm was a badge. Most of the black enamel had flaked out of the letters stamped into it around an embossed seal, but Anne could read them. They said; *Ailchester Police. Detective.*

"You folks don't want to go mixing in with no police work," the other, the one who held the gun said. His voice was a thin, almost apologetic whine, but it held some quality that made Anne's skin crawl with dread. "Leastways in

Ailchester. If you wasn't new here, you'd know it ain't healthy." His face was too long for its width. There was almost no space between his pale eyes and his yellow teeth were so crowded in his narrow jaw that they bent, some in, some out, overlapping. "How about it, Hen?"

Hen's chuckle was humorless, and somehow evil. "Ain't healthy is right," he grinned. "And how." He glanced down at the shuddering form in the snow. "Ask Dan Collins here if you want to know."

The prone man moaned. "Shut up!" Hen growled and his leather-booted foot thudded into the fellow's ribs. "Or tell us what you done with it. That's all we want outer you."

"Damn it," Peter blurted. His fists were clenched at his sides and a little heart-shaped scar at the left corner of his mouth went white. "*That's* not police work! Arrest him if he's a crook, but don't torture him."

"Sez who?" The detective's lids slitted. "Who the hell d'you think you are anyway?"

"That's not the point. Look here, mister detective. If you don't pick that injured man up and take him where he can get medical attention, I'll report this to your chief."

"You'll report…" A muscle twitched in Hen's cheek. "Now you don't want t' do that, feller." He looked worried.

"Right. I don't want to do it, but I will if you make me."

"If I make you, huh. As how?"

"By doing anything more to harm him,"

"Yeah?" The detective's foot moved again, to plant a heel on an outflung hand, curled and flaccid in the snow. "Like this?" The heel dug down, twisted. There was a crunch of broken bones. There was a scream, thin and high and animal-like, from a suddenly writhing form on the ground.

Corbin choked out an exclamation and started forward. The taller man's gun muzzle jerked up a little with trigger pressure. "Peter!" Anne cried and he halted.

The one called Hen hadn't moved. "Th' name's Stanger," he grinned. "Henry Stanger. Now go ahead an' report me to th' chief." He jabbed a gloved thumb at his companion. "Meet Chief Jason Kest of th' Ailchester Police."

CHAPTER TWO
SHOTGUN HI-JACK

ANNE CORBIN had been warm with their tramp around the base of Savin Ridge, their climb to its summit from behind, taking a shortcut home. Now she was shivering. Deep lines dug into Peter's face, joining the ends of his mouth to his nose. There was a hard ridge of knotted muscle along the edge of his jaw and his nostrils were pinched. Jason Kest showed his yellowed teeth in what might have been a smile were it not for the icy lack of expression in his eyes.

"At your service, Mister Peter Corbin," he said. "What was it you wanted to tell me?"

"Nothing," Corbin answered, very softly. "I've changed my mind."

"Well, I got something to say to you." The apologetic whine was still in Kest's voice, but Anne sensed that he was virulent as any reptile. "You just come into town. You rented yourself the Gordon house on Elm Street. You got yourself a job in the Fulton Silk Mill, keeping books. You bought a mess of furniture from the Bon Ton Store on Depot Square. That all looks like you expect to settle here. Is that right?"

Peter's mouth was a thin, pale line, but he nodded assent.

"That's fine," Kest continued. "Ailchester's a fine town for a young couple to settle in. It's a fine town to work and to bring up kids. You'll get along swell here—providing you don't run foul of the law here. The Law in Ailchester is Jason Kest. Do you get me?"

"I understand what you mean."

"All right. You tend to your knitting and I'll tend to mine. There's a path through the woods right here. It'll take you out on Hampton Highway and if you turn to the right you'll see Ailchester in front of you."

"Goo'bye," the brute-faced Stanger cooed. "It was a pleasure t' meetcher, I'm sure."

Corbin's head snapped around to him, and sinews in his neck corded. He took a short step forward.

"Come on," Anne said hastily, tugging at his arm. "We've got to hurry or Faith will scold us for keeping dinner waiting. Come on, Peter."

He went with her into the forest's damp shadows. Leafless underbrush crackled against their knees, kept on crackling even when they found the overgrown path Chief Kest had mentioned. The smell of loam, of fungus, rose musty about them.

"He knew an awful lot about us," Anne said.

"Too much. Where we're living, where I'm going to work; even where we bought our furniture. Ailchester's not a small enough place for things like that to be common gossip."

"I'm afraid, Peter," the girl whispered. "I'm afraid of him."

"I wonder what his game is? Look here, Anne. Keep on going. Make as much noise as you can."

THE HOUSE THAT TERROR BUILT 215

"What…" the girl began, but her husband was gone. He was slipping back the way they'd come; a drifting, silent shadow in the dimness. That year of hiding in the woods on Lane Hill had taught him woodcraft as necessity alone can teach anything. Not a twig snapped as he went, not a bush crackled. Behind him, going towards the Highway, Anne threshed loudly enough for two.

Corbin shrugged against a tree bole very near the margin of the forest, peered around it. Stanger was kneeling beside his victim, was rubbing a handful of snow into his cheeks. Collins was thinly dressed for the weather. He was collarless. His countenance was bruised, netted by scratches, unshaven, but there was nothing of viciousness in it. He was hardly older than Peter himself.

"Damn," Stanger grunted, settling back on his haunches. "How the hell are we gonna make this mug tell us where the stuff is? He's dead to th' world."

"That's nice." Kest's left eyelid twitched. "You had to kick him in the belly the minute I got my gun on him. You had to get in my way so he had a chance to run. You had to show off how hard you are, busting his hand, so he'd pass out. I'd like to put some lead into you, you lumberhead."

"Well, I thought…."

"You've got nothing to think with. Cripes knows how long he's going to be like that. We can't stick here all day, someone else may come along. We'll have to take him in now, and work on him when he come out of it. Pick him up and come on."

STANGER BENT, heaved Collins' inert body to his shoulder. As he came to his feet, lifting the flaccid burden almost effortlessly, he grunted. "I don't like them two seein' us give him th' works. I don't like the shape of the Corbin guy's puss. He's the kind that gets ideas."

"You leave them to me." They were starting away, Collins' head and arms dangling down Stanger's back, his left hand blue and swollen to twice its natural size. "Corbin might get into our hair if it wasn't for his wife. She was scared to death and she'll see that he keeps his nose clean. If she don't, I'll take care of him."

"An' mebbe you don't know how t' do that," the detective chuckled just as they passed out of earshot. "Remember that time...."

Peter Corbin could hear no more, but for a long moment he remained as he was, his brow furrowed. They were going to his right. They were going away from Ailchester, towards where Savin Woods swung around the end of the ridge. They were not taking their prisoner to the grey granite jail in town!

There might be some reasonable explanation for that. Above the trees, just where the white shoulder of the ridge thrust into them, a triangle showed what might be the corner of a roof. Where there was a house, there would also be a road, and the lawmen might have parked a car on it. But why had not Kest directed him and Anne that way, instead of sending them along that dim, easily lost path through the woods?

Why was Stanger so perturbed over having been observed brutalizing Collins? Corbin had had too much experience with small town officers not to sense something out of the ordinary in this. What was it the detective and Kest were so eager to locate?

The devil! It was none of his business....

"He threw it into the woods, Peter." Anne's voice was suddenly at his shoulder. "Let's go look...."

"Anne!" His fingers dug into her arm. "What's the idea? I told you to go ahead, so they'd hear you and be sure we weren't anywhere near."

"I went almost to the road before I started back. They couldn't have heard me coming back, because you didn't." A merry dimple dented her cheek and there were teasing lights in the greyness of her eyes. "I'm as good an Indian as you are. But they may be returning soon to look for whatever it was Collins had that they're after. We can tell exactly where he was when he threw it by the marks in the snow where he fell down, and he was too weak to throw it far. Come on. Hurry."

They shouldn't get mixed up in this, Corbin thought. Kest and Stanger were dangerous. Both he and Anne had suffered too much at the hands of the police to chance stirring up trouble with them again. But they had suffered too much from unjust operation of the law to refrain from interfering with injustice at the hands of the law. It would do no harm to see what it was Collins had undergone so much to keep from the cops. If it were the loot of some robbery they could turn it over to Kest. If it were not....

"All right," Peter said. "Come on."

They kept within the protective screen of the brush at the forest's edge, but they kept near enough to it to be able to follow the plain trail of Collins' desperate crawl. Opposite the spot where the man had first fallen, they stopped.

"He threw it to the right," Anne said. "Over this way."

"No," Corbin disagreed. "But let's not waste time arguing about it. You look over there and I'll look where I think it went. We don't want those two heroes to find us here if they take a notion to come back."

He heard his wife moving through the brush. He pushed dried withes apart, working away from the woods' edge.

There was a fresh scratch on the bark of an oak, low down. There was a glint of metal among its roots. Peter bent, and came up with something small in his hand.

HE STARED at it, his call to Anne unuttered. This couldn't be what Collins had endured brutal torture to keep secret. It was only a key, and it was not some intricate, irreplaceable device but an old-fashioned, plain shanked, door key. Any lock that this fitted could be opened with a hairpin.

"Give that to me or I'll blow you apart!"

Peter twisted around to face the thin, gasping voice. A shotgun thrust at him from between two gnarled trees, not five feet away. It was held by a woman. She was hatless and her hair was draggled over her hunger-sharpened face, so that her black and feverish eyes seemed to peer from behind a matted screen. Her cheeks were colorless save where some lashing bough had wealed it with angry red. A tattered coat of mangy fur hung from her shoulders, but beneath its frayed hem, her feet were bare and bruised and bleeding.

"Give it to me," the demand came again. "As God is my witness I'll blow you apart if you don't." The shotgun's barrel shook with the trembling of the hands that held it. She was panting, as though she had been fighting through the brush. Was it exhaustion or madness that ran in long shudders through her scrawny body?

"Just why should I give it to you?" Peter asked, his voice steady as his eyes. The gun might go off at any instant, the way the woman's finger was chattering on its trigger. It could cut a man in half at this close distance, and its spreading charge would riddle everything for yards around. Where was Anne? Was she within range? "Is it yours?"

"Is it mine?" Hysterical laughter spilled from the woman, laughter thin-edged and half mad. "No. It's Dan's. But he's starved me and froze me on account of it, and so I guess I got a right to it. And even if I ain't, this shotgun gives me the right. Are you going to turn over the key, or do I take it from your body?"

The name of Kest's prisoner was Dan Collins and this woman must be his wife. The apparently worthless key, then, actually was the thing the cops were after. What strange value was attached to it that it should be the center of such a maelstrom of violence?

Peter shrugged, smiling. "Your argument seems irrefutable," he said. "I...."

A mackinaw-sleeved arm shot from behind the woman! Its hand grabbed the gun barrel, jerked it up. Flame belched into the branches above. Corbin leaped across the space between, through a shower of snow clots, wrenched the shotgun from its owner's grasp, flung it away.

Anne had filtered around through the woods, had come up silently behind the woman, who was now struggling in her grasp. "Please," Anne said, "don't fight so hard. We won't hurt you. We'll give you the key if you can prove you have a right to it." There was gentleness in the way she said it, and compassion. The Collins woman was suddenly quiet.

"And if you can't prove it's yours, we'll turn it over to the police," Peter put in. "We...."

"No," the woman cried sobbing. "Not to them. Not to Kest. He'll... Oh God!" she broke off. "Hear that? They heard the gun go off. They're coming!"

There were faint shouts in the distance. Corbin turned to peer out into the open. Three black forms were moving swiftly across the white slope of Savin Ridge. The shapes of Kest and Stanger were unmistakable. The other—he was too short to be Dan Collins....

"Quick," the woman clawed at Peter. "Quick. Get away from here." The hysterical shrillness was back in her voice. "They mustn't know you have the key. I'll try to get away too, but if they catch me I won't tell them about you. Keep it for me. Come to my house tonight, on the highway, near the fork. Kate Collins. But go now. Oh, hurry. Hurry!"

She darted away. "Come on, Peter!" Anne blurted. The Corbins were sliding away through the black, twisted shadows of the woods. They were taking advantage of every bit of cover, were springing from stone to stone in the forest loam to avoid leaving footprints.

"Damned if I can make out what that's all about," Peter grunted. "But there's one thing I'm certain of. I'll be damned if I'll give up the key to that damned brute, Kest, 'till I've had a talk with Kate Collins."

"There's trouble coming, Peter," the girl trotting at his side whispered. "Trouble for us. I'm afraid. I'm dreadfully afraid."

CHAPTER THREE
RENDEZVOUS
WITH DEATH

I**T WAS** warm in the kitchen of the little house on Elm Street. It was bright with the light; the yellow light of electricity, wavering red light peering through slits in the front of the big coal range. The splash of sudsy water and the clatter of dishes being washed were sounds that were cheery and familiar. It didn't seem possible that this morning a man had crawled, racked by pain, through snow, only to be caught and hammered with bruising fists. It didn't seem possible that not four miles away, a woman had stood barefooted in the snow, a shotgun in her shaking hands and hysteria spewing from her twisted lips.

None of these things would have seemed possible to Peter Corbin if there had not lain, on the cleared table at which he sat, a common door key, brand new.

"I can't make it out," he muttered. "What could there be about this thing that is causing so much commotion? Faith," he looked up. "You've heard the story. Have you got any ideas?"

Faith Parker handed a dripping soup plate to Anne's towel-encumbered hands and looked up.

Faith was flat-breasted and acidulous of countenance. Her fingers were gnarled and workworn, her tiny, birdlike eyes wrinkle-lidded. Long ago she had taken the place of Anne's dead mother, a servant in the old Marsh house and far more than a servant. When the girl had been doubly bereaved and her whole world had crashed about her ears, Faith had remained loyal even knowing Anne had become a thief. She was all of the girl's Laneville childhood that remained to her, and she was all of that childhood that mattered.

She was no servant here, but a friend who labored for the love of those whom she served.

She answered Peter Corbin now, her voice thin and querulous. "That Collins is a crook of some sort, and the key is the evidence that will prove it on him. If I was you, I'd turn it over to them two cops and sleep easy. Haven't you had trouble enough already without having to go out and look for more?"

"No." Anne had rubbed the plate to a lustrous polish and put on a stack of others. "Kate Collins is no criminal, and she has suffered terribly for whatever that key represents. Kest and Stanger are brutes. There isn't any good in them at all. We won't give them the key until we are convinced they have a right to it."

"I agree," Peter responded. "I'm going to hold on to it, at least until I've had a chance to talk to the woman."

Faith's fingers plucked at her apron. "Them policeman are nasty customers, and they're bound to get hold of it. They're liable to arrest you for being mixed up with Collins, and if they do your fingerprints will be taken and sent to the G-Men's file in Washington. There's another set there, that tells you're a convict escaped from the penitentiary at Bolton. You're not a hankering to be dragged back there, are you?"

"No!" Anne gasped, the color draining from her face. "That mustn't happen."

"I wouldn't stay there long," Peter laughed. "You both forget that Zander's confession in Ryan's presence clears me of sabotaging that dynamo. Ryan will come to bat for me, and...."

"No he won't," the older woman broke in. "He can't."

Corbin's head lifted to her, and he saw that in her expression that squeezed his heart with sudden dread. "What do you mean?" he asked quietly. "You know something you haven't told us."

Faith's countenance was the color of death. "Yes," she mumbled. "I didn't want you youngsters getting upset, so I been keeping it from you—but now I see I got to tell you. When you asked me for the newspaper this morning I told you it didn't come, and you didn't bother about it no more. But it did come. I burned it in this stove before you two come down for breakfast."

There were grim, hard lines about Peter Corbin's face now. "What was in it, Faith, that you didn't want us to see?"

"There was a story about an airplane accident, near Laneville. Everybody on board was killed. One of them was Fulton Zander and another was that cop, Ryan. They were the only ones in the world that could prove you innocent of what you was sent to prison for. Of what you're supposed to stay there four more years for."

The crackle of the coals was the only sound in the room. Peter was a rigid statue, fear coming back into his eyes; fear that he had thought behind him forever—the terrible fear of the hunted. A grey mask crept over Anne's face, hazing its ruddy freshness.

AND THEN, quite suddenly, the girl was smiling. "It's all right, my dear," she said, moving to her man, covering his bronzed, capable hand with her slim, white one. "It's quite all right. You said yourself, this morning, that no one from Laneville can ever trace us here. All we have to do is give the key to Kest, and we have nothing to be afraid of."

"Give the key…" Corbin repeated dazedly. And then strength came back to his voice: "I was beaten up exactly the way Kest and Stanger beat up Collins, Anne dear. The cops hammered me till I was a whimpering, spineless thing, and I was guiltless of any crime. I hate, not justice, not the law when it works justice, but those who are supposed to serve justice and work injustice instead. Something, some instinct deep within me, tells me that's what's happening in this case. If I didn't have you to consider, I'd risk going back to Bolton Pen to fight for that man we saw so brutally treated, for that woman we saw standing barefoot on the frostbitten ground. But if you say so, I'll give up the key and…."

"No, Peter." There were tears in the girl's eyes, and the same fear that had come into Corbin's, but her little chin was firm and determined. "No. Not till we're sure...."

She stopped suddenly, her eyes widening. The knock at the front door that had interrupted her was repeated, loud, demanding. "Someone.... But we don't know anyone here. Who...?"

"Best way to find out is to go see," Faith snapped. She went out of the kitchen. Anne moved to the door out of which the old woman had gone, peered out into the foyer.

Hinges creaked and there was the rumble of a man's voice. Anne's head jerked around, her pupils dilated. "It's Kest and Stanger, Peter! Somehow they've found out that we have the key, and they've come for it."

Corbin snatched up the key, jumped up. His glance darted about the room. The flour can? No. It was the first place anyone would look. He darted to the sink, dropped the small object into the opaque, soapy water in the dishpan....

"Couple of men to see you, Peter." Faith was in the doorway again. "They're awaitin' in the hall...."

"No we ain't," Hen Stanger growled, pushing her into the kitchen. "We're comin' right in." Kest ranged alongside of him as he halted and stood spraddle-legged just inside the door.

Faith sniffed disdainfully, and went back to her sink. Her hands plunged into the water and the dishes rattled. Corbin's dismay did not show in his face, but the heart-shaped scar at the corner of his tight mouth was white.

"Come in, gentlemen," he said. His low tone emphasized the word 'gentlemen' just a little. "Come right in and make yourselves at home."

"They didn't wait to be asked," the old woman sniffed. "Drat this water! It's got cold. I'll have to heat some more and I've let the fire die down." She lifted a lid from one of the holes in the range top, made rattling noise as she shoveled coal into it. Faith Parker could show her contempt for those she disliked in numberless irritating tricks like that one.

"Where is it?" Stanger demanded when the noise had died down. "Let's have it—quick!"

Corbin looked blank. "Where is what? I don't know what you're talking about."

"The hell you don't. Spill, feller. Where is it?"

Peter's eyebrows lifted as he turned to Kest. "Is it your usual custom in Ailchester to employ lunatics as detectives. I...."

"I'll lunatic you," Stanger snarled. He pounded towards Peter, his hamlike fist swinging. Anne screamed and Corbin ducked the blow, crouched to defend himself. But Kest's hand was on the detective's shoulder.

"Cut it, Hen!" he said sharply. And then, "Frisk him."

Stanger growled, but his hands were open when they reached for Peter. One went into his trouser pocket and Corbin grabbed his wrist. "Wait a minute," he panted. "Where's your warrant for this? You need one or your actions are against the law."

"I told you once I'm the law in Ailchester," Kest whined.

"That doesn't make it so. You might beat up a man out in the fields where you think yourself unwatched, and get away with it. But there are two witnesses here and I don't think the people of Ailchester will stand for any proceeding like this." Corbin's frank blue eyes caught and held the other's lustreless ones. "Call off your dog, Kest."

THERE WAS no movement in that kitchen for a long moment. There was only a silent battle of looks. And it was Kest's that dropped.

"Let him go, Hen," he yielded. "But that don't mean we're quitting, mister. I told you to keep your nose clean and I… Holy Smoke! I got it!" He whirled, darted to the sink. "It's in the dishwater!" His hands were on the pan, were lifting it. The soap-filled water poured over the edge.

"Don't you break none of my dishes," Faith Parker cried out. "Or I'll…."

Kest caught the dishes as they started to tip out of the basin, slid them to the sink bottom. Cutlery clattered. The pan was empty. Kest was poking a long finger into it, and a pulse was pounding in Peter Corbin's temple.

His eyes sought Anne's. He was asking her forgiveness. Kest wouldn't be satisfied with recovering the key. He would arrest Peter, and….

"Hell," Jason Kest grunted. "It ain't here."

"If you are quite through playing bear in my kitchen"— it was Anne who recovered first—"would you mind leaving us? My husband and I prefer a quiet evening at home to the sort of entertainment you have been furnishing us."

Kest looked around at her, and his lashless lids were slitted. "We'll go now. But you and your husband ain't through with us. Not by a long shot. Nobody ain't had the laugh on Jason Kest that ain't laughed out of the other side of his mouth by the time I was through with them. Come on, Hen."

They tramped out of the door and out of the house. "Peter!" Anne exclaimed. "What happened to it? You did put it in there. I'm sure I saw you."

Corbin spread his hands wide. "I certainly put it in there, and just as certainly it wasn't there when Kest emptied the pan. I can't understand what became of it."

"Is this what you're talking about?" Faith Parker had the stove-lid off again, and she was fishing inside. Her clawlike hand came out and the key was in her fingers.

"Faith!" Anne snatched it from her. "How did it get in there?"

"I put it in there when I put the fresh coals in. It lay on top of them and they ain't caught fire yet. Coal takes a long time to get hot, but them lummoxes wouldn't know that."

"Kest is no fool," Peter answered, his brow still creased with puzzlement. "He guessed that I'd hidden it in the dish-pan, and I can't understand how he did."

"The same way I did," Faith chuckled grimly. "By that splash of soap suds on your sleeve. He knew that with two women in the house you wouldn't be washing dishes, and the only other way it could have gotten there was if you threw something in the water."

"I'll be damned!" Corbin grunted, staring down at the wet spot on his shirtsleeve.

"Well," the wrinkled spinstress continued, "are you ready to give in now? You came within an inch of going back to Bolton that time, and the next you won't get out of so easy. Those birds know you've got that key and they're bound and determined to get it from you."

"*How* did they know it?" Anne whispered. "There was no snow in the woods and the ground was frozen hard. Even if they'd found our tracks and followed them, they would have been here long ago."

"The woman told them," Faith grated. "That Kate Collins you're so worried about."

The girl shook her head. "Not she. Not unless they...."

"Used the same methods on her as they did on her husband." Two grey spots showed on either side of Corbin's nostrils. There was wrath in his low growl. "I'm going out there to see, and, by God, if they have...."

"Come along. What are we waiting for?" Anne started out through the door.

"No, Anne! You're staying here. You're going to hide that key so they'll have to tear the house apart to find it. Faith! See that she doesn't follow me."

"I'll see to that," the spinstress promised, grimly. She'll stay here."

CHAPTER FOUR
FRAMED!

SOMEWHERE IN the distance a tower clock boomed eight times. There was no moon, but the snow on the high banks through which Hampton Highway had been cut had an eerie luminance of its own. In that weird light, the hovel, set far back in the angle where a narrow, uncleared road debouched from the pike and climbed into the thickening woods, seemed doubly lonely. It was cloaked with an ominous blackness, an ominous silence.

Peter Corbin paused, his lips tightening. This was the only fork in the highway within ten miles of Ailchester. This must be the house the Collins woman meant. But surely if she were there she would be showing a light. Perhaps not. Perhaps she wanted the shanty thought deserted while she waited for him to come.

He shrugged. It would do no harm to try the door. His heels rang too loudly on the frost-hardened shoulder of the road. He made too much noise climbing the bank. There wasn't anyone around to hear the sounds he made, why worry about them? Why worry about the marks he was making in the snow? Kest and Stanger were already suspicious of him, and the fact that he was visiting Kate Collins would not make them more so.

The door, of paintless, weathered boards, had no knob. There was only a rusted hasp screwed to it, meant to be fastened by a padlock. But it was not. It was folded back against the door. The padlock hung in its iron loop in the jamb. Corbin fingered it. What could this hovel contain valuable enough to be protected by so heavy a lock?

A thought struck him. He fished a small flashlight from the pocket of his lumber jacket, let its light fall on the keyhole. No. The key over which there was mysteriously so much to-do would never fit into that zig-zag slit. He flicked off the light, tapped softly on the door. There was no response.

He tried again, rapping a little harder. The door swung inward, creaking, but only blackness showed in the widening slit.

Peter waited. There was no hint of any human presence, no sound of movement, within the house. But behind him there was the hum of a car coming along the highway from the direction of Ailchester, nearing swiftly. A sudden impulse sent him through the doorway, closing the door softly behind him.

The thick boards shut out all sound. He was swallowed by absolute lightlessness, thick and oppressive. The air was musty with odors, of body sweat, of stale cookery, of machine oil. There was one smell that threaded the others, acrid. It lifted the short hairs at the nape of his neck, feathered his spine with a chill ripple. It was the stench of burned flesh.

"Hello," Corbin whispered into the throbbing darkness. "Is anyone there?"

No answer. No stir. But he had strangely the feeling that he was not alone in the hut. Elusive, ascribable to no impression on any of the five familiar senses, the feeling was undeniable. Somewhere in this dark house there was another than he.

The flashlight was still in his hand. His thumb moved the switch in its slit and a narrow shaft of white light shot out, dust motes dancing in it. It struck out of the blackness a rusted, ramshackle stove, moved to a drab wall that was merely the inside of the house's outer boards. A few ragged garments hung from nails driven into the wood.

Beside these was a window, tightly covered by a board shutter across which an iron bar was clamped. Queer, Peter thought, and his light moved further.

It impinged now on something in the center of the room that was utterly incongruous to the squalor everywhere evident. It was a sturdy work bench, in prime condition. An expensive metal lathe fastened to its top gleamed with assiduous care. Polished tools were carefully racked, but there were threadlike metal shavings on the bench top, bits of broken metal.

The light drifted on, touched a rickety chair whose cane seat hung out of its bottom, touched dirt-grey bedclothes hanging over the edge of a decrepit iron cot, moved to the upper surface of that cot.

The half-naked form of Kate Collins lay there. Her ankles were lashed to the iron tubing that made the foot of the bed, her arms were pulled up over her head and lashed by the wrists to the bed's head. Her eyes were open, but they were no longer glittering fiercely. They were glazed, unseeing. They were the eyes of death.

Corbin muttered an exclamation, moved across the room, on stiff legs, to the side of the cot.

Wealing the cheeks, the forehead of the woman, cicatrizing her abdomen, were long, yellow-white blisters! The blisters of burns! And the agony of those burns was frozen into the contorted, dead face, into the twisted limbs.

Peter Corbin's skin was an icy sheath for his body. He knew now how Kest and Stanger had found out he had the key. He knew....

"Hold it, Corbin!" Jason Kest's whining voice said behind him. "Hold it just like that. I've got you covered."

"Caught in th' act!" That was Henry Stanger's coarse accents. "By Jingo. Caught in th' act." Handcuffs jangled as he came toward Peter.

PETER CORBIN paced the stone floor of a jail cell. Five paces to the wall, turn, five paces to the other wall, black lines flitting over him that were the shadows of bars cast by a vague light in the corridor outside. Turn, and five paces back. The stink of disinfectant in his nostrils. How well he knew that endless pacing, that prison odor, how infernally well! He would know them again, for four maddening years—for how many additional years because of his escape?

They couldn't convict him of killing Kate Collins. How could they, when he had not killed her? Her body had been cold, stiff with *rigor mortis.* She had been dead for hours. He could prove an alibi for those hours. He could prove it only by Anne's testimony, and Faith's. Would a jury of strangers believe his wife, his friend? They must. They had to! It couldn't be possible that an innocent man could be framed with murder. But he'd been framed with another crime once, what had happened once could happen again.

It didn't make much difference whether he was acquitted of the killing or not. He was going back to Bolton and this time there would be no escape. They hadn't taken his fingerprints yet. They hadn't even booked him. Kest had whined something about there being plenty of time, the Judge was out of town over the week-end. He would be back Monday morning and that would be the beginning of the end.

Thinking like this would drive him mad. Think of something else. Of the fact that he had seen no other prisoners in the cell block. Where was Dan Collins then? What had they done with him? Had they left him in that house at the north end of Savin Ridge? Why? He was not legally a prisoner, that was certain. Their suspicions, his and Anne's, of Kest and Stanger were confirmed.

Anne! If he were sent back to Bolton Pen she would....

Corbin's pacing stopped, abruptly. There were sounds in the corridor outside, the opening of a door, the rattle of keys, the thud of approaching footfalls. Another prisoner.

No. Hen Stanger appeared at the cell door. "Here's someone t' see you, Corbin," he grunted. He was sliding a key into the lock. There was another man with him. Short. A bland, round face chinned by a clipped, grey vandyke beard. His overcoat, black and luxurious, cut in an old-fashioned manner, his derby hat square-topped. This was the man who'd given Peter his job, Friday afternoon. J. Thomas Fulton, owner of the factory that gave employment to three-quarters of Ailchester.

He was inside the cell, and Stanger had locked it again, was going away. "I'm sorry to see you here, Corbin," Fulton was saying. "I've come to see if there is anything I can do for you. You see, I feel like a father to all my employees. We're all one big, happy family at the Mill and I'm the father. I stick to my children even if they've been bad."

The corner of Peter's mouth twitched. "I don't want anything from you." The resentment he felt was puerile, but he could not rid himself of it. "I can take care of myself."

"Oh come now," Fulton smiled benevolently. "You haven't been here long. You can't know the best lawyer to employ, for instance, I can recommend one. I can advise you."

"What advice can you give me?" That was better. The man was, after all, well-intentioned.

"Well, I... Phew. This odor is sickening. I wonder does that window open?"

"I think it does." It would be cold in here with it open, but perhaps he could think more clearly with fresh air in his lungs. Peter crossed to the aperture, thrust up the sash that framed thick glass in which a heavy wire net was embedded. A blast of icy air came in, and with it a clamor of boyish voices.

CORBIN STARED out past the two black bars that crossed the deep stone embrasure. Depot Square was white with snow. There was a snowball fight going on out there, a fort just below this window being defended against the onslaught of a dozen shrieking youngsters....

"That's better," Fulton said behind him. "Infinitely better."

Peter was staring at the point where one of the bars entered the stone sill. It was pitted with rust there. An hour's filing would cut through it, and his slim form could get through without touching the other bar. But he had no file. Kest had made sure of that.

"Listen to me, Corbin." Peter turned back to Fulton. "As I was saying, I can recommend a lawyer; but he wouldn't be able to accomplish much if Chief Kest is determined to convict you. Kest's influence in Ailchester is great, very great. However, I've been talking to him, and I have an idea that we can get him to be lenient."

Corbin's eyebrows lifted. "Yes?"

"Yes. There is a small matter of a key that seems to have set him against you. I am persuaded that if you were to adjust that, you would find it easier to get out of your difficulties. Much easier."

Sinews corded in Peter's neck, and a pulse throbbed in his temple. The key again. The policeman would go to any lengths to get hold of it; to torture, to framing a man for murder. Before she died, Kate Collins must have told them that he was coming to her, and they had laid for him. Their testimony that her body was rigid when they found him in the hut would go far to clear him. They would give that testimony if… he gave them the key.

"I don't know what you're talking about," he said slowly. "A key? Please explain."

Fulton shrugged. "I'm merely repeating what Kest said to me. I haven't the least idea to what he referred. But think it over. My earnest advice is to think it over. Conciliating Kest is your best bet. Meantime, nothing more can be done till Monday. I'll see that my attorney comes to you then, if you are still here. Goodbye, my boy, and good luck."

"Goodbye." Corbin's tone was musing. "And thank you."

Fulton called Stanger to open the door. It was locked again and the two had gone off. The cold was numbing Corbin. He started across to the window to close it.

If he gave up the key, he thought, the murder charge would be withdrawn. Why not? He reached up to the sash.

Why should he sacrifice himself, sacrifice Anne's happiness, for some quixotic idea of revenging a woman whom he had seen for the first time this moon? He would....

Abruptly he wasn't thinking any longer. He was staring out through the window, into the Square, and a muscle was twitching in his cheek.

The boys attacking the snow fort had worked nearer. One of them, a little taller than the others, but just as slender, just as active, had brought a picture back into his memory. A snowy night just like this, in Laneville. A slim lad stealing furtively through deserted streets. A boy just like that one, but he had known it was not a boy. He had known it was the girl he loved, Anne Marsh, disguised and on her way to the final episode of her long battle to accomplish Justice outside the Law.

She had looked just like that.... The lad threw a snowball. It arced high into the air. It was larger than most. It was coming straight for the window through which Peter stared! It dipped. It was going to miss....

Corbin's hand darted out through the bars, clutched the snow missile. As he pulled it in, the boy below waved an arm. Peter's heart pounded against his ribs.

The window was closed. He was at the front bars of the cell, was listening intently. Voices rumbled far off, in the jail office at the end of the corridor. There was no intimation of any living presence nearer.

He retreated to the window. His fingers dug into the icy ball, split it open. There was something hard inside, wrapped in wax paper. The something hard was half of a triangular file, and there was another paper, white, twisted around it.

Corbin's trembling fingers got the white paper open. His eyes devoured the neat, copperplate writing:

"After midnight the Square will he deserted. I'll be behind the Depot waiting for you, till dawn. Anne."

CHAPTER FIVE
THE END OF THE ROAD

BREATH HISSED from between Peter Corbin's teeth, and the faint rasp, rasp of his file stopped. The clock in the Town Hall Tower bonged twice. He had not dared work at the window bar till there was no longer anyone in the Square who might spy him. That had been nearer one than midnight, and it had taken him longer than he figured to file through the bar. But it was done now.

His fingers closed on the end of the rusted iron rod. He gave it a jerk and he heard it crack. He got his feet against the wall and pulled toward him, the muscles in his back tightening, torn with pain, the muscles in his thighs quivering. Slowly, with infinite slowness, the bar started to bend, inward.

The Town Hall clock struck the quarter-hour before the bar was bent sufficiently to let Peter through. His muscles were weak and painful, his hands were bleeding. He poked his head through, looked out. The plaza lay absolutely vacant under a brooding sky. He could hear no footfalls, no intimation that all Ailchester was not bound in deep slumber.

He was rigid, sending the tentacles of his hearing back into the dim reaches of the jail. There was sound here, long and rasping. His lips moved in a humorless smile. That sound was a snore. Stanger, in the office at the end of the corridor, was snoring.

The end of the bar plucked at Corbin's coat; he was squeezed between the stone window frame on one side, the remaining bar on the other. Anyone less lithe could never have made it. But he did. He got through. He hung for a moment, by his hands from the sill, dropped the ten feet to the ground. Jarred and shaken, he paused not an instant but darted across the snow-covered Square, a flitting, silent shadow.

He reached the shadows that lay against the depot, merged with them. He went around the deserted building. From the blackness lying between freight shed and the station a whisper came to him.

"Peter! Thank God. This way, Peter. Hurry!"

The next moment Anne was in his arms, his lips hot upon hers, her body, warm and feminine despite the youth's clothing that disguised it, crushed against his. Her gloved hands clung to him desperately, and then they were pushing him away.

"No, Peter. Wait. Put this sweater on and this cap. Hurry. There's going to be a freight along in two minutes. We've got to be down by the watertank so we can climb into a car while it's stopped."

"Into a car! What…?"

"We've got to get away from here. Far away. I won't have you go back to prison." She was sobbing. "I'd die if you did." Her hands tugged at him. "Come, Peter. Hurry."

He took her thin wrists in his fingers, held them gently but firmly. "No, Anne," he said. "We can't do that. If we run away now, we'll keep running forever. Fear will go with us, and it will always be between us. We will get to hate each other.…"

"No!"

"Yes. The only way is to stay here, to fight this out. To beat Kest and make a place for ourselves here in Ailchester. And I've got an idea that we can do it. Where's the key?"

"I—I've got it here. I had it hidden, but when I came to meet you I took it along. I wasn't going to let them have it. Here." She had fumbled at her clothing and now the cold metal was pressing into his hand.

"Collins had a metal lathe in his house, and there was a broken key on the bench. That told me the secret of *this* key." Peter moved along the side of the freight shed to where a faint green luminance from a signal light filtered past its corner. "It told someone else that secret, too; told them it was a key they must hunt for. Look."

He held the key's shank in one hand, its top in the other, twisted the top. The metal turned in his hand. "The shank's hollowed out. It's really a tube. This top unscrews to open it." It came free. "And inside—there's this." Corbin drew out a tight roll of paper from the key's hollow shank. It rustled open in his fingers. It was onion-skin paper, tissue-like but strong. There was no writing on it. There were only lines....

"Got it!" Peter exclaimed. "It all ties up." He thrust the paper into his pocket, twisted to Anne. "Listen, honey. I've got places to go and things to do. You go home and get to bed, so that when Kest comes looking for me you can swear you know nothing of my escape."

"No, Peter. I'm going with you. I'm...."

"You're doing exactly as I say. I'm not taking any chances on your getting hurt." He pulled her to him, bruised her lips with a fierce, almost desperate kiss. "Now go."

Anne whimpered protest, but she went. Corbin got into the sweater she had brought him, pulled the cap low over his brow, and moved away, too. He kept to the railroad till he was past the town, circled to the left, reached Hampton Highway and crossed it into the dark and brooding woods.

IN THE darkness of the big house on the shoulder of Savin Ridge someone moaned. The shadow that had flitted up stair after stair from the basement paused and was still for a moment. Then it was moving again, soundless, along an unlighted corridor. It reached a door, folded against it.

"Water," a pain-shot voice gasped from behind that door. "Water."

"Come to, have you, Collins?" someone purred. "If I'd been sure that you would, I should have been saved a great deal of trouble."

"You!" The first voice screamed weakly. "Oh God! You!"

"Yes, my friend, I. You didn't think you could beat me, did you? You're convinced by now, I hope. Because I should hate to be put to any more trouble getting from you what you know I want. You'll tell me now, won't you? You'll draw it for me."

"Go to hell."

"Still obstinate, eh? Well, I think I can persuade you. You see this, Dan Collins? It's an electric cigarette lighter. When I plug it in here, like this, and press this button, the filament grows red-hot. You see? Now if I press this on your skin, it would not be very comfortable, would it?"

"Damn you!"

"Damn me if you like. Scream if you like. There is no one around to hear you. Do you think if you scream anyone will hear you, Dan Collins?"

The door swung open. "Maybe he doesn't! But I would have heard him." A lithe figure sprang through the doorway. "If I'd waited!" It reached the one of the two who in that room was erect, smashed the cigarette lighter from a hand numbed by surprise, dug savage fingers into terror-paralyzed biceps and pounded the little man against the wall. *"Mr. J. Thompson Fulton!"*

Eyes goggled from a vandyke-bearded face that was no longer bland. "Corbin!"

"Yes. Peter Corbin. Not safely locked up in jail for you to offer freedom to in exchange for the plans that you have tortured for—murdered for. The game's up, Mr. Fulton."

"Murdered!" Collins, blood-masked and ghastly, jerked up to a sitting posture on the couch where his crumpled form had lain. "Who…?"

"Your wife, Kate," Peter flung at him over his shoulder. "Tortured to death. You'd have done better to sell him your invention, Collins, than to have tried to hide it from him."

"Sell it to him!" The man's voice was a shrill squeak. "Sell him the work of five years' hell, starvation, despair, for what he offered me when I could get a half-million for it from his competitors!"

"And ruined me." Spittle dribbled into Fulton's beard. "Ruined me either way. You worked five years on a damned invention that would put my product off the market. It took a hundred to build up the Fulton Mills, a hundred years and three generations. Rather than let it be smashed, the life's work of my grandfather and my father, the livelihood of a thousand men, a thousand families, in Ailchester I'd…."

"Torture, Fulton?" Peter broke in. "Murder?"

"Torture," The bearded man whispered. "Murder." Black lights crawled in his pupil-dilated eyes. "I didn't intend to at first. I promised Kest ten thousand if he got the plans from Collins. He said he'd get them by tonight. And then he brought Collins here, made me hide him here."

Peter knew the man was playing for time, but he had to get the whole story, so he only said, "Go on," when Fulton paused.

"Then there was the shot outside, and we rushed out. The woman got away, and Kest told me it was Kate Collins, that she must have the plans. He said he'd get them from her. But I didn't trust him any more, I told him I'd attend to that myself. I followed her to their hut, offered her money. She refused."

"So you tortured her and killed her!" Peter nodded grimly. "You're a filthy rat, Fulton. Let's have the rest of the story before I give you a dose of your own medicine."

Fulton quailed before the look in Peter's eyes and, whatever he may have been thinking, he evidently decided that Peter meant what he said.

"She had screamed something about a key before she died. I understood what she meant when I saw what was on the lathe bench. I phoned Kest that you must have it, told him to get it from you. I didn't know what to do about the woman. I just left her there, came back here to think it out.

"Collins was still insensible, was scarcely breathing. Then Kest 'phoned me that he hadn't gotten the key from you but had arrested you for the murder of Kate Collins. I saw my way out. I'd get the plans from you, but I wouldn't help you. You'd be convicted of the murder and I'd be free. But you were stubborn. My only way to get Collins' device was to get it from him. I worked over him to bring him back to consciousness, and just as I succeeded, you...."

"Lift them my friend." The command came from behind and it was the whining voice of Jason Kest. "Grab for the ceiling before I put lead into you. I kind of thought you'd make for here when I came to relieve Hen and found you'd skipped."

Peter's hands released Fulton, shot up over his head. He turned, slowly, to see the Police Chief standing in the doorway, his bull-nosed revolver steady in his hand.

Corbin was rigid. "You heard what Fulton said. You're an officer of the law. You know it's he whom you should arrest for murder."

"Yeah," Kest grinned. "I heard him, and I might still arrest him. But I've always had a hankering to be partners in the Fulton Mill and for a half-interest in it, I might listen to reason. You see, it might be arranged that you got shot trying to get in here after escaping, and that Dan Collins there was helping you and got killed too. How does that sound to you, Mr. Fulton?"

"A half-interest?" Fulton licked his lips. "To you!"

"It's better than the hot-squat."

"Well..." Muscles tightened under the man's cheeks. "Well..." He was going to give in, and that meant death for Peter. "If you won't take less...."

Peter's thigh muscles exploded, hurling him at Kest. He was upon him, was pounding him to the ground with flailing fists, was wrenching his gun from him; his gun that had not been fired because just before Corbin had jumped, a heavy pair of fire-tongs had crashed against the back of the police officer's head....

Wielded by Anne, by the girl who had suddenly appeared behind him and struck, her approach soundless as a phantom's.

Peter leaped up, whirled to Fulton, Kest's revolver in his hand. "You won't have to make that bargain," he snarled. "Don't worry any more about it."

FULTON AND Kest were safely bound, and the Corbins were waiting for the State Police to come from Hampton to take them away. "I thought I told you to go home," Peter chided Anne.

"As if I could when I knew you were going into danger." Anne was still dressed as she had been in the Square, but the dimples that dented her cheek were never owned by a boy. "I trailed you and I saw you go into the basement here through the window you forced open. I was afraid you'd hear me, so I waited outside, but when I saw Kest drive up and unlock the door with his skeleton key, I followed him in. What I can't understand, though, is how you knew to come straight here."

"There was something fishy about Fulton's coming to see me in jail. When I saw the plans that were hidden in the key, I knew why he had done that. I remembered the third man that came out with Kest and Stanger when Kate Collins' gun went off and it was easy deduction to figure that he must have been Fulton, and that Collins was being held prisoner here.

"But that's all over, my dear. We have only one problem left to decide. You wanted to leave Ailchester tonight. I'm ready to go with you if you say the word."

Anne fingered a button of his coat. "You said that if we run away from here, fear will be always between us and we'd grow to hate each other. Let's stay, Peter. Because here there has never been anything but love between us."

TWIN SHADOWS OF THE NIGHT

NOT EVEN THE SHADOW OF AN
INCOMPLETED JAIL SENTENCE
COULD DETER YOUNG PETER
CORBIN AND HIS DARING WIFE,
ANNE, FROM RISKING THEIR LIVES
IN A HAZARDOUS SKIRMISH
WITH THE LAW! FOR THEY WERE
DETERMINED TO WIN JUSTICE
FOR THE DOWNTRODDEN PEOPLE
OF AILCHESTER, IN SPITE OF
A CRIMINAL TYRANT AND A
CROOKED CHIEF OF POLICE!

CHAPTER ONE
THE CHIEF
DECLARES WAR

THE SETTING sun dropped below a cloud. Its
low rays streamed through the windows of the
Fulton Silk Mills, laying shadows over the bookkeeper's
desk at which Peter Corbin was working. Corbin stiffened.
Small muscles knotted along his blunt jaw, and the little,
heart-shaped scar at the corner of his mouth turned grey-
white. In his blue eyes came a look of brooding fear.

The shadows that striped the white ledger page on which
his pen poised motionless were narrow and long and evenly
spaced. Cast by the iron rackets of a high fence outside,
they were exactly like those thrown by prison bars!

Peter's thin, sensitive nostrils flared. Abruptly the hush
of the office, deserted but for him, seemed the hopeless
silence of a jail. The drab plaster wall from which his shelf-
like desk jutted appeared to take on the texture and tint of
grim, grey granite. Other walls seemed to close in about
his slender, lithe frame.

The space between the wall in front and the wall behind
him was only six paces! In his mind he began again his
endless stepping off of those six paces, back and forth, back
and forth, thinking endlessly again of how he had been
framed for a crime he did not commit, hate growing within
him for the man who had framed him, for the Society
whose Law had thus been misused against him.

Over two years ago he had escaped from Bolton Pen, but still its cells waited for him, grim and implacable. The black shadows of penitentiary bars still lay across his soul, and the dread of discovery, of return, went with him, day and night....

"Peter!"

The clear, silvery voice shattered the imagined cell Peter Corbin's fear had erected about him, as once that same voice had shattered his hard hate for all humanity and transformed it into hate only for the unjust who use the Law to perpetrate injustice. He swiveled around. A girl was coming toward him between two rows of unattended desks. Her slim, small-boned body was the personification of lissome grace. Close-cropped, tawny curls clustered about the pert-featured oval of her face.

"Anne!" Corbin exclaimed, sliding from his stool. "Anne! What on earth are you doing here?"

"I came to get you," she answered. "When you 'phoned home you'd be working a little late I knew that meant half the night if I didn't come down."

She reached him. His arms went around her. "Anne," he breathed. "Wife o' mine." He held her tightly, so tightly she could not help but feel the quivering of his body against her soft curves. She saw the shadows on the wall, and swift understanding leaped into her cool, grey eyes.

"Come on," she said, pushing him away from her with gentle hands that somehow clung. "Put your big book away. If we hurry we'll still have time to take in a movie after supper." The thing to do was to bring Peter back into the routine of everyday living that people know who do not live in fear. "Please, darling. I walked across town and I'm starved."

A smile crept across Corbin's sultry countenance, and the poise of his head was once more jaunty. "Okay, honey," he consented. "We'll hurry. We'll take the shortcut through the Sump and a taxi from Hampton Boulevard."

"A taxi! Peter! It's forty-five cents to Elm Street and we can't afford—"

"I said a taxi, Mrs. Peter Corbin, and a taxi it's going to be."

AS PETER and Anne closed behind them the back gate in the factory fence, a colorless and stealthy dusk was already settling over the expanse of refuse-strewn cinders Ailchester calls the Sump. In the grimy half-light, small huts, paintless and askew, looked more like the abodes of some race of ancient gnomes than civilized habitations. The odor of garbage floated about the bedraggled shacks. Here and there a few ragged children scrabbled lackadaisically in heaps of ashes and debris, their pinched faces old and wan.

Breath pulled in between Anne's teeth. Peter grasped her arm, steered her to a path that wandered off toward the railroad embankment on the other side of which was the tree-lined, gleaming main thoroughfare of Ailchester.

A pot-bellied little girl in a tattered dress yelled some obscenity at them. Her eyes peering through a covert of tangled hair like the eyes of some sick beast, a woman held a puny limbed infant to a brown, withered breast, she made no attempt to cover with her rags. A hoarse shout came from behind the shack in whose doorway the nursing mother stood, and then a thin wail threaded the dusk with pain.

Anne stopped short. "What was that?" she gasped.

If only the crash of glass
would lure Chief Stanger away
from that open window....

Her husband shrugged. "Seems to be a usual thing
around here. Nobody's paying any attention to it. So don't
you bother about it."

The cry sounded again, like the exhausted scream of
some small creature caught in a trap. It was cut short by
the spat of flesh on flesh. Anne pulled away from Peter,
darted around the corner of the hovel.

"Anne!" Corbin yelled, "come back!" The patter of her feet was the only answer and he went after her, cinders crunching under his heavier soles. He passed the gaping side-boards of the shack, saw another behind it. Anne was snatching at the upraised arm of a barrel-bodied, thick-necked man. Before him cringed an old woman whose grey, stringy mop all but hid a face like a skull covered with wrinkled parchment.

"You brute!" the girl exclaimed. "Striking that old lady!"

"What the hell," the man grunted, heaving around as Peter pounded up. "She'd of scratched my eyes out if I—" He broke off. His small, heavy-lidded eyes got smaller still, resting on Anne's countenance. His blue jowls lumped. "Well," he mouthed, "if it ain't my friend Mrs. Corbin again. And *Mister* Corbin! Are you two fixin' to get in my hair again?"

He was in civilian clothes, but 'cop' was written all over him: in his thick-soled brogues, his gnarled, banana-fingered fists, in the black derby shoved so far back on his head that it seemed to cling there by virtue of some minor miracle.

"Looks like you make it necessary for us," Corbin answered him. "The first time we met, you were brutalizing a starving man half your size." The shack door was abruptly filled by a huge mass composed of a rolled-up mattress from rents in which mouldy straw trailed; a bundle of grimy sheets, and dirt-crusted blankets. A broken chair perched on top of these and the whole seemed to be moving under its own power. "Now you're slapping around a woman old enough to be your mother. You seem to be rising to lofty heights, Detective Stanger."

"*Chief* Stanger to you." The old woman wailed again, and went to her knees in the dirt, her taloned claws gathering the bedraggled household furnishings that had collapsed and scattered. "Chief Henry Stanger of the Ailchester Police." Stanger chuckled, the sound humorless and somehow evil.

A HUGE Negro was now revealed in the doorway, his overalls sweated, eyes rolling in his black countenance to focus curiously on the group.

"Chief!" Anne exclaimed. "Did you say Chief?"

"You heard me," Stanger grinned, thick-lipped. "You two fixed it pretty fer me all right. You put Fulton in the hot squad fer bumpin' off Kate Collins an' got Chief Kest a fifteen year rap fer bein' accessory after the fact. But you didn't get nothin' on me that could stand up in court. What I did, I did under orders from my boss, an' I wasn't supposed to know what it was all about. So the Town Council give me Jason's job when he went up to the Big House. Which means it's me that's the Law in Ailchester now."

The bull-necked cop paused. His pseudo good-humor drained from his florid countenance, was replaced by steel-hard, glowering menace. "That's a good thing fer you to not to ferget, just like I'm not fergittin' Jase Kest was my friend, nor what yeh done to him."

It was a declaration of war, definite and ominous. Peter Corbin went cold. He knew too well what weapons a law-officer could use in such a war, and he knew the one crushing weapon Stanger had and was not yet aware of it. The thread by which the Damoclean Sword was suspended over the Corbins' hope of a happy, normal-life was fraying. The faintest zephyr of chance would snap it.

"All of which," Anne Corbin broke the long minute of throbbing silence that followed Stanger's pronouncement, "doesn't explain the way you're treating this old lady. What has she done to you?"

The officer's piggish eyes shifted to her. "Not that it's any of your look out," he grunted. "But Mame Salt ain't done nothin' to me. I'm jest carryin' out the law by evictin' her fer non-payment of rent."

"Rent!" the girl gasped. "For this?" Her amazed gesture swept over the malodorous Sump. "You don't mean these people pay rent for living here! Why, that's a crime."

Stanger licked his lips. "The Law don't say so, and what the Law don't say is a crime ain't one. The Law says anyone owns property's got a right to be paid by anyone livin' on it, and my job's to see he gets paid or else—"

"But—but I'm sure if the owner of this land came down here and saw what it's like he wouldn't make them pay."

A strange sound, something between a hen's cackle and the neighing of a spavined horse, interrupted her. It came from the toothless, twisting mouth of the old hag. "Try an' get somethin' from Benton Courtney," she spluttered. "Unless you're young an' purty."

"Benton Courtney!" Corbin ejaculated. "The owner of the Bon Ton Department Store!"

"An' all the land between this side of the tracks an' Alewife Crick. Dumps an' swamps it is, but Benton Courtney kin squeeze diamonds out of it fer the gals he plays with. Five dollars a month he gets for these dumps, an' if you're a week late it's get out." Her cackling laugh made the twilight hideous, as if anything could make more hideous that hell of desolation.

"LISTEN, STANGER." Peter Corbin's voice was quiet and calm. "Let me get this straight." That voice was too calm, Anne thought, seeing the pallid spots that pitted the skin either side of her husband's nostrils. "Mrs. Salt owes five dollars rent, and for that she's being dispossessed?"

"Right."

"And she'll be permitted to remain if Courtney gets that five dollars?"

"Nope. Not unless Jim here gets a dollar an' a half. He's started his job an' the Law says—"

"Six and a half, then."

"Fer six and a half, in cash, old Mame kin stay here till the first of next month."

"We'll worry about next month when it comes." Peter had a thin wallet in his hand, was fumbling within it. "Here's a five dollar bill." He produced it. "Anne, I'll have to ask you to lend me the dollar and a half—"

"Nev' min' dat, mistah," the black put in. "Ah reckon ah kin get along widout it." He bent, as if to hide his face, and started gathering the stuff on the ground in his long, simian arms. "Ah better git busy an' take dis junk back in."

"I want a receipt, Stanger," Corbin clipped. "I believe the Law you talk about so much entitles me to one."

Speechless, the Police Chief produced a book of forms from his pocket, moved to the wall to use it as a desk while he went laboriously to work with the stub of a pencil. From rheum-rimmed sockets Mame Salt's faded eyes peered at her benefactor, her deep-graven wrinkles channeling the ready tears of age and feebleness. Peter turned to Anne, a whimsical half-smile twitching his lips.

"I guess you win, honey," he murmured. "There isn't going to be any taxi home for us tonight."

"And no movies, tonight or for a long time to come." The girl's eyes were shining. "But if I read the signs a-right we're going to be too busy for movies. The first of next month is only three weeks off." Anne knew what was in her husband's mind, and in her heart there was glad approval.

But there was also a grey dread in her heart too, and a chill of fear in her veins. The routine of everyday living that ordinary people know was not for Peter and her, these two who had for those who use the Law for their own mean ends a bitter and driving hate.

CHAPTER TWO
CASING THE LAY

BENSON COURTNEY was one of those small men who are very tall in their notion of then of own importance and who try to impress that personal esteem on others by a pompous walk and an imperious manner.

At precisely four in the afternoon of every business day Courtney would issue from the ground-glass door of his private office on the Bon Ton Store's second floor, and parade his black cutaway coat and the grey-trousered little paunch it revealed, his triangular little beard, his silk-ribboned pince-nez and his grey-spatted patent leather shoes, through his department store.

During this triumphal progress the pouchy black eyes behind Benson Courtney's glittering spectacles were not occupied solely in observing the working of his enterprise. They were quick to note a well-turned calf, a temptingly rounded bosom, a coquettish glance, whether these were the property of salesgirl or patron. If the ensemble of which calf or bosom were part happened to be more than ordinarily intriguing, Benson Courtney did something about the matter, or tried to. It is remarkable in how many cases his attempts met with success—or perhaps not remarkable when one recalls that Courtney was about the wealthiest man in Ailchester, and his generosity to the aforesaid intriguing ensembles was well-known to everyone.

See then, on the third afternoon after the events just related, this sleek-feathered cockerel strutting down a crowded aisle of his private barnyard. A tactful half-step behind him paces Hartley Alden. He is gaunt and grey-haired, and stooped. He is like a silent shadow, following Courtney around. He has been Courtney's shadow since the time the Bon Ton Store was a hole in the wall on Pine Street, Alden its only clerk.

"I'm packing them in today," Benson Courtney remarks. His voice is light, almost feminine. "It just shows you what brains and a knowledge of feminine psychology can accomplish, in spite of the recession." White, soft-cushioned, his hands dry-wash one another. "Look at the crowd around that table of silk nightgowns for instance. If I hadn't used the phrase 'spun platinum for golden bodies' in my ad, would those women have come flocking

"Yes, Mr. Courtney," Alden murmurs, omitting to mention that the nightgowns in question are being sold at half their real value, and that it was he who unearthed the manufacturer who had to take a staggering loss on them to obtain badly needed cash. "I mean no, Mr. Courtney."

The knot of bargain-seekers parts. A slender girl breaks from it. She has a gleaming nightrobe in her small hands and as soon as she is in the open she holds the robe against her measuring it for size. The day is hot and her close-cropped, tawny ringlets are hatless. She has a minimum of underthings beneath her sleeveless, low-necked frock, and this is completely covered by the lustrous nightrobe. As Benson Courtney sees her, the latter seems to be all she has on.

The silk shapes itself to the delicate curves of the young girl's body. The pale rose of her dress, glimmering through the gossamer fabric, seems to have the very sheen of blushing, pearly skin. An indrawn breath hisses sharply between Benson Courtney's teeth and over Hartley Alden's fleshless and sharp-featured face flits a shadow of dismay.

COURTNEY HASTENS his steps a bit, his sensuous lips pursing. The gown drops from the tawny-haired girl's fingers. Her right hand goes to her eyes. She sways and her left hand gropes blindly before her for support. Benson Courtney's arm slides around her waist just in time to save her from falling.

"Oh!" the girl whispers. "I—I feel faint." Her blue veined lids lie closed over her eyes and she nestles confidingly against the vandyked little man. Faces are turning toward them as he gently presses her toward a counter stool.

"Now, my dear," he purrs solicitously. "You'll be all right in a moment." He helps her to seat herself, and holds her head against his pouter-pigeon chest. "Alden," he snaps. "Stop standing there gaping. Get a glass of water. Hurry."

"Yes, Mr. Courtney," Alden murmurs. He has picked up the nightgown, and he puts it on a counter before he glides away.

The girl's eyes open and Courtney is looking down into grey, bottomless depths. "I—I'm better now." She seems not to be too sure. "It must have been the heat—and the crowd. Oh!" Abruptly she realizes her position and tries to straighten up, but Courtney's palm on her warm, satin-soft cheek, his arm about her shoulder, prevent her. "If—if I could just sit here and rest for a minute."

The expressions of the clerks and shoppers crowding around indicate their thoughts: "Just see how democratic the great man is, taking care of the girl himself." But Benson Courtney pretends not to be aware of this as he says, "Not here, my dear. Come to my office. It's airy there and cool, and you'll be more comfortable."

He slides his hand down the girl's bare arm and cups it under her elbow, helping her to rise. Perhaps because she is still dazed by her attack of vertigo she makes no effort to resist.

They go across the floor of the big store and behind them trails Hartley Alden, a glass of water in one bony-jointed hand, the girl's pocketbook in the other. He cannot see Anne Corbin's face and Courtney is too absorbed in his own pleasant speculations to watch it, so neither notice the secret smile that touches her small red mouth.

That smile was wan and shy as Anne settled down on the cushioned sofa in the great man's private office. "This is very kind of you," she ventured. "But I'm putting you to an awful lot of trouble."

"Not at all," Courtney smiled back at her. "If it weren't for your distress I should tell you what a real pleasure it is to have you here. It isn't often that this drab room is brightened by such a presence."

"Oh," Anne objected. "I don't think it's drab at all." She glanced around at the pastel-hued walls, on which hung three vivid Van Goghs; the oriental rug; the massive desk of carved mahogany. The couch on which she lay and two deep-seated club chairs were protected by slip covers of gay-colored chintz. Curtains at the wide windows were of the same material, the tints of the design reversed. "I think it's very lovely, and in such nice taste too."

The door through which they had entered stood open, the bustle of a busy office coming in through it. Benson Courtney was too experienced a hunter to flush his quarry till he was certain of his aim.

"Thank you," he responded to the girl's compliment. "I like pleasant surroundings." Only a flicker of his eyes pointed the reference. "And now, young lady, you just lie there and rest while I work. A nap will fix you up."

"Just a few minutes," Anne murmured, shrugging into the pillows, apparently quite unconscious of the tempting picture she made. "If you're sure I won't disturb you." Her voice trailed off drowsily, and her eyes closed.

Courtney stood above her for a long moment, his hands washing one another. The mask dropped from his face and it was the countenance of a satyr, glittering-eyed, humid-lipped.

AT FIVE-THIRTY ringing gongs announced the end of the Bon Ton's business day. Benson Courtney's glance went to the girl on his couch. She stirred a bit, but the half-curled hand flung across her eyes did not move.

He watched the slow, even rise of her bosom, small lights crawling in his narrowed orbs. If Alden didn't make too much noise when he brought in the cash that had been taken in since the bank closed at three....

At five-fifty Alden's lank, stooped form darkened the doorway. His dour gaze drifted to the couch as he came softly across the deep, silky rug to Courtney's desk. He put a heavy canvas bag on the desk, his expression that of one who has bitten into an unripe persimmon.

"One thousand, two hundred and thirty-seven dollars and sixty-two cents," he announced. "A good afternoon's business."

"Well do three times as much on Saturday," his employer remarked, dry-washing his hands, "with that furniture sale." He rose. "Well," he asked, "what are you waiting for? Why didn't you close and lock the door as you came in?"

Alden gestured to Anne. "What about *her?*"

Courtney's eyes got hard and his nostrils flared. "Can't you see that she's asleep?"

"But—"

"But nothing. You're an idiot, Alden. You've been an idiot for twenty-five years."

"Yes, Mr. Courtney," the other murmured. He went back to the door and closed it on the noises of the departing office force. By the time he returned to the desk and lifted the canvas money bag from it Courtney was at the wall opposite that before which the desk stood, his pudgy hands tugging at a portrait of a young man in brilliant blues and yellows.

The young man folded outward on one hinged edge of his frame. The patch of wall thus uncovered was a little lighter in shade than that around it. Otherwise it appeared the same as the rest, but when Courtney's white, plump fingers pressed on it a square of the plaster retreated below the general surface and then slid sideways. Where it had been was the gleaming black surface of a safe door, a numbered dial silvery upon it.

Alden, coming up behind the boss, was not watching this process. He was looking at Anne Corbin. She had rolled over, and all he could see of her head was its back, russet high-lights flecking her curls. The lines of tension in his face eased.

The safe door was open. Hartley Alden placed the money bag within the orifice behind it. The door closed again and Van Gogh's young man resumed his former position.

"Good night, Alden," Courtney said significantly. "Be sure you're on time tomorrow morning."

Hartley Alden said, "Yes, Mr. Courtney. Good-night, Mr. Courtney." He unlocked the room door. The outer office was deserted now. Perhaps because Alden's fingers slipped from its knob, the door slammed sharply. Anne Corbin sat up with a start.

"Oh!" she exclaimed. "It must be terribly late." Her pupils widened. "How long have I been asleep?"

"Just long enough, my dear," purred the little man with the vandyke and the spatted shoes. "I'm free to leave, and to ask if you would be kind to a lonely bachelor and have dinner with him."

"DINNER!" ANNE'S hand went to her breast. "It's nice of you to ask me, but I can't. I live way out on Hampton Highway and mother—"

"You can telephone your mother and tell her you'll be a little late. Tell her that you just heard there's going to be a sneak preview of a Charles Boyer picture at the Swan Theatre tonight and you must see it."

"But she'll find out there wasn't and—"

"There really is going to be one. I'm a part owner of the theatre and so I know. Well, that's settled. You're going to have dinner with me, and—"

"In these clothes? Without a hat?"

"My dear girl!" Courtney brushed that objection away with a gesture. This was going to be easy, almost too easy. "How silly of you to be worrying about clothes and hats when we have a storeful at our disposal. I know just the hat that will suit your winsome beauty." He caught her hands in his, tugged her to her feet. "Come on. We'll get you all dressed up and then we'll be ready for fun."

Anne's eyes were dancing now, her small face crinkled with a mischievous smile. "All right. But if I'm going to try on hats and dresses I'll have to fix my hair and powder my nose and everything."

The implication of intimacy set Courtney's pulses hammering. "There's a lady's room right outside the big office, to the left. Don't keep me waiting too long, my dear. His arm moved to take her within its circle, to press her close to him, but somehow she evaded him. She was out of the room He heard the door of the outer office open and dose "This is my lucky day," he hummed, taking a comb and hand mirror out of his desk drawer to preen himself.

Anne Corbin scampered down a flight of stairs and went swiftly between long rows of counters that with white dust sheets thrown over them were somehow ghostly in the dimness. Her footfalls echoed loudly in the vast, unpeopled reaches of the big store. Abruptly her heart thumped her ribs! What if all the exits were already locked and she couldn't get out without Courtney's aid?

Her alarm was unjustified. A man was standing at the door to which this aisle led. He wore a broad-brimmed straw hat, but she recognized him as the grim-faced Alden. He seemed a little startled at seeing her, but he opened the door for her, silently. She went out into the sun and bustle of Depot Square and breathed a sigh of relief.

She might not have been so relieved had she been aware of the conversation going on behind the door out of which she had just come.

"That the gal you 'phoned me to come an' spot?" The inquirer was a wide-shouldered, bull-necked individual, coming out from behind a sheeted showcase where he had ducked at the first sound of Anne's approaching footfalls.

"Yes," Alden responded. "That's the one. You'd better get after her quick or you'll lose her. I haven't anything to give you on her, not even her name. There was nothing in her bag to tell that or anything else about her, which was one thing that made me wonder what her little game is."

Henry Stanger made no move to follow Anne. "There ain't no hurry," he chuckled, the sound humorless and evil. "I don't know what she's up to, but I know who she is. Somethin' tells me I'm gonna enjoy keeping an eye on Mrs. Peter Corbin a hell of a lot more'n I did checkin' up on yer boss' other skirts."

"*Mrs.—!*" Alden exclaimed. "It's the old badger game then."

"No," Stanger drawled. "No-o-o-o. Somehow I don't think it is. But whatever it is I'll make damned sure to find out, an' then…." His piggish eyes leered from between their heavy lids and something very unpleasant crawled in them.

CHAPTER THREE
STANGER PROWLS ALONE

FAITH PARKER'S long nose twitched with indignation as she thumped a plate of fragrant lamb-chops on the table in the kitchen of the Corbin home. " 'Tain't enough you come in late," her acid voice complained. "You got to take nigh half an hour scrubbin' yourself. How do you expect me to have your vittles right?"

"I'm sorry, Faith dear," Anne Corbin put her arm around the older woman's thin waist and hugged the flat-breasted, scrawny form to her. "But I felt—unclean."

Peter Corbin's nostril flared. "Damn it!" he exclaimed, "I shouldn't have let you do it. There was some other way we could find out what we need to know without your letting the old roué paw you."

"He didn't, Peter." Anne seated herself in the chair her husband was holding for her. "It was just the slither of his voice, and the way he undressed me with his eyes. Ugh!" she shuddered. "But I knew I could handle him. It was the other man who frightened me. That Hartley Alden. He almost caught me watching Courtney open the safe."

"He did!"

"But I fooled him." Her mischievous twinkle was not confined to her eyes, it danced all over her face. "I turned my back to them and watched them in my little magnify-ing mirror, which I'd palmed in my hand. I read the combi-nation and everything, Peter. We're all set."

"Good girl!" Corbin exclaimed. "I—"

"Fool girl, I say!" The way Faith put the heaping platters of mashed potatoes and string beans down was eloquent of her disapproval. "But you're the bigger fool, Peter Corbin." The dried up, wrinkled spinstress had been Anne's nurse, foster-mother and faithful friend from infancy, spoke with the freedom of her long service. "Everything's going along so nice after that first scare we had, and now you're looking for trouble. You're forgetting fingerprints are on file in Washington and the minute they're taken again anywhere the keepers from Bolton Pen will be around looking for you."

The color drained from Corbin's face. "You're right. Faith," His hands tightened on the edge of the table. "But when I think of those people on the Sump—"

"Why don't you think of the girl you say you love," Faith cut in, her nose twitching like an agitated rabbit's. "Think of how Anne will feel when they take you off to serve that three years that's still coming to them. Think of her all alone, grieving for you, longing for you. Isn't it enough her life was burned to ashes once, without your doing it to her again?"

Peter's mouth twisted, as though with almost physical torture. "Let's drop it, Anne." His tone was thick, choked. "We've found security and peace, and—"

"Peace!" Anne's cry interrupted, and then she reached across the table, laying her slender, white hands over his bronzed, strong fingers. "Yes. We have a lovely home, warm and clean and comfortable. We have the best of food, good clothes, a soft bed at night. And you have work so that we can keep all these. But what has Mame Salt got, and how long can she keep what she has? What has that woman got who was suckling her sick baby? Will there be any peace for us in our soft bed, or will our sleep be troubled with dreams of the misery on the Sump? Will there be any peace for us on the first of next month, knowing that Benson

Courtney's collectors are out there, that Henry Stanger is waiting, with his Negro helper, to toss Mame out on the dumps with the other garbage? Is that the kind of peace we want?"

Faith Parker turned away. The young people would have to think out their problem for themselves. She had said her say and now she felt very much in the way. She went to the backdoor, making her excuse a pail of refuse that was not really ready to be put out on the kitchen porch.

"Is it, Peter?"

There was challenge in Anne's grey eyes as they caught and held her husband's blue ones. She read a question in their agonized depths.

"Yes," she answered him. "I am ready to endure even that. I am not afraid."

He broke into a boyish smile. "That's settled, then."

"ALL SETTLED." Anne picked up her fork. "Look, Peter. The best time is Saturday night. It's their busiest day, and the bank closes at noon, so there will be something worth while in the safe. Courtney's office is wired, but I studied the system and I know how to beat it. We'll—"

A scream shrilled in through the backdoor. It cut off with the thud of a body against the outer wall.

"Faith!" Corbin exclaimed, leaping from his chair. He beat Anne to the door by a single stride, dashed out into cool darkness. He twisted to the right, made out a pallid form shoving itself feebly up from the porch floor.

"A man," Faith Parker gasped, "listening at the window— There he goes!"

Peter spun in the direction of her pointing hand, discerned a bulk of blacker darkness moving across the darkness of the back yard. He leaped the porch steps in a single bound, flung himself after the intruder.

A hedge rustled as the dim form merged with its black wall. Corbin reached the barrier, thrust at it with his hands to break through. A hard fist exploded against the side of his jaw, pounded him to the ground. Feet thudded as Peter floundered, half-dazed. He heard Anne's cry, "Peter!" and he was on his feet again, was ploughing through the leafy wall. He came out on the other side just in time to see a shadow flit out of the street end between his house and his neighbor's.

It took him only seconds to reach the end of that alley, and come out on the narrow, flowered-bordered sidewalk, but there was no one fleeing down Elm Street. There was only a burly form strolling toward him, derby hat clinging to the back of its head by virtue of a minor miracle.

"Hello!" Chief Stanger said, coming up to the staring Corbin. "Havin' trouble?"

"Where did he go?" Peter gasped.

Stanger's thick lips pulled away from yellow teeth. "Where did who go?"

"The fellow who ran out of this alley."

"Nobody run out uh there. I would of seen him if he did."

Muscles along the ridge of Corbin's jaw knotted. "Look here, Stanger! Maybe you don't like me, but I'm a resident of Ailchester and I'm entitled to the protection of its police. Some prowler in our back yard sloughed my maid and conked me. I chased him out of here. You must have seen where he went and it's your duty to arrest him."

"My duty, eh," Stanger mused, a slow grin spreading over his knobbed countenance. "Sure it's my duty to arrest prowlers. Show him to me and I'll put the cuffs on him in half a shake of a lamb's tail. Where is he?"

"Where—you go to hell!" Corbin turned on his heel, stalked stiff-kneed away to his own front gate and up the path to the door that was opening to show Anne's slim silhouette against the dim light from the foyer.

Chief Henry Stanger of the Ailchester Police chuckled. "Kinda hot under the collar, that boy." His face sobered. "But it's too damn bad that female hadda come floatin' out on the porch just as I got there. I'd like to know what they think they're goin' to do about the Sump.... Well, I'll find out, you kin lay yer bottom dollar on that, an' when I do it's just goin' to be too damn bad fer Mr. an' Mrs. Peter Corbin. Just too—damn—bad."

SATURDAY NIGHT the Bon Ton Store stayed open till nine, and the Swan Motion Picture Theater till eleven. It wasn't till a little after midnight, more than two hours later than its usual wont, that Ailchester settled into hushed slumber.

With the cessation of sound and movement along Hampton Boulevard and in Depot Square, the Sump stirred and came alive. From its festering hovels, crouched, ragged shadows crept forth. They crawled through back streets, drifted through narrow alleys. Like so many human vermin they sought out the refuse cans and debris heaps behind the white-painted little cottages of the town, retrieving here a half eaten loaf of stale bread, there a bone to which some shreds of meat still adhered. Sometimes great good fortune would turn up a discarded bed, a corroded pipe or even a battered water tank of copper that could be sold for actual cash.

From another section of the town, but just as shadowy, just as furtive, two other prowlers of the night had made their way to Robin Avenue, on which the western wall of Benson Courtney's emporium of trade fronted. They whispered together in the mouth of a lightless alley now, peering watchfully up and down the lifeless block.

"It's that second floor nearest the boulevard," Anne Corbin murmured. "Now remember what I told you about the wiring; one connection is at the right hand upper corner, a half-inch in and just a little less than an inch down. The other is at the left hand lower corner, an inch up and an inch in."

"I've got it all right, honey," Peter replied in the same low tone. "Don't you worry. I've got everything you told me down pat. Look—!" He jerked his hand to where on the lower floor, a window was illuminated briefly by a yellow glow. "The watchman is downstairs. Now's my chance,"

"Be careful, my dear," the girl sobbed, pulling him tightly to her. "Don't take any chances. The instant you hear me whistle 'Thanks for the Memory,' drop everything and run." Her lips found her lover's, stayed there for a second. And then she was extricating herself from his clinging arms. "Go. Hurry."

Flitting across the street on soundless feet, Corbin's lithe frame was black as the midnight that brooded about him, his hands black-gloved, even his face soot-masked under his tight black cap. So completely black he was that when he reached the shadows lying along the Bon Ton's facade he became at once a part of them, indiscernible even to the girl who watched him with wide and burning eyes.

Benson Courtney himself had directed the designing of that wall when the store was built. As might be expected from a man who wore spats and hung a wide black ribbon from his glasses, the stone had been tortured into many ornate arabasques. Peter's soft-shoed feet found these excrescences as easy to his climb as though they had been placed there for that purpose.

BLACK-CLAD AS he was, he might have been some shadow detached from those below and skimming upward along the dim wall. In minutes he reached the window Anne had pointed out. Its sill was wide, its frame, of stone blocks, deep. Peter Corbin was no longer even a shadow as seen from below.

The sharp spiral of his drill made only a soft whisper of sound as it bit into the wood of the window's sash; an inch down, a half inch in at its upper right corner. The auger's metal grated on other metal and instantly Corbin pulled it from the hole, bent to the lower left corner to repeat the operation.

That took only a half-minute more, and the drill vanished in the interstices of Peter's garment. The hand which cached it came out now with a coil of wire and flipped it open. There were clips at each end of this wire, spring clips that went deftly into the holes the drill had made, their jaws biting the wires within the tiny wells.

The corners of Corbin's mouth lifted in a tight-lipped smile. The alarm that guarded Benson Courtney's private office now was short-circuited. When he opened the window there would be no break in the current to bring the watchman up from the lower floor, or Stanger's cohorts from the police station across Depot Square.

The window still was locked, but a wafer-thin blade made short work of that final barrier. The sash slithered up in its frame. There was no longer any shadow on its sill....

In the alley below Anne Corbin tensed, abruptly, at a shuffling sound to her right. Someone was coming from the direction of the Boulevard. Her skin an icy sheath for her quivering body, she thrust her head past the edge of the alley's maw where she lurked. Something grotesque, misshapen, moved along the sidewalk toward her. It

paused, changed form, came on again. It was like something hideous, unhuman, that had formed out of the night.
It reached the pale glow of a street lamp—and Anne
laughed softly.

The apparition was Mame Salt, the old woman of the
Sump, her already contorted body rendered gargoylesque
by a big bag poised on her shoulder. She looked like the
witch out of Hansel and Gretel, hobbling along, stopping
now and then to examine a bundle of sweepings set out in
front of a store, angling to the gutter at every infinitesimal
glitter that might possibly be a dropped coin.

Mame mustn't see her. Anne pulled back into her cover.
The shuffling came nearer. The hag was dimly outlined
against nightglow. She stopped, bent, although there was
nothing there that might promise her treasure trove.

"Hsst," Anne heard. "Hank Stanger's hidin' in the alley
behint ye." The woman's words were the merest breath. "He
was afollyin' you an' yer ol' man. He kinda lost ye, but now
he's located ye an' he's watchin' to see what ye're up to." She
was gone on the final word, shuffling away north towards
Pine Street.

The girl's lips puckered to whistle 'Thanks for the
Memory.' No sound came from them. First this was
because her squeezed lungs could not find breath for it.
And then, when air did wheeze in through Anne's tight
larynx, it was panic that silenced her, panic and despair
running gelid through her veins.

If she gave Peter the agreed-upon warning, he would
come out of that window and down the facade of the Bon
Ton Store. And this was precisely what Henry Stanger was
waiting for!

CHAPTER FIVE
CAPTURED!

PETER CORBIN dropped catlike from the window sill to Benson Courtney's oriental rug. Only sky glow tempered the blackness of the room, but Corbin needed no light. So vivid had been Anne's description, so accurate the plan she had drawn and so carefully had he studied it that he was as familiar with it as with that of his own bedroom. He went straight to Van Gogh's portrait without a single glance around him.

If he had stopped for that glance he might have noticed a spark of luminescence low in the baseboard of the wall at the right angle to that on which the picture hung. But even if he had, he would in all likelihood have thought it merely the reflection of some vagrant beam on a nail's polished head.

Be that as it may, Corbin lifted his gloved hands to the portrait's frame and opened it out from the wall as though he were opening the painted door of a doll's house. He pressed the plaster thus uncovered. It went in the fraction of an inch, slid sidewise. The front of the Bon Ton's safe was revealed, and the numbered dial whose combination Anne had read. Peter's deft fingers took hold of the dial, started twisting it....

Anne Corbin bit her lip to still the whimper deep in her throat, thinking swiftly. She must get Stanger away from here somehow in the next three minutes. It would not be longer than that before Peter reappeared at the window across the street and started climbing down the department store's wall.

Would the policeman follow her? She laughed throatily, as though some idea had just occurred to her, peered out into the street and started moving. She ran north on Robin Avenue toward Pine Street, seeking to draw the hunter away from the Boulevard. She was almost to the further corner before she glanced over her shoulder and saw no bulky form following her. The edge of the alley mouth was jagged, indeed, by what might be the outline of a human figure, but Stanger was too shrewd to be lured away by her subterfuge.

He knew that Peter had started out with her, and he wanted to know what had become of the man. The girl had too obviously been a lookout

Anne sobbed, slowing to a stop. If Peter were caught he would rot in prison, and she—life would end for her. There was no balancing of values in her mind at that moment, no reckoning of a paltry punishment for herself as against a return to Bolton Pen for the man she loved. She saw a loose cobblestone on the sidewalk and she saw the gleaming plate glass front of a pharmacy. She stooped, snatched up the stone, and flung it crashing through the drugstore's window.

"Hey!" she heard a hoarse shout. "Hey, you!" She saw Stanger's barrel-like bulk surge out of the alley mouth and twist to come running toward her. She turned too, started to run. The cop's heavy footfalls slowed. He was hesitating. Anne made as if she stumbled, went down to her knees. Stanger's thudding steps hastened again. The girl shoved herself to her feet, staggered as if hurt, went around the corner into Pine Street. But she had delayed too long. The policeman's footfalls were right behind and they were coming far faster than she could run.

THE SPLINTERING crash of glass came clearly into the office of the Bon Ton's owner. Corbin's head jerked to the window, but the little safe door was open, and he'd already seen the money bag, there for his taking. His fingers closed on it, lifted it out. It was heavy with coin and packets of bills.

"All right, guy," a voice said. "Grab for the ceiling before I plug yuh."

Breath whistled from between Peter Corbin's teeth as he spun around to the sound. His arms went above his head and as though his fingers were frozen on its neck by startlement the bag of loot went up with them. That crash of glass must have covered the click of a lock, for the office door was open now and framed within it was a tall, lanky man from whose hand a blue-nosed revolver shouted very steadily, and very ominously near the prowler.

"I thought Alden was nerts yesterday when he fell for that electric-eye dingus," the lantern-jawed watchman grinned. "But I guess I was wrong. It flickered a light downstairs to tell me someone was in this room, so I guess it set off an alarm acrost the square in the police station, like Alden said it was supposed to do."

"Electric eye?" Despair was a murky cloud rolling within Corbin's skull, but he did not forget to speak with the thick-lipped intonations of the negro he hoped his blackened countenance made him appear. "Whut dat, man?"

"Some kind of light you can't see that goes across in front of that wall and does things when a smart burglar like you walks into it." Very faintly sounds came into the room, thuddings, the trample of many feet. "There they are by jingo!" the watchman exclaimed. "The cops. They had a key and they're comin' upstairs. You'll have plenty of time to study about black light in the calaboose, my friend."

THERE WERE high hedges along Pine Street, in front of sleeping cottages and Anne thought despairingly that if she could hide behind them she might still escape. But Stanger was too close to her for that.

"Halt," she heard his yell. "Halt or I'll shoot."

She stopped, turned. He was still too far away for her to make out his face in the murk here, but she could make out his bulky form. His arm bent, tugging his gun out of its shoulder holster. Just then a grey wraith swooped out from behind a hedge, hit the sidewalk right in front of Police Chiefs flying feet Those feet struck whatever it was, swept out from under the cop. He plunged forward, falling.

Other grey, half-seen figures were pouring out of the darkness, from lurking places in shrubbery, from the openings of auto driveways. They were piling atop Stanger, making a weird, tossing mass beneath which his lewd oaths were muffled. Anne, gaping, caught sight of a scrawny arm flinging up out of the mass, rags fluttering from it. She saw a hollow-cheeked face, its toothless mouth open and laughing. A stench came to her, the smell of unwashed bodies, of starvation-rotted flesh, of garbage.

Taloned fingers were clutching her arm. "Run, dearie," a cracked voice jabbered in her ear. "Run home quick as ye kin." It was the cackling voice of a witch out of Hansel and Gretel, the voice of Mame Salt.

"What—how—" Anne Corbin stammered.

"I saw you was in trouble," the hag gibbered, "an' I got holt of my frien's thinkin' mebbe we could help ye. Mebbe we ain't worth much, us from the Sump, but we don't forgit them as is good to us. Now you run along quick. He ain't seen yer face yet, so if ye git away 'fore he gits loose ye're okay."

"But—but Peter—"

"He kin take care of hisself, if I knows anything about men. Go. Fer God's sake go!"

THE MUFFLED sound of the police squad was nearer. They must be halfway to this floor now. "Hey!" the watchman exclaimed. "That bag. Drop it!"

Peter Corbin dropped it—with a sweeping forward motion of his arm that sent it hurtling straight at the snouting gun. In the same moment his thigh muscles exploded, catapulting his hundred and forty pounds of sinew and muscle across space in a flashing flying tackle.

The metallic bump of the revolver and the thud of two bodies striking the floor were followed at once by the sharper crack of knuckles on bone. Corbin's fist spatted again on the watchman's jaw, and the black-clad youth was leaping to his feet. The money bag was in one hand as he switched the key to the inside of the door, pulled it shut, and locked it. He was fastening the bag to a hook at his belt that had been prepared for it as he darted across the floor to the open window. His hands were free when he leaped upon its sill.

A heavy fist hammered on the door. The glass panel shattered under the impact of a nightstick. A hand appeared in the opening, groped for the keyhole. The key wasn't in it. It took perhaps a minute more for pounding gun-butts to break the lock.

The cops surging in found an unconscious watchman stretched on the floor. They found a safe door hanging open in a wall, a window tight shut and jammed, so that it was a little while before they could look out.

By that time the street below was empty of life or movement. Peter Corbin was halfway across town to Elm Street, and the withered crone that had met him in the mouth of the alley where he sought Anne, and whispered to him that she was safe, was chuckling to herself as she climbed the railroad embankment with her ragged cohorts.

"**NEARLY SIX** thousand dollars," Benson Courtney moaned, the next Monday morning, his head propped in his hands, his elbows on the massive desk in that gayly decorated office of his.

"Five thousand, seven hundred and ninety-three dollars," Hartley Alden murmured, "and sixty-three cents—to be exact."

"You're an idiot," Courtney snapped. "A penny-counting idiot."

"Yes, Mr. Courtney," the other responded.

"Get out of here! Get out and attend to business. I don't want you hanging around."

It's four o'clock, Mr. Courtney. Time for your tour of inspection."

"Damn my tour of inspection," the vandyked little man snarled. "It's an asinine stunt."

"Yes, Mr. Courtney." The shadow of a vinegary smile drifted across Alden's face. "Then I presume you wish to take up the usual real estate matters at this time."

"The hell I do. You attend to them. I always do what you say anyway. You never seem to be able to do anything of your own volition."

"I'm sorry. There is one matter which I must bring to your attention. Concerning the Sump—"

"Another beggar squealing about his rent. Throw him out. Call Stanger and have him thrown out."

"There is no one to be thrown out, Mr. Courtney. In fact, there will be no one to collect rent from left on the Sump after the end of this month."

"What!"

"Exactly. I've just been informed that from somewhere our tenants out there have scraped together enough money to buy a plot of land out west of Ailchester. They're going to put up a community house there and farm the land. I understand an individual called Corbin, Peter Corbin, is arranging with the Federal Government for seed for them, and a loan with which to buy equipment and do their building."

"Corbin? Who the devil's he? Never heard of him."

"Neither did I, till today. He's a bookkeeper in the mill, a nobody. But Chief Stanger seems to know him. And to have something against him. Stanger said something about getting Corbin if it's the last thing he ever does. Corbin and his wife."

Courtney's soft hands were tearing a blotter to shreds. "Help him, Alden. Help him any way you can to get this Corbin and his wife, too."

Again there was the flicker of a secret smile in Hartley Alden's fish-like eyes. "I wonder," he murmured, "how easy that's going to be. You didn't find it so easy to get the wife when you tried it yourself."

"What!" his employer spluttered. "What was that you said?"

"Nothing important, Mr. Courtney, nothing important."

"You're an ass, Alden. A blithering ass."

"Yes, Mr. Courtney," Hartley Alden murmured.

ABOUT THE AUTHOR

ARTHUR **LEO ZAGAT** (1895–1949), like fellow writer Erle Stanley Gardner, was a lawyer who forsook his profession in favor of the uncertain life of a pulp magazine writer.

A veteran of the First World War who attended City College of New York and Bordeaux University, Zagat graduated from Fordham University Law School in 1929, with the intent of practicing law. But it was the beginning of the Great Depression, and so he turned instead to writing with his fellow lawyer, Nathaniel Schachner.

Their first collaboration, "The Tower of Evil," appeared in *Wonder Stories Quarterly*, Summer 1930. Ten others followed, all appearing in the top Science Fiction titles of the era, *Amazing Stores, Wonder Stories* and *Astounding Stories of Super-Science*. They also sold to *Weird Tales*. In 1934, Zagat struck out on his own, branching out to write for Popular Publications magazines, where he made a name for himself writing detective stories and contributing to Popular's trio of weird menace magazines, *Dime Mystery Stories, Horror Stories* and *Terror Tales*. Thus he became known as "The Horror Story Man." He was also prolific in *Detective Tales, Ace G-Man Stories* and *Strange Detective Mysteries*.

When he had more than one story in a magazine, Zagat used the pseudonym of Grendon Alzee—the last name a play on his initials. For Culture Publications' sole entry in the weird menace sub-genre, *Spicy Mystery Stories*, Zagat wrote as Morgan Lafay.

He is said to have written as Anton York, which was the name of the hero of Eando Binder's famous story about an immortal. Curiously, Arthur Leo Zagat was known to some of his colleagues as Leo, but to intimates as "Bob."

Very few series emerged from his typewriter over a 20-year writing career comprising an estimated 500 published stories. His longest and most famous, Doc Turner of Morris Street, ran for nearly a decade in the back pages of *The Spider*. It was one of the most popular backup series in any similar pulp magazine. Featuring the ministrations of kindly old inner-city pharmacist Andrew "Doc" Turner, it was inspired by Zagat's period of working at his father's pharmacy while attending Fordham.

Zagat's stories starring Steven "Tiger" Carlin appeared in Street & Smith's *Detective Story Magazine* in the early 1940s. Carlin was assisted by an elderly neighborhood druggist, Richard Frost.

Red Finger had a much shorter run, of course. But he was the closest to a pulp superhero that Zagat ever penned.

Zagat was also known for his fantasy serials written for *Argosy*, among them, "Drink We Deep," "Seven Out of Time" and the "Tomorrow" stories featuring a boy Tarzan named Dikar battling Japanese invaders in a future conquered America. He also appeared in *Blue Book*.

During World War II, Zagat served as Chairman of the Pulp Writers' Section of the Authors' Guild, a branch of the Authors' League of America, where his legal background proved invaluable. Zagat left to join the Office of

War Information, dividing his time between his New York apartment and his desk in Washington, while continuing to turn out stories. After the war, he taught short-story writing at New York University and was heavily involved in tutoring returning soldiers in the art of fiction writing. He subsequently founded the Writers' Work Shop for Veterans.

A lifelong resident of the Bronx, Arthur Leo Zagat died of a heart attack on April 3, 1949, at the age of 53. Of himself, he once wrote: "I have had no adventures in far lands. I have worked in a drugstore. I have sold insurance from door to door. I have ridden in the subway and walked the city streets with eyes and ears open. I have read Mother Goose… I do not think of myself as an artist. I am a trades-man, a merchant of tales. It is the way I make my living, and I behave towards it as any man behaves towards his means of livelihood."

www.ingramcontent.com/pod-product-compliance
Lightning Source LLC
Chambersburg PA
CBHW020543020726
47494CB00006B/1895